The Lost Daughter

A Jean Brash Mystery

DAVID ASHTON

TWO
ROADS

www.tworoadsbooks.com

First published in Great Britain in 2017 by Two Roads
An imprint of Hodder & Stoughton
An Hachette UK company

1

A CIP catalogue record for this title is available from the British Library

ISBN 978 1 473 63229 5
Ebook ISBN 978 1 473 63230 1
Audio Digital Download ISBN 978 1 473 64072 6

Typeset by Hewer Text UK Ltd, Edinburgh
Printed and bound by Clays Ltd, St Ives plc

Hodder & Stoughton policy is to use papers that are natural, renewable
and recyclable products and made from wood grown in sustainable
forests. The logging and manufacturing processes are expected to
conform to the environmental regulations of the country of origin.

Hodder & Stoughton Ltd
Carmelite House
50 Victoria Embankment
London EC4Y 0DZ

www.hodder.co.uk

David Ashton was born in Greenock in 1941. He studied at Central Drama School, London, from 1964 to 1967, and most recently appeared in *The Last King of Scotland* and *The Etruscan Smile*. David started writing in 1984 and he has seen many of his plays and TV adaptations broadcast: he wrote early episodes of *EastEnders* and *Casualty*, and twelve McLevy series for BBC Radio 4.

inspectormclevy.com

PRAISE FOR THE JEAN BRASH
AND INSPECTOR McLEVY SERIES

'Here is Jean Brash centre stage in all her splendour – clever, cheeky, generous, alluring, hard-headed, yet prone to the occasional burst of crazy romanticism, an old friend who is full of surprises. I find her as irresistible as McLevy does: she's my favourite character and David Ashton's writing is as delicious, elegant and compelling as she is'
Siobhan Redmond (Jean Brash in BBC Radio 4's McLevy series)

'Ashton is an old hand at milking the Old Town, New Town and Leith for their maximum atmosphere, suspense and air of criminality. That, combined with the intriguing premise of a crime-solving brothel-keeper, makes *Mistress of the Just Land* a most diverting page turner'
Herald

'David Ashton impeccably evokes Edinburgh so vividly that you feel the cold in your bones and the menace of the Old Town's steep cobbles and dark corners'
Financial Times

'An intriguing Victorian story . . . elegant and convincing'
The Times

'McLevy is one of the greatest psychological creations and Ashton the direct heir to Robert Louis Stevenson'
Cox, CBE

By David Ashton

THE INSPECTOR McLEVY SERIES

THE JEAN BRASH SERIES

TO MADDY

Now you are in the book.

Chapter 1

Who is it that can tell me who I am?

King Lear

Leith, April 1883

The baby was howling blue murder. Jean could see that; she could also see that it was a girl baby, for the creature was naked as a mason's nail.

What was a naked baby doing in a bawdy-hoose? For Jean could also note that they were both in her boudoir – a cradle of frills and lace that Hannah Semple often likened to a spider's web. The woman had a damned cheek; Jean Brash, Mistress of the Just Land, did not remotely resemble a spider plus the fact there was not a man of woman born who had ever lain in that bed except for yon Italian lawyer ensconced unannounced and see where it had got him.

Thrown out on his lughole. *Arrivederci.*

The baby howled again. It was now quite purple in the face, which was a wee bit alarming, and Jean supposed she'd better pick the thing up.

Mind you, this was definitely not *her* baby, even though not long born by the looks, because Jean would surely feel the after-agonies of birth and there was no sign of any slidey placenta to say nothing of the nine months of watching your veins bulge out all

1

over the place as if they were kale worms: surely she would remember that?

Queen Victoria was forever having progeny but that had stopped when her husband died. Albert, by name, was the source of such fertility. A sad loss.

To tell truth, babies were not Jean's speciality. When they were at a distance, cocooned inside a perambulator, buried under protective layers, she could manage an appropriate cooing noise or even a guarded wave, but that was about her limit.

Anyhow, who'd want a bawdy-hoose keeper, even if the venue were the best in Edinburgh, waving at your child? Albert and Victoria for certain sure would have drawn the line.

Another howl, though it was more of a yowl this time, as if the poor wee mite were losing conviction.

She bent down, girded her loins, and picked it up. The thing went quiet immediately as Jean held it close to her breast after the manner illustrated in the best household magazines. It began nuzzling at the opening in her nightdress, mouth opening and closing like one of the exotic fish that Jean so admired.

But the fish were slouching in her garden pond; this was closer to home. A more insistent nuzzle. *My God, was the creature hungry?*

That would explain the howling of course but she had nothing to offer bosom-wise. She could go down to the kitchen below and get some milk and a sugar biscuit – that was always possible – but the baby had its head right inside the nightdress and was sucking at what she could only surmise was a nipple.

Her nipple.

The sensation made her feel a wee bit rubbery and Jean felt herself being drawn to the bed; that little mouth had a power all of its own, like a leech or a limpet, and her legs were turning to jelly as if she were wading through a peat-bog. She only just made it to the bed before collapsing on to the sheets, where she lay stupefied while the baby sucked and chewed. *It must be getting something but God alone knows what . . .*

There was a sharp nip of pain. Surely the thing didn't have teeth already, or was it a vampire, maybe?

Jean looked down at the top of the baby's head. A few strands of hair, dark in colour, stuck to the scalp. Sweat maybe had caused that, coming out of the womb was surely no joke; no, the thing couldn't be a vampire. It was too small, too vulnerable. She felt an odd stab of tenderness to go with the nipping. *Oh, to hell with it.*

So Jean Brash just lay on her side and let nature take its course in the filmy paradise of her boudoir, the delicate gauze curtains moving gently in a breeze of sorts as they hung round the bed. Jean must have left a window open again, Hannah Semple was forever gnashing at her about that: you never knew, said the old woman, what might fly in unannounced through the gap.

Was that how the baby had got in maybe, planked there by the stork?

Once a madman who thought he was the natural son of Robert Louis Stevenson had come in through that window and damned near killed Jean, whipped her with his cane till the flesh wept blood and would have dealt the death blow but for an interruption that sent him back through the window and over the garden wall.

Divine intervention.

Or rather Hannah with a cut-throat razor when Jean, with her last remaining strength, threw an empty perfume bottle through a pane of glass to signal that all was not well in the boudoir of Madame.

Inspector James McLevy had tracked the madman down and the assailant killed himself inside a church, hurtled down from on high to hit the flagstones like a rotten apple.

But that was another story and the baby seemed to be asleep now. Jean surmised she'd better follow suit and therefore closed her eyes.

Enough was enough.

'Mistress!'

Jean was jolted awake to find the indignant face of Hannah Semple glowering down at her like some Notre-Dame gargoyle with a grievance.

'It's near nine o'clock in the morning, are you jist going to lie there lik' a lump of coal?'

'I beg your pardon?'

'You heard,' replied Hannah, unmoved by the icy tones of the erstwhile sleeper. Then she was taken aback to see the said mistress turn and wildly shake the pillow beside her, turning it this way and that while scrabbling about in the bedclothes.

'Where's the baby?'

'Whit?'

'I had a baby visit, where is the thing?' The pupils of her green eyes were dilated and swivelling from side to side uneasily.

'I warned ye about them oysters last night,' came the stolid response. 'But you would eat a whole dozen.'

Late the previous evening, Jean had closeted herself in a side room with some male visitor that she herself had let in the front street door, and the pair had consumed twenty-four of the best pan-door shellfish plus a bottle of champagne between them before the fellow slid off into the night.

For sure it wasn't Jean's young lover: that mannie walked like a

Highland bullock, this gent was light on his feet and skipped out like a spring-heeled lamb. The Mistress had been a touch thoughtful afterwards but at this present moment she was plain carnaptious. 'Oysters be damned,' she muttered. 'I had a baby beside me.' She gazed down and pressed the sheets with her hand as if trying to find a trace left by the strange arrival.

The two women looked at each other while a crow in the garden outside complained about some matter of corbie concern.

'It would be a dream, Mistress,' said Hannah soberly. 'A dream of some kind.'

'But why about a baby?'

Hannah had no answer to this as Jean felt round about her waist and then looked down reproachfully at her breasts, which were certainly full enough but not with anything resembling milk.

'It was hungry. A girl.'

'Weans are aye hungry.'

Neither woman had ever borne a child. Hannah had only met one decent man ever in her life and he'd been shot dead at a gambling table.

And Jean Brash? A bawdy-hoose keeper waddling around like a duck? Not much chance of that.

But behind the thought lay a darker one. Of her own lost childhood. The fear of what? A repeat performance?

She could not remember the baby's face, just the little mouth opening and closing around her.

Jean rose from the bed, wandered over to the open window and looked out at the garden of the Just Land.

Spring had finally arrived after a dull, drookit first three months of the year, and the buds of bushes, trees and flowers were cautiously poking forth their heads like cave dwellers coming out into the light. Plookie Galbraith had mown the lawn yesterday and managed not to lose any limbs, which was a miracle in itself, so there was still the sweet scent of cut grass.

All was serene. Ornamental peacocks like debt collectors prodding beaks into the ground; the aforesaid exotic fish disturbed the surface of the pond, their sluggish equivalent of a salmon leaping mightily in the air as it launched upstream to spawn; her beloved roses also paying tribute with a wary budlike unveiling to the watery April sunshine as its rays dispersed a morning haze that still clung like a cobweb from the early dawn.

Had all inclined towards the window they would have witnessed a woman in her prime, red hair tumbling over the ruffed shoulders of a silk nightdress, green eyes to match the emerald tones of the cut grass and a skin smooth as the milk she had failed to collect in her dream. Pretty as a picture.

All was serene.

So why did this beauty feel a lurch inside as if the earth were crumbling beneath her feet?

'We have a bawdy-hoose tae run, the girls are still in their scratchers, and you havenae had your breakfast.' This from Hannah Semple, who was by no means pretty as a picture but keeper of the keys of the Just Land.

Jean nodded. Back to the real world.

Chapter 2

There was never yet fair woman
But she made mouths in a glass

King Lear and his three rivalrous daughters lolled restlessly in the railway carriage, each with murderous thoughts in mind.

The train on its way from London to Edinburgh Waverly Station, a long journey through the night that was nearing its end taking at least treble the running time of the play itself.

Alfred Tyrone lifted a regal chin and reviewed the theatre company that occupied some of the compartment. He caught sight of a hawklike profile reflected in the carriage window, jet black hair long and straight, the nose also long, hooded eyes to flash emotion and a wide slash of a mouth that hid his least admired facet – small teeth, some of them slightly discoloured from the many cigars inhaled and, did he but know it, a little congested near the gums, producing an occasionally acrid odour similar to burnt cork.

Had he risen from the seat, Alfred would have measured over six feet to the naked eye and, aside from somewhat spindly shanks, proved himself to be a fine, upright figure of a man with a voice whose timbre could be heard from here to John o' Groats.

Master of all he surveyed.

King Lear in clover.

His sister Bridget, who would not welcome the comment that she had been dealt a poor hand in the family queue for striking countenance – being thin featured, eyes set a smidgeon close together, skin somewhat dry and flaky, perfect casting for Goneril, malevolent older daughter of the King, but far from ingénue material – glanced at her brother opposite and wished to puncture his massive ego with a sharp hat needle or poisoned bodkin. They were twins by birth who did not remotely resemble each other and that, in some way, added insult to injury.

The six feet of length that served Alfred so well did Bridget no favours at all, emphasising that she was flat-chested, bony hipped behind the corsetry, and still a virgin. Almost. That was another story.

Alfred had always been the favourite, the beautiful boy, handsome man, the gifted one – not as gifted as he and the whole family thought but gifted enough, in their opinion, compared to her. An eagle to her dowdy pigeon.

She was, in fact, the more *sincere* actor, but he took up more space and gobbled up attention. Bridget was relegated to performances of 'character' though she had once heard Alfred describe them as 'born spinsters'. Mind you, Goneril was no old maid. Perhaps she ought to take a leaf out of the character's book?

One day she would kill Alfred, put out his eyes and, with them, play marbles in the gutter.

The woman sitting beside Bridget was rather pretty, fair-haired to the sister's stringy brown tresses, and her own murderous inclinations were scattered like stray seeds in the wind.

Melissa Fortune – a name conjured up to replace the real one – had hitherto played the sweet leading parts of the company, tremulous innocence being her speciality. This was augmented by full lush lips and a slender willowy figure hinting at pliable corruption. However, now she was condemned to Regan, other homicidal daughter of His Majesty, and though there was the promised pleasure of male humiliation and other assorted cruelties that she might relish, Melissa had been spurned from her rightful execution because of that little bitch.

The fact that Cordelia, the heroic offspring of King Lear, dies in the play was of little compensation. Like a Gorgon, she would live anew at the next performance.

How dare she usurp the rightful queen?

The fact that Melissa was a shallow creature who lived her life in the manner of a skittery seabird on the surface of the deep ocean of existence and cared only for her own gratification, should not overlook that she might well be capable of inflicting death. Providing she did not break her fingernail.

Emilia Fleming, seemingly asleep, nestled beside Alfred, not at all overly close to excite gossip but near enough that he might be aware of a certain fragrance of sweet cologne, could sense the hatred from opposite and it excited her to the very bones. She loved hatred, looked down on love unless used as a tool, and adored their bastard child of lust.

Her body, though clothed to the latest fashion, was small and rounded. There was a rumour in the company she might be double-jointed, and dark hair with auburn tints tumbled down her face and neck, tendrils escaping as if wild and wanton, framing the gypsy cast of her countenance. Not pretty exactly; more sensual and spoiled, like a bruised rose.

It was said she came from Newcastle and there was the slightest tinge of that accent to her speech but the girl kept such history to herself.

The past is a shadow that haunts us; and can be no more shaken free than a shadow. In the absence of light, it still remains hidden. Biding time. And lurking under Emilia's excitement of what might be looming ahead was a shuddering fear from what lay behind.

For a moment she swivelled round to see if *he* was watching – her lover, her killer-to-be. He had warned her that he might have to take a life or two in Edinburgh and her only response was 'Can I watch you, Billy?' Then they had laughed, neither knowing precisely what the other meant. And neither caring. Not yet.

Time would test whether this might offer pretence, like a role upon the stage, or a harder reality.

Until then, they would delight together.

Billy Musgrave saw her turn. He fingered his gold earring as a memory of her naked body danced across his mind. Double-jointed. Twisting like a corkscrew.

He had a gold tooth to match that earring and a grin like a basking shark.

The young keelie would have made a wonderful Edmund, the bastard son and arch manipulator of evil in the play, but was, due to his inability for stringing the Bard's words together and even had he, a thick Leith accent rendering them incomprehensible to delicate English ears, relegated to that of the main stage helper.

In fact, stage manager, for Billy was clever with his hands and knew how to work effects and machinery. An unwitting disciple of Archimedes, he pulled levers and changed a world upon the stage.

As Billy gazed out the window at a sea he had never bathed in, being baptised in the Waters of Leith along with all the other wild boys of the parish, it must be said of him that, again like Edmund, his instincts for evil were *impeccable*.

At the front, where every leader of men should be, Alfred allowed a vision of Henry Irving to enter his mind and conjectured how the great actor would look fallen from the battlements in *Hamlet* to break his neck and lie there on the stage, all animal magnetism fled.

The cast would gather round to gaze downwards at the dying prince. How sad, thought Alfred, how *desperately* sad it would be. But of course, the show must go on.

He lit a cigar, tried to forget the perils of precipitate finance and puffed out a cloud of obscuring smoke as the train rolled on, taking them all to a terminal conclusion.

Chapter 3

I am even
The natural fool of fortune.

The human ran, the animal followed, both hurtled onwards by terror – the boy, a lank, disjointed figure, sallow pockmarked face crunched in panic. All his life it had been like this; moments of promised joy broken by persecution and pain.

The small dog yelped and, as the pursuing footsteps grew louder and nearer, it darted away in front, little legs driving piston-like as the beast disappeared into the morning mist of the cobbled, twisting wynd.

Vinegar Close, in fact.

Leith was fissured by these conduits, narrow alleys that gripped close upon entrance like a hand around the throat or so many cracks in a chamber pot; slots of ambush gouged out of the damp walls of a warren of crumbling buildings that housed families ten to a room like a nest of insects, rustling and writhing together in the night. Near the harbour, salt air stinging the face, they resembled a giant hive that crawled with scuttling humanity.

One of which was Plookie Galbraith, whose large feet slipped and crashed his body against the mildewed wall.

Good that wee Raggie Biscuit got away, they cannae injure the beast now – he has his wee collar, that'll save him.

But what such fragmented thought had forgotten was that in the absence of one target another might appear all the more enticing.

As Plookie lurched onwards, the side of a leather boot clipped at his heels and the boy fell flat on his face, wind hammered out of the body.

A primitive superstition: if he lay face down they would go away because if he could not see them, they would not be there. What you cannot see cannot hurt. Only God sees everything. And He never interferes.

The same foot flipped Plookie over as if he were a dead rodent. Eyes held shut: it might still work.

Then a cruel dig at skinny ribs goaded him into vision. Bob Golspie. That was bad enough but standing beside his large hulking frame was Niven Taggart. Jack-a-dandy. Dressed well – a real gentleman you might think but that was as far as it went.

It was said the devil had almond eyes, slanty, cold and yellow. Niven was Satan's double. He smiled thinly and ground the toe of his fancy boots deeper just below the ribs, forcing a gasp out of his victim.

'Where ye goin' in such a hurry?' he asked.

'I – I – didnae want tae be late.'

Bob Golspie laughed. With his broad flat face you could easy mistake him for an Eskimo. You could also think he was a fat cheerful soul but that would be a mistake. Yet at least his violence was casual, he would swat at you like a fly. Niven was just born evil. He could walk into a low tavern and folk would feel a chill in the backbone as his slight stiletto figure slid inside, a baleful spirit.

Plookie had seen the two of them waiting on the corner and shot off another way but he must have left a trail of some kind because here they were.

And so was he. Open-eyed.

'Ye work for Jean Brash now, I hear?'

A casual question riddled with danger, Niven's eyes like icy pinpricks.

'Aye – I help wi' the horses. And the grass.'

'She must pay ye well.'

'Not much.'

The toe dug in again. Plookie winced and tried to play daft. Bob laughed. Niven looked bored.

'Empty your poche.'

Plookie sat up and did so, making a good job of it, turning the dirty pockets inside out. Some coins fell on to the cobblestones. Small change. Bob scooped it up.

'Ye get paid every week?'

'Not much. Shillins. Wee coin.'

Niven suddenly hauled Plookie up off the ground with a slim arm like a steel bar, sliding out from a hidden harness the large hook-knife that was his preferred weapon. Taken from a lascar seaman, it was feared amongst the street keelies as a hellish cutter; it could operate both at close quarters and from distance. He had a butcher friend who kept it sharp. Niven paid for such diligent labour by cutting up the animal carcasses – he had become quite an expert in dismemberment.

As he had proved to himself not ten hours ago on a moonlit harbour. Up and through.

The hook now rested just under the boy's groin and Plookie tried to keep the fear from showing on his face.

Play daft. Play stupid. Pray to God.

'Don't mark him,' said Bob quickly. 'We don't want Jean Brash tae know.'

'How come?'

'She has friends, Niven.'

'Such as?'

'Jamie McLevy for a start.'

The policeman was one person in Leith who knew the wynds better than any of the keelies and he was also a thing to avoid, like the Canongate pox.

'She has her ain street folk as well,' Bob continued. 'Best leave her. She's Queen Bee.'

Niven smiled. He had his own thoughts on that, yes, his own private thoughts as he pulled Plookie near enough that the boy could smell some kind of scent.

Did Satan wear cologne? Barber's scent, maybe? Niven was clean-shaven, not a hair on his face, smooth, small featured like a baby. Till you got to the eyes.

'How much does she pay ye?'

Plookie thought to lie then thought again. If Niven found out, he'd be a gutted herring. But how could he find out?

'On the Friday. Seven shillings.'

Liar – it was ten. And he had saved. And hidden. One day he wanted a place of his own. Out of the wynds.

'Every week. Ye come tae us. Give us half. Ye don't cheat or I'll rip your guts like a pig's bladder. Ye get paid. Ye give us half. For safeguard. That's fair, eh?'

Niven's gang operated a system where they 'protected' the denizens of Vinegar Close and their surrounding area from a violence that the keelies themselves would mostly inflict and generate, though there were other invaders that might seek to intrude.

Other gangs.

It is a mark of humanity that no one seems to be able to remain where deposited. As a dog will mark out its territory with copious urine, so they cross invisible lines of conflict and then kick hell out of one another. Nations, tribes, Napoleon, Alexander the Great, or even a bunch of keelies in the wynds of Leith.

'Fair. Aye, dead fair,' came the gormless answer.

Niven looked narrowly at Plookie Galbraith. It was hard to believe that the boy was so glaikit a specimen as presented – otherwise how come he had lived this long?

Last night Niven had watched a man die. A single strike. A secret kept. No one knew but him. Something that would give him a name amongst them all was on the approach, but you cannot neglect day-to-day proceedings.

'Don't mark him, eh?' he asked.

Bob nodded solemnly in response.

'Whit about this?'

Niven jabbed the heft of the hook-knife sharply into Plookie's midriff to double him over at the sudden pain.

While Bob laughed, Niven bent his face close again.

'I'm watching you, Plookie. One mistake. That's all I need.'

Wide-eyed fear. Don't wet yourself. Only the one pair of trews for all weathers.

'And one day I'll be calling you for a deed tae perform wi' Jean Brash. One day.'

The boy nodded. Mouth agape. Slaver if it helps.

Then Niven strutted off followed by Bob while the other straightened up slowly and tried to stop any sudden tears forming in the eyes.

All his life Plookie had been battered by people like Niven. His gangling frame had no strength and no violence of intent. All his life.

And now he had a chance with Jean Brash. He had not long ago stood out in the pouring rain for her to spot out a pair of killers she had in mind to track down, and the woman never forgot a favour. That's what she had said anyhow.

Plookie had been summoned to the Just Land; auld Hannah Semple had glowered at him and Angus the giant coachman had shaken his head. But Angus was from Aberdeen; they were a miserable collection up there.

And Jean was unmoved. She had been working in the garden and was wearing an old coat that somehow managed to look graceful on her body. Or rather, as happens with beauty, she loaned out grace and the coat was indebted.

'He will help round the place and especially with the horses,' said she to Angus. 'He likes animals.'

A whimper from below brought Plookie out of his thoughts. The dog had returned and rubbed itself as if in apology against his thin ankles.

Plookie bent down and lifted the animal up to lie against the side of his neck and nuzzle in for comfort.

Raggie Biscuit. A good pal. Mongrel tae the bone.

While the dog shivered gratefully, Plookie's fingers threaded round its collar, a rough piece of cloth that he had fashioned himself. As long as that held, all was safe. He had put a wee bit of paper with the dog's name inside and, greatly daring, had added the rider, *belongs tae the Just Land.*

For the first time in their lives, he and his pal had a chance. But he would have to find a way through the mess. He couldnae tell Jean Brash about the pain in his gut, about this persecution of the innocent – she would think him weak – not to be trusted wi' the horses.

What did Niven mean, *a deed tae perform*? That did not sound right. Not right at all.

And how could Plookie find a way?

A church clock struck the half-hour and he tumbled the dog to the ground where it growled happily enough.

Time to go. They would pass a big bake-hoose where the foreman Tam Duncan aye gave Plookie a poke of raggie crumbled biscuits for the dog.

How it got the name.

'Come on, wee man,' said the boy, clenching his hand into a fist of sorts. 'We have work to do.'

Chapter 4

When the mind's free,
The body's delicate

There were moments when the Just Land gave birth to a curious innocence. Jean looked at the girls as they squabbled over the morning laundry of a bawdy-hoose and felt like a somewhat compromised mother hen.

The flock comprised eight working magpies plus big Annie Drummond who added weight as a peacemaker when Hannah came down too hard. Besides an ability to conjure a sentimental tune from the piano of an evening to the newly replete or yet ravenous clientele, Annie could also, like the best magician, make six cream buns disappear in a blinding flash.

Companions to the magpies but birds of a different feather were Lily Baxter and Maisie Powers, who plied their trade in the cellar depths, dishing out a variety of well-merited physical flagellation on the bare behinds belonging to various captains of industry. The two were prepared to lower their standards and insert the odd high court judge, surgeon or landed gentry, but for the most part preferred the exploiters of human labour as a target for painful remonstrance. Since God in his infinite wisdom allowed these capital fellows to wax and prosper, it seemed only right, to Maisie, that she redeem their wicked ways by, at times, prostrating them far from gently across the Berkley Horse, and then leathering hell out of them.

Upon request, of course.

Who knows why these fine and decent lords and masters wished to be punished – they led an exemplary life and other than a slight tendency to lay up treasures upon earth rather than heaven, were model citizens admired beyond measure by their impoverished workforce – yet for some reason they found the action of yoking pain to pleasure well nigh irresistible.

So they suffered and rejoiced. Shrived in blissful agony. Worth every penny.

And paid on completion to Mistress Brash. The horse, being a contraption of cuffs and wooden struts to hold the body in place, did not need payment or feeding.

Maisie was a sturdy, well-built harbinger of such ministrations, while her companion-in-arms, Lily, was a bundle of good-natured energy. Deaf and dumb from the womb, a grin never far from her face, she tiptoed through depravity as a child playing hopscotch – and every night entwined her pocket Venus of a body around Maisie before they drifted off to a well-earned respite.

Sister of Mercy.

This morning, in common with all the other girls, they were flapping the damp sheets at one another before pegging them out on the line.

It was Jean's decree that no matter how wild the night before, after a strong breakfast round the big table in the kitchen where gossip mingled with the porridge, the girls decamped to the wash-ing house where, fluttering fingers or not, the previously washed bed linen was put through a wringer the squeezing rollers of which at times put a thoughtful gleam in Lily's eyes, and then, weather permitting, hung out on the rope to dry. This was the signal for all kinds of mischief but under Hannah's stern eye, wherever a clod of muddy grass cuttings was thrown it had best never land on the sheets.

A practical side to all this: it was a chance for both Jean and Hannah to observe the morale of the troops, for, like it or not, they were an army of sorts, or perhaps more accurately, a family.

Each magpie was examined by the doctor every month and the clients were sheathed up like an Egyptian Mummy when the vital moment reared its head.

Plus the fact that no matter the shenanigans, one hint of violence from the client towards a girl and he was out on his ear, courtesy of an elegant escort from Jean, a twitch of the razor from Hannah or a boot in the behind from Angus should the fellow not take a hint.

Better pastoral care could not have been taken of these young women were they novices in a convent.

Yet it was a dangerous life, as Jean well knew from her own bitter past. She had witnessed violent and abusive acts with lethal results as she rose through the ranks of the frail sisterhood. One face in particular haunted her: a wee Inverness lassie, her face cut to ribbons by a jealous rival. She herself had been a young magpie then and had thrown her body over to protect the victim, but it was too late. This was not a Sunday school.

And so as their laughter rose to the sky along with the crows, the girls were keenly scrutinised for any tensions without or within.

The Dalrymple twins were, as usual, peas in a pod. An odd symbiotic pair that truly seemed to be the one person split in twain. They finished each other's sentences and men without turning a hair.

'Nettie Dunn is pittin' on the beef,' Hannah muttered aside to Jean. 'Eats like a horse.'

'Takes all sorts,' replied her mistress sagely. 'What was it that Dumfries farmer used to say?'

'Ye want a cratur ye can find in the dark,' recited Hannah.

While Jean smiled at the idea, the aforesaid Nettie turned with a face full of cheek to demand, 'Mistress, when are we getting our pictures painted?'

'Ye'll get damn all paintit except your impudent neb,' Hannah retorted. 'Get back tae work!'

The girls giggled and did so but Nettie had raised a sore point. Against the old woman's strenuous advice and warnings of doom, Jean had agreed to let a female painter shortly enter the hallowed portals and depict the magpies in portraiture.

Sketches and more detailed drawings, not obviously of the girls in full flow but on the wing as it were. Resting after honest toil or preparing to later engage in same. There would be, however, no trace of a patriarchal hand. Or face. Not that the clientele would welcome that event.

Seeing their lustful faces framed in a gallery might not add much to familial or conjugal bliss should the good wife be on hand.

The fact that the painter in question was daughter to a man of the cloth cut no ice with Hannah. Was the woman, Sarah Baines, though teaching art at a fine girls school in St Andrews, not of a Sapphic mode?

At least the Mistress had described her so; Hannah had quite a few other words that came to mind.

And was she not also cheek by jowl with the headmistress of that same school, one of those women who were aye bursting to get equal rights for their sex?

As far as the old woman was concerned, if that's what they wanted, they could damned well work for it the same way she did. Ye get nothing for nothing.

But Jean was intrigued by artistic notions and furthermore, on the nothing-for-nothing principle, had been promised by Sarah that a certain bawdy-hoose keeper might likewise be immortalised, and if the drawing proved true then further emblazoned in oil. Full length, of course, fully dressed, and dignified as hell. A lady of fashion. Mistress of all she surveyed.

And was she not embroiled deeply in the arts already as regards a rough-hewn sculptor, Jack Burns, who was forever trying to persuade her to model as a naked goddess? He had seen then worshipped at the unclothed human version and therefore proposed a deification of sorts.

For some reason being chipped at in effigy by a stone chisel in a draughty studio where the only warm place was a small coal fire if you discounted Jack's narrow wee palliasse on the floor and even then you needed two bodies at full tilt, did not inspire a similar inclination in Jean.

So she kept art at arm's length and the warm circulation of Mister Burns close to hand. Allowed him to visit her private room in the Just Land at times yet only for a candlelit meal and he never stayed the night.

Her bed was her own nest. The odd newborn baby might drop in now and again but that was in dreamland.

At arm's length is aye the best, let folk too near and they'll tear you limb from limb.

Though art was an insidious wee devil and there was something else in which she had recently invested so this afternoon she might take Mister Burns on a little trip.

The city of Edinburgh itself was going to celebrate this spring by a festival of sorts where many cultural recitals would be enacted with the mooted high spot a gala performance of *King Lear* – 'buggerlugs', as Hannah pronounced when Jean described the rough plot of the play to her. 'The man's an eejit.'

The notion of hard-earned bawdy-hoose money going anywhere near arty-crafty pursuits would have given the old woman a fit of the sulphur jaundies, so Jean had kept this secret for the moment though later on this day she might slip away to see the investment for herself. Hannah notwithstanding.

Yet despite any such caveats, trade was good, culture in the air, the birds were on the wing and surely nothing could go wrong?

Except that Jean had heard rumours from her people on the street that there was trouble, bad trouble, mooted between the keelie gangs and possibly something planned in Leith that had little to do with art.

That would be a criminal act. A criminal act would involve James McLevy – on the side of justice.

And somehow her name had become involved, even though she had made it her business to carefully separate herself from a previous life outside the law.

This included, if you were to believe vile rumour, fire raising, insurance swindles, pocket-delving of respectable citizens, justifiable blackmail and, to top the bill, arsenic poisoning of a certain violent procurer, evil swine, and business partner, by the name of one Henry Preger.

A malevolent bastard who deserved to die, yet surely not by the fair hand of Mistress Brash?

But that was long ago, this was now.

Her visitor of last night would have wished to involve Jean in a felony of some proportion but she had hushed him there and then with the following advice.

'Don't even tell her. Don't even begin. Leave it lay. Drink your champagne. You look handsome as a prince, Erik my bonny fellow – stay that way and get back on the boat.'

Hannah heard the same rumours as Jean and had carefully sharpened the edge of her cut-throat razor.

While Maisie Powers, despite her usual rough housing with Lily, had a deep worry nagging about her wee brother Richie who had an easy smile but wicked ways. He was going to the devil – a process easy to begin and hard to stop for the small of stature – and hanging out with some nefarious keelies.

April is a dangerous period – things that have been dormant for a length of time start poking up. A sudden outcry from the girls signalled that they had spotted the tall figure of Plookie Galbraith trying to sneak in by unlocking a side gate near the stables. They enjoyed the boy's red-faced confusion but there was no malice in the teasing and Jean waved him onwards.

'Angus is waiting,' she called, voice cutting through the crisp, sheet-drying air. 'And so are the cuddies. Clean out that stable.'

'And ye're late!'

The boy waved awkwardly to acknowledge Hannah's admonishment and shot off out of sight, followed by his wee scabby mutt of a dog.

'Wha was it in the Bible, had a' they plagues. Boils and god knows all whit kind o' suffering?' asked the old woman out of the blue.

'Job, I think,' answered Jean. 'Why?'

'That laddie reminds me o' such a person.'

A somewhat sweeping statement and had Hannah known the good book more intimately, she may have been assured that Job was eventually rewarded by the Almighty.

Mind you, that was after going through eternities of pain and tribulation.

And the Bible has its moments of inaccuracy.

Chapter 5

Things that love night
Love not such nights as these

Edinburgh, February 1844

In her bedroom, she bent over the basin and tried to contain the bile that was forming in her throat. A young woman attempting to be brave in spite of the nagging fear that twisted in her heart.

Outside there was a storm, rain battering on the windows like a bad conscience.

He had told her it would be safe. He was older, wiser, she was not to worry but he was from a lower class, an employee. If her mother and especially her father knew what had been perpetrated by his trusted helper? But she loved him. Or did she? She had to love him.

And Dermot had told her that the stars shone out of her eyes, the Irish charm of him. Though what would he say when she confessed that love just brought up your breakfast and was now staking a claim to supper as well?

It might merely be a sickness, an ague, something she had eaten, but this had lasted too long. Each morning, a disgorged meal. Thank god she had a family reputation as a small eater. For a moment her lips twisted in humour at this idea but then the bile rose again.

Of late, such sick disappeared down the privy but this occasion, due to the unwelcome time of night, the upstairs was occupied. Her

*father Thomas took an inordinately long time to have a bowel move-
ment and the girl was afraid if she went downstairs she might inad-
vertently vomit before gaining sanctuary. Like the cat being sick. But
cats made a low growling noise; she just covered her mouth like a
proper lady.*

*And the housekeeper Margaret had been eyeing her with some
suspicion. The old woman had a nose for any kind of scandal and
regarded herself as a cut above the serving classes though the girl could
sometimes smell a trace of cheap whisky on the breath.*

Everyone in this house had a secret.

*The girl retched quietly and mopped her face with a cloth that she
would have to smuggle out and jettison into the bushes when she took
a healthful walk in one of the parks. Every inch the young lady. But
what to do with the contents of the bowl?*

*The door opened out of the blue without so much as a knock and
Margaret was standing there. For a moment there was a chill silence
while the storm howled like a soul in agony outside. It was February,
a grim wrenching time of the year when spring seemed a promise not
to be kept, darkness lay over the city like a funeral pall and stray
lights from the street lampposts provided insufficient relief as slates
whirled off a neighbouring rooftop to crash in pieces on the cobblestones below.*

Of course her family roof was safe and solid.

Storm proof.

*Finally the old woman spoke. 'Are you over, Miss Jennet?' Jennet
was a pet name she had used all these years when addressing her wee
charge, who was now a young woman with a lifelong quandary.*

*The girl nodded. She could not meet the other's eye as the old serv-
ant passed by her, picked up the heavy basin, draped a napkin from
the sideboard over the guilty contents and walked back to the door.*

There she turned, the affected tones at odds with such brutal truth delivered.

'You should have never let him near. A serving employee. A hireling. Not even a white collar, Miss Jennet. Irish to boot.'

With that remonstration she was gone. Leaving the girl to look at her image in the mirror, above where the basin had been set.

For the young lady's toilette. So that she might form herself into an acceptable young female adjunct to the family of Thomas Shields, bookbinder.

So Margaret knew. One servant knew, and the other who visited the house to pledge his time and allegiance to her father was most definitely aware that rules as well as hymens had been broken.

To what consequence? All her life she had fought against these rules but had never found support, only stony faces. Until Dermot. Until the day he had laid his hand upon her back. Lightly. So lightly, you could scarce believe the touch.

And that touch bred others. At first in the home here and then in his lodging room with the sounds of squalling children piercing through the thin walls. When she should have been walking in the park.

Their laughter together had conquered all. But laughter fades like the morning dew.

Her dark auburn hair was sweaty, a fleck of the sick even stuck to a tendril, the light sage-coloured eyes set wide apart and staring into the glass.

Her father had a book – the poetry and songs of Robert Burns – a gift from an employer of his craft. As a child she had been forbidden to see inside that volume lest the sentiments within corrupt, and of course it drew her like a magnet. One poem that caught her eye, a hurried eye in case she was discovered, 'Aye Fond Kiss'.

Had we never lov'd sae kindly,
Had we never lov'd sae blindly,
Never met or never parted,
We had ne'er been broken-hearted.

A violent gust of wind rattled the window. She looked out into the black nightscape and could see the spinning lights on the masts of the ships as they whipped perilously through the angry distant ocean.

At the mercy of something beyond their control.

Chapter 6

Allow not nature more than nature needs,
Man's life's as cheap as beast's

Leith, April 1883

A small crab scuttled along the shingle as the spray rose from an angry departing tide bullied by a hidden moon in the morning sky that tugged it about as a child would some loving mother fast running out of patience.

The crab came up against an ashen lifeless hand where it lay at the end of an outstretched arm, the fingers bleached with salt water, invading the whole body through pores that were still open for business.

The flesh was soft. It would deteriorate as all things do when left to linger by an absence of life.

While the crustacean poked out a claw to establish possible avenues of edibility, a slack mound below the bent thumb in the palm of the hand offering a starter of sorts, this contemplation was broken by footsteps on the shale crunching towards the inert repast.

Off went a disappointed segment of marine life and upon the scene came Inspector James McLevy and Constable Martin Mulholland.

The wind whipped in off the sea to hit them both amidships

but caused no resulting lack of balance. Neither did it shift the corpse.

The policemen made an odd pair. One – the inspector – might have been mistaken for a grizzled merman though instead of a crown of tangled seaweed he sported a low-brimmed bowler and in place of pronged trident an old service revolver tucked away in a reinforced inside pocket. The eyes were slate-grey and deep set, countenance parchment white and the whole assembly not unlike a Roman ruin that still held a few historically valid nooks and crannies. His body was square, solid, with surprisingly dainty hands and feet; however, there was an indefinable sense of barely contained violence always ready to erupt.

As far as the criminal fraternity of Leith were concerned, this incipient ferocity was only too often defined especially when backed up by the second arrival. Mulholland was more akin to a lighthouse than a mythical sea-creature. He did not so much tower over folk as loom. His face was open and candid as a farm-boy's, with clear blue eyes, and the guileless whole might lull the witless into thinking him an easy mark. That would have been an error of judgement. Unlike the inspector, he had little fat to spare, body lean as a greyhound, and his chosen weapon was a self-fash-ioned hickory stick that came down like the Hand of God, though it was rarely followed by exaltation, more often a sojourn in Leith Station's flea-ridden cells.

At this moment, however, neither man had need of physical exertion. A dead body may cause mayhem in the future but at the present it just lay there – an empty mussel shell.

Silence. The wind whipping, a distant seagull shrieking out a warning that justice was in the vicinity.

Mulholland finally spoke, a soft Irish lilt that cut against the terse reported circumstance.

'An old fellow on the shore found him – well, to be truthful, the dog did. Chasing a ball.'

'Whit kind of ball?'

'Golf. The old fellow had a mashie niblick. He hit the ball, the dog chased it.'

'Whit kind of dog?'

'West Highland terrier.'

'Small, then?'

'That's established.'

McLevy grunted. This was supposed to be his day off; he had stayed up the night before drinking bad coffee and poring over some forensic papers, then on a whim popping over to peruse Edgar Allen Poe's *A Descent into the Maelstrom* before falling into an uneasy sleep peopled with maritime wraiths being sucked into the gaping maw of a big monster with bloodshot eyes. That the monster bore a passing resemblance to his own Lieutenant Roach did not, even in the wildness of the dream, escape the inspector's notice.

He had been awakened by Mulholland calling up early doors to his attic window and, in consequence, looked like an unmade bed. Yet it was his own fault – McLevy had aye insisted if a dead body with mysterious intimations was found in his parish, then he was to be informed.

Night or day. This was the day section.

'Where's the man with the dog?'

'At the station. Out of the cold. Where he came in to report the finding of a cadaver.'

'Does he look like a slaughter merchant?'

'Not remotely.'

'That's a pity.'

The reason for this line of questioning was only too clear for such dyed-in-the-wool observers of inflicted death. The man's saturated coat gaped open and the pale white shirt was ripped and torn apart where an implement of some sort had been stuck into his body, just below the ribcage, then ripped upwards. It had been pulled out further on the journey up and, from the looks of it, kept a large portion of various organs for company, some oddments of which undoubtedly belonged to the heart.

Losing the heart in romantic novels often causes pain and tribulation but, in this case, the process may have gone a little too far.

Romeo eviscerated.

They both knelt down to investigate further while seagulls shrieked and the departing tide paid no heed. Gentle probing of the pockets of the clothing yielded nothing at all – empty as the grave – there were no rings on the dead fingers, no watch, no chain, no pocket book, nothing that might provide identity. It would seem the corpse had desired to keep his secrets.

'A bad wound,' said Mulholland solemnly. 'Surely you don't need to cause all that mess just to kill a man?'

'Some folk just like tae make a guddle.'

With that summation, McLevy leant back and scrutinised the face of the corpse. A tidy well-kept countenance despite the buffeting no doubt received, for the sea has little mercy. The hair silver, neatly parted, eyes a washed-out pale blue, and the open mouth disclosing teeth that certainly put the inspector's own to shame, which resembled tombstones in an abandoned graveyard.

McLevy lifted up the flaccid hand and weighed it as a pawnbroker would an item on the counter.

'How long d'ye think him to be swimming wi' the herring shoals?'

'Not too much damage. From last night, maybe?'

'Maybe.'

McLevy peeled back the sleeves. No marks on the wrists and he'd wager the same for the ankles.

'No attempt to load the body down, no rope marks, nothing to send it tae the bottom feeders.'

'The killing may have been done in a hurry,' ventured Mulholland.

'Or the killer didnae care. *Gloried* in it.'

It always worried Mulholland when the inspector went off into one of his *dwams* – eyes half shut in a reverie, with the killer, as if McLevy was somehow tuning into a murderous mind. What caused the constable a measure of disquiet was the idea that one day McLevy might not tune out again.

'Whit if this was – some kind of – challenge?'

'Challenge?'

'Uhuh. As to say, see what I've done – put that in your pipe and smoke it.'

'I don't see how you get to this conclusion.'

McLevy flipped the coat aside to display what his sharp eyes had noted earlier: a large smear on the inside of the lining that had survived the soaking.

'Whit d'ye make of that?'

McLevy's eyes were open and innocent and such warned Mulholland that he had best beware, there was nothing the inspector liked better than to lead his subordinate down the path of misconceived conclusions.

The smear was on the opposite side to the wound and – wait – the shape of it told a tale.

'It looks like – you would say it was a blade of sorts must have hacked that damage. Sharp edge. That mark has a clean edge.'

In fact now that Mulholland remembered, as McLevy undoubtedly had already done so, some three years ago in an axe murder case a similar incident had occurred.

'As if the weapon had been wiped upon it,' the constable pronounced.

'Uhuh. Took you long enough. Ergo?'

Mulholland uncoiled to full height and adjusted a police helmet which on top of his caped figure looked, as his superior had told him many times, like a pea on top of Ben Nevis – but the motion gave him time to think.

'A man cool enough to swab clean a murder implement, if he wanted to get rid of a body, would have done so.'

The inspector straightened up also, a thick heavy overcoat wrapped round him like a bearskin.

'Exactly. He believes himself out of reach. Too clever by half. Arrogance can be a weak spot. I should know.'

He suddenly let out a great howl of laughter to send seabirds and shore life scuttling.

Mulholland did not bat an eye. It was a long shot to assume such a conclusion but experience over many years of murder and mayhem had taught him that McLevy's long shots were sometimes worth a wager. And to tell truth, life had been a touch dull recently, thus here was spring providing them both with a new-laid murder.

There was further commotion as a heavy carriage slowly lumbered across the shingle drawn by a couple of unenthusiastic but hefty horses.

'Here comes the carry wagon,' observed the constable. 'We can get this fellow back to the station cold room and examine at leisure.'

'Aye,' replied the inspector. 'The police surgeon may break the habit of a miserable life and discover a wee thing useful.'

Yet still McLevy would not budge.

'Whit do you think tae the clothing?'

'Well enough tailored. Let's hope there's some labels.'

'They have a foreign cut. The clothes.'

Mulholland blinked.

'I didn't know you to be a sartorial expert, sir.'

The inspector ignored this slight upon his own mode of dress, where garments often seemed to have been flung willy-nilly at the presented body. He peered down once more at the white face. Despite saturation, the features were sharp and pointed, well groomed, even handsome.

'Foreign,' he said. 'It is my belief this man is foreign.'

'How do you get to that?'

'Instinct.'

The inspector swallowed hard and his face registered discomfort and longing. 'I could use a cup of decent coffee.'

'The only place to provide such is Jean Brash. You're forever saying she makes the best in Edinburgh.'

'This is a murder case, Mulholland,' the inspector retorted sternly. 'Coffee can wait!'

With that contradictory statement he turned abruptly and left the scene, to be followed by the loping figure of Mulholland.

The two young policemen on the carry wagon were waved towards the victim and nature would then be left undisturbed by the machinations of men, until the next time.

Yet had the corpse been able to voice agreement, he would have indeed confirmed that McLevy was correct. He was indeed from another land and last night had encountered two people. One he had charmed in vain, the other he had not charmed at all.

That particular failure had killed him.

Chapter 7

The art of our necessities is strange

The theatre troupe of Alfred Tyrone, alias King Lear, had in truth performed in and been confronted by many outlandish venues. They lived by the skin of their teeth and the show presented to the world at large, that of a successful travelling company, was at least as good if not better than the production of the play itself.

Somehow Alfred managed to scrape up the money from various penny-pinching deals with venial promoters to pay his charges a pittance of sorts and in every city find them a cheap lodging house while he, it must be said, resided in better class hotels with his sister Bridget, who flatly refused to lower her high standards.

By hook or by crook, all managed to exist and even have a reputation for theatrical quality, but it was a thin covering, like a bat's wing.

Yet for Emilia Fleming there was a wild excitement in this life – she revelled in the uncertainty – and her sojourns with Billy Musgrave in the lower depths of a town or city had their own dark deep pleasures.

The deeper she plunged, the better delight.

They had performed in dank spaces that were once thriving havens of culture but the legitimate stage was fast losing ground in face of opposition from the 'free and easies' – the 'music halls', the 'harmony rooms' – all of which had sprouted up in the back rooms of the taverns and public houses and as a result the groundlings no longer came to fill the theatres. It cost too damned much and they could get better entertainment for the price and swallow of a beer.

Is it a mark of civilisation that the heights of artistic endeavour must involve an equally high admission fee? Or is someone just coining it in?

These niceties aside, the company – consisting of the three women and two older actors who had to portray all the other male parts in the play – were, contrary to the craft, lost for words when they happened upon their latest venue, Billy Musgrave leading the way. Alfred had supplied Billy with the whereabouts, already gone on ahead and left them all to follow on once they had dumped baggage at the lodging house or, in Bridget's case, at the Royal Hotel Princes Street.

This they had accomplished. And here they were.

In front of a tent.

A large tent it must be admitted but pitched at a flat expanse of scrubby green grass on Leith Links, with a cold unforgiving east wind whipping across from the not too distant sea, carrying also a faint rotting odour from the nearby slaughterhouse in Salamander Street.

The wind strained against the surface of the tent as if demanding entry as Billy pulled a door-shaped section of canvas towards him and ushered them through.

Inside was a hive of activity, with Alfred's voice ringing out over the hubbub. He was standing on what might have been a stage, or at least one in the process of construction if you squinted hard enough, and declaiming an excerpt from the storm scene of the play.

> Blow, winds, and crack your cheeks! rage! blow!
> You cataracts and hurricanoes, spout,
> Till you have drench'd our steeples, drown'd the cocks!

The workmen, hammering, nailing, clattering iron against wood, paid not a blind bit of notice but in answer, another voice, a high-pitched piping effort, sounded refrain from a far point of the enclosure.

'I hear every word, sir. Clear as a bell!'

A small, slightly effeminate man darted forward from the shadows and clapped hands together enthusiastically. He was then introduced by a lordly Alfred to the company as Kenneth Powrie, a theatrical impresario who had his roots and office in Edinburgh and, as part of the city's brandishing the masks of tragic and comedic arts in their springtime festival, was about to unleash this stellar production; not quite in the open air, for that would be foolish in the biting aforesaid wind, yet in a hitherto unprecedented fashion.

They would set the city ablaze with admiration and the crowds would flock in like new-born lambs.

Previous blazes when three main Edinburgh theatres had been burnt to the ground by fire during the last five years, hopefully not an act of God from a disgruntled deity at the quality on offer, had to a certain extent dictated this groundbreaking venture.

Kenneth was a tiny elfin creature who seemed to bubble with energy and charm but behind that was a shrewd and capricious personality though not necessarily a trustworthy one. Not exactly a liar but perhaps a man who might entertain many versions of the truth.

A Sagittarian by birth star.

Yet he had a winning smile, wavy brown hair, eyes twinkling with what seemed like genuine enthusiasm as he kissed the ladies' hands, exchanged a manly grip with both older actors, waved an egalitarian gesture towards Billy and led them all to where Alfred's proud figure had taken stance exactly centre front of the newly erected stage.

'Where are our changing rooms?' Bridget asked her brother.

'They are – in construction.'

To augment this answer, further hammering came from behind a hastily erected white sheet that obscured some other workmen who were putting various wooden partitions upright at the very back of the tent.

'By tomorrow,' interposed Kenneth, 'you will not recognise this setting. It will be – transformed!'

They looked around. The workmen were in the process of laying down the planking that would form a rough floor but for the moment the place resembled an empty barn.

'The seating will arrive tomorrow,' Kenneth announced. 'Fit for a king!'

Bridget sniffed and the two older actors John Wilde and Barnaby Bunthorne looked down at their feet as if the woodchips below might suddenly burst into flame. Yet to give them credit, neither was alarmed or surprised.

Amongst his many parts, Barnaby played the Fool to Lear and John had his eyes put out on a nightly basis as Gloucester; they had both been through the mill and still survived to tell the tale.

Melissa yawned as if she'd seen it all before but was aware of covert appraisal from a few workmen. She stretched her shapely arms in the air and announced that she was hungry. A girl needs sustenance.

Where lay the little slut? she wondered for Emilia was nowhere to be seen. Then a figure appeared beside Alfred and also declaimed above the racket.

> Good my Lord,
> You have begot me, bred me, lov'd me; I
> Return those duties back as are right fit,
> Obey you, love you, and most honour you.

Kenneth let out a little chirruping sound of approval as Alfred smiled indulgently but there was a seductive edge to this delivery from the erstwhile Cordelia that the Bard may not have necessarily intended.

The clamour stilled a little as the workmen took note of this bold hussy who had clambered up at the back of the stage and relished attention garnered from the watchers. A study not lacking lustful elements.

Emilia, who had loosed the straps of her bonnet and shaken her head to unleash the rich mane of hair, stamped her foot on the bare boards as she assumed the third position of speech delivery, taking a deep breath that emphasised a generous bosom in the petite figure. There was something about the impudence of Emilia's stance that provoked a desire to squeeze the breath out of her, see if those gypsy eyes might tighten in surprise at the strength of an embrace.

Kenneth smiled admiringly but a thought was running through his head that if you dressed the girl according to taste, she might well bring in the crowds. There was a certain sensual quality to her that attracted the eye – and where rests the eye, so desire follows; and where desire lays its head, there's money to be made. Thus art and commerce shake each other by the hand, with a little carnality to season the exchange.

Alfred, whose libido was mostly concerned with a reflection in the glass, nodded gravely at his pupil and then raised arms up into the air as if receiving the acclaim of an unseen audience.

Billy Musgrave grinned at the faces on the workmen as they fidgeted and scuffed around. What they imagined, he had already accomplished.

Of the two older actors, one cared only for the bottle and the other preferred alternative avenues.

And on the distaff side?

Bridget sniffed, a hiss escaped the lips of Melissa that might have put an onlooker in mind of Cleopatra's asp, and in the crevices of the grass a female cockroach paid no heed to such antipathy while carrying her eggs low to the abdomen as she scuttled to avoid the planking being laid above.

And then an event happened that changed the game.

The flap of the tent was thrust aside by a strong manly hand that might possibly have known acquaintance with the odd cold chisel, and a woman entered.

Odd shafts of sunshine were coming through the various gaps in the tenting and one, as if ordained, lit the figure like a well-aimed spotlight.

Her outdoor coat was lavender-blue, a bonnet in the French

style perched upon the shimmering red hair, and she looked every inch the Queen of Leith.

'Mistress Brash – Jean Brash, as I live and breathe!'

Kenneth gave a little hop of delight in the air, and the cockroach made good her escape.

Chapter 8

Time shall unfold what plighted cunning hides

As they approached the tent, Jean had been struck by a curious feeling of anxiety.

To avoid what would no doubt have been an indignant outburst from Hannah Semple, she had manufactured an errand of sorts but was conscious at the same time of a depth of annoyance with herself. Why should it matter if she hazarded some paltry funds to support the bedraggled arts?

Where was the harm?

Yet she knew the old woman would see more than that – to a distance beyond these questionable assertions.

'Ye're a bawdy-hoose keeper, always will be; never more, never less.'

Was that Hannah's voice in her head or more likely her own pronouncement?

Although Jean attended many of the societal soirees of Edinburgh city and could mix with the best of them, pinkie crooked as she sipped the hellish coffee, there was always this feeling of withheld judgement.

Unspoken but like a vein of prejudice running through the surrounding atmosphere. And what she found so hard to bear in herself was the need to 'belong', to be accepted by folk that she for the most part detested.

Do we not, all of us, feel this pendulum of need and resentment, as if what we are by nature is never enough?

The other source of unease for Mistress Brash was the man walking beside her. Jack Burns was younger by some years, a sculptor by profession, and affected a somewhat bohemian style of dress. Of late he had adopted the wearing of a battered straw hat, which might well have suited Vincent van Gogh in the fields of Provence but positioned itself strangely on the streets of Leith.

He was also Jean's lover, not particularly skilful but possessed of an ardent stamina though she sometimes had to educate him in the nuances between flesh and stone. He was intelligent, a talented artist, and provided he lay supine and she took the high road, there was always hope of improvement though she had noticed of late that he was prone to take credit when she let loose a yell of scalding release.

It is ever a delusion of men to consider their appendage the Mons Meg of deep desire.

This was the first time Jean had allowed them to be seen together in the public eye. If you can call picking him up in her closed carriage and rattling through the streets to Leith Links a flamboyant display.

Why had she brought him? Moral support, or just someone to hang on to in the slippery grass?

If he was aware of her discomfort, it showed not a whit as he marched along, a handsome brute, half a head taller than her own decent height, a man among men.

He grinned at her, opened the tent flap, and in she went. Ready or not, here I come.

Inside was another world.

Jean felt herself a character in a play that had entered a madhouse. Bits of rope hung from above, workmen stood and gawped at her like waxworks, a tall man on what looked to be a stage had flung his arms aloft and was frozen as if in a tableau while behind him there was a motion as if another body had just hurtled from the arena.

It seemed a moment petrified in time with a haunting feeling of menace, as if something had been disturbed and was looking for blood.

Then Kenneth Powrie called out her name and a kind of normality reinstated itself.

The men went back to work, Kenneth darted forward to kiss her gloved hand with a flourish, nod affably to Jack who tipped his straw hat, and then she was introduced to the company as an angel who had flown in from heaven to provide financial succour for this looming tragedy.

While Jean smiled and nodded as if she were minor royalty, part of her, just as she would in the Just Land, was appraising the faces before her. In her own domain she could calculate the contents of a client's pocket book with one swift glance; this was a more difficult task but far from full pockets have their own signature.

Kenneth of course she knew of old, his father had been a crafty old bugger of a lawyer and when he died, it had been revealed to his distressed widow that there was not a penny to be found in the house or anywhere else. All gone up in smoke at various gambling dens or – and this is where Jean came in – expensive bawdy-hooses.

The widow followed soon after into the vale of death, no doubt to track her husband down though his afterlife destination might differ to hers, and the son was left to scrape a living wherever possible. This involved various failed business ventures but somehow Kenneth always popped up like one of his father's discarded champagne corks. Such was his charm and *joie de vivre* that Jean inevitably found her own business acumen sidelined and ignored when invited to save an educated orphan from financial stormwinds.

This was his latest foray and, since it chimed with some desires of her own, the die was cast. She could at least hope to trust him not to swindle her as regards the money but if she broke even it would be a triumph. However, she would be there in all her glory on the first night and could thumb her nose at the Unco Guid who held their position in respectable society as unassailable as that of the Creator in heaven.

The two actresses were presented by Kenneth and as is the manner of women, all met but warily. As one cat will circle another to discover what might attract or repel so polite nods were exchanged and while they catalogued Jean, she returned the compliment.

Bridget reminded her of a disillusioned wife who waited only to find her husband's latest betrayal, and Miss Fortune put Jean to memory of a certain treacherous seductress who had plied her trade at the Just Land and stolen a priceless pearl necklace from her mistress.

Rachel Bryden was the harlot's name and she had ended up on a boat bound for South America and a rough harbour bordello in the city of Buenos Aires, accompanied by her equally vile lover Oliver Garvie, heading for the male equivalent – the pair had tried to make a fool out of Jean and suffered her reprisal. With a little help from James McLevy. And the moral of the tale? Never come between a woman and her pearls.

This actress had the same willowy body, evasive eyes and deceit-ful invitation as Rachel. Or was Jean letting an old remembrance colour her judgement?

Melissa's eyes had drifted past Jean to gauge the worth of Jack Burns, who stood a little way back, having been introduced to one and all. Jean sensed this but did not worry – was she not his goddess, after all?

'Mistress Brash,' a sonorous voice broke into her rumination. 'What an honour to find a patroness of such beauty and elegance. An honour indeed!'

Alfred Tyrone bowed his noble head earnestly over her hand and then straightened up to gaze soulfully into her eyes.

Jean's lips twitched in a returning smile. The man was an actor, every inch, and there was something about him that amused her greatly. Bombastic, egotistical but somehow – himself. As cock on top of the midden will crow as if upon a throne, so this man appreciated himself to high heaven.

In fact – even taking into account the two older specimens behind, one dissolute, the other like a worn-out peacock, and a younger man further away with a gold-toothed grin that was vaguely familiar – the whole company amused her.

Or rather – enlivened Jean.

As if somehow she found their existence, their mode of living outside society, had a resonance with her own.

Would that be the reason why she was so attracted? A bunch of vagabonds, only accepted at a distance? Whatever it was, she felt at home in this chaos, this subversion of normality.

'The honour is mine, Mister Tyrone,' she murmured in response. 'The public must be entertained.'

Not by a flicker in the hooded eyes did Alfred reveal what

Kenneth had informed him as regards Jean's particular branch of entertainment.

'I have lived my entire life by that very dictum, Mistress Brash, and I assure you that this will be an awe-inspiring spectacle of theatre!'

'Yet I would have expected a larger company,' said Jack out of the blue, a trace of mischief in his voice.

'We are astonishingly versatile, sir,' was Alfred's smooth response, echoed by Kenneth's 'Astonishingly so!'

Jean recognised a bluff, a nod and a wink of sorts from miles away but contented herself with a reply of, 'I am sure you will fulfil your obligations.'

However Jack was not finished, encouraged by a complicit smile of acknowledgement from Melissa.

'To my recollection, *King Lear* has three female characters, do you not agree, Mistress Brash?'

'That is correct, Mister Burns,' Jean answered, nettled that somehow her knowledge of the play was in question. 'Of the same family. Two evil, one not so.'

She shot him a look to signal that if he wanted to stay vertical, he was going the wrong way about it.

Alfred noticed the implied absence of a third female member for the first time.

'An accurate supposition, madam.'

He frowned, as if he had divided his kingdom in vain. 'Where is our Cordelia?'

'She was on the boards with you, brother,' said Bridget, a certain biting emphasis to her words. 'Sharing the limelight. Do you not remember?'

They all looked at the stage, which was empty and bare as the blasted heath itself.

Alfred ignored the sibling sarcasm and almost bawled out above the renewed clatter of the workers, 'Emilia, where art thou? Come forth if you please!'

For a moment nothing took place as if someone had missed their cue for entrance but then a small figure emerged from the far side of the platform and walked towards them.

Billy Musgrave grinned as she passed him by but Emilia did not seem to notice. Her awareness was fixed upon the visitors, face white and features not holding their usual challenge and sultry impudence.

Alfred gestured her to join the company.

'May I present,' he intoned as if a master of ceremonies, 'our latest and most welcome addition – Miss Emilia Fleming – a Cordelia par excellence!'

He extended a hand towards Jean Brash to indicate where Emilia should direct her humble attention.

Jean smiled.

Emilia lowered her eyes, and then the moment was broken by a dreadful scream of pain.

One of the young workmen, perhaps distracted by all the pulchritude on display, had misdirected a claw iron and instead of hauling up a bent nail, the claw had slipped and buried its sharp edge into the flesh of his hand. Surprise as much as pain had caused his cry but the blood spouted as if he had cut a vein. The boy held out his hand as if fascinated by the sight of his own gore and the red liquid streamed down his clothes and spattered over his workmates.

Alfred turned pale. He had been up to his elbows many's the time in stage blood but the real stuff was a different and nauseous matter.

Bridget was made of sterner stuff. She moved swiftly towards the suffering youth, ripped a piece from a concealing sheet that was hanging nearby and bound it tightly around the hand, wound it over between thumb and palm and then tied a tight knot to hold it in place. This seemed to do the trick; flesh not a vein had been severed, the blood flow diminished to a trickle and the young man mumbled his thanks.

Bridget turned back to her brother and said crisply, 'When – if I may ask – do we begin rehearsals?'

'The conditions are not ideal,' was the solemn response.

'The conditions are *never* ideal.'

The acrid tone produced a slight wince from Kenneth but Alfred had a pachydermal hide to insulate an artistic soul from a sister's barbs.

'Indeed!'

He raised his arm aloft as if desiring a benison from heaven and rallied the troops.

'Now – this very moment – the play's the thing!'

A quote from *Hamlet* not *Lear*, but any port in a storm, as he nodded majestically to Jean and then turned to lead his company towards the moribund stage.

As they straggled after him, Kenneth bringing up the rear like a sheepdog on the lookout for strays, Jack Burns tapped the straw hat a little down over his eyes and murmured, 'I think, Mistress Brash, it is time we quit the scene. We both have work on hand.'

Jack was going to have an exhibition of pieces at his studio as part of the artistic plethora and the Just Land was always open for business.

Yet Jean did not move for a moment. The uneasy feeling she

had experienced on the way here had returned and been deepened in some mysterious way.

The blood that marked her moment of meeting with Emilia Fleming had disturbed something in her psyche. Or was she getting too damn fanciful with all this arty-crafty nonsense, as Hannah Semple would no doubt say?

She nodded and led the way out with Jack, one glance spared towards the stage, following.

As the company clambered up, Melissa Fortune also sparing a glance to the side, Emilia was the last to take her place.

She wiped her lips with the back of a sleeve and looked down to where her nails had left deep indents in the palm of a hand.

But no one could know. No one could tell. She had spewed up into a corner and the emission was not copious. To flee the stage behind Alfred was, thank god, not difficult. He took up so much space.

And she had held on to her nerve, looking into that woman's eyes. The workman's blood had helped tremendously – it must be an omen of some kind. She almost laughed aloud at that idea but her insides were still knotted.

But Billy could sort that out – he would have her dancing on the head of a pin. They could corrupt each other till the cows came home and she always had her blessed pipe to numb the pain.

Her name was called from above, and Emilia joined the rest. All friends together. The play's the thing.

Although it does, even as far back to the Greeks, seem to produce one death after another.

Chapter 9

Lieutenant Robert Roach peered down at a naked forked carcass laid out on the cold slab and wondered, as he did now and then, if it might have perhaps been best had he remained in the undertaking business.

With a more respectable class of corpse.

His father had been a well-respected funeral director who laid out the dead with deference and decorum; many a grieving partner of many a departed soul had been comforted by the sight of their former household associate lying at peace, immaculate, with no suggestion towards the less attractive traits of character that had occasionally disfigured the living personality. Penny-pinching, crabbit disposition, belier of delights – such as the men thought of the women – and dull, dreich, weaselblown, torn-faced scunner – such as the women thought of the men.

It is one of the miracles of God that both such dissimilar specimens can exist together, like two shipwrecked sailors clinging to a spar of wood and who, even in that precarious position, manage to produce offspring that will, in time, find another ship that's heading for the rocks with appropriate companionship.

Roach's younger brother had taken up the burden of titivating the cadavers with a joviality that was never far from his nature and

Robert, to his parents' relief and bewilderment, had allied himself to the forces of law and order.

Why?

A mystery to him then that had continued to this very day. Perhaps it was his terror of things changing – for to the lieutenant the only accepted variation in circumstance was a misplaced drive on the golf course – and the law is a great preserver of the way things must always be.

Straight as a gallows rope.

All of that aside, here he was in the mortuary cold room of the Leith Police Station looking at a dead man who was by no means titivated, but in fact, resembling a badly ploughed field by dint of a lacerating gash that split his body all the way up on the left-hand side.

On the right-hand side of the remains stood the bane of Roach's life, one Inspector James McLevy, whose grumpy demeanour would not be improved by events that were yet to be revealed, and his looming fellow conspirator, for the two were as thick as thieves, Constable Mulholland.

Roach did not enjoy wrecked ribcages and sea-brined viscera. His wife, presently embroiled in the approaching festival of art, had recently dragged him to a gallery of religious painting where one, a grisly decollation of John the Baptist, had disturbed some previously digested breakfast kippers. This sight put him in a similar frame.

The lieutenant had a delicate alimentary system and age had not improved its sensitivity.

Age rarely improves anything save well hung steaks and good wine.

'Well well,' said Roach, stifling an inconvenient eructation. 'Man's inhumanity to man, eh?'

This quote from the Bard of Ayrshire elicited no response from the brooding McLevy.

'Mayhaps the police surgeon could shed some light, sir?' offered Mulholland.

'There's a big enough hole,' muttered McLevy. 'Even Doctor Jarvis couldnae miss it.'

Roach ignored the slight upon his surgeon. Though Jarvis annoyed him almost as much as he did McLevy, it would never do to let the inspector know that they might agree upon something.

'Identification?'

'Nothing on the body,' Mulholland replied, 'But—'

'Labels,' interjected the inspector.

'What?'

'On the clothing. In Dutch. It is a language with which I have some acquaintance.'

'How so?'

'The poisoned pig.'

Roach searched his memory, then remembered with a slight shudder the case of a man whose large behemoth of a pig had snouted up a neighbour's vegetable patch. In revenge, the neighbour poisoned the pig. In retaliation the man killed the neighbour and then sowed him up inside the hide of the pig, which he had skinned. A grisly affair, but what had it to do with the case?

'Neither of the combatants in that particular stramash were Dutch,' he remarked. 'Canongate and Leith Walk, as I recall.'

'I was talking about the pig.'

Roach stared at McLevy, whose face was stolid without a trace of irony or humour as he added, 'The pig came from Holland.'

In the silence there sounded a timid knock at the door of the room but no one paid it any heed.

'I assume that is your idea of humour, McLevy,' said Roach coldly. 'Now tell me, if you please, what is a man from Holland doing with his insides splashed out all over the parish of Leith?'

Then another thought struck him. 'And what in God's name has it to do with labels?'

'The clothes of the corpse had labels, sir,' the constable chipped in before the pair got going again. 'In a foreign language. Dutch, the Inspector tells me.'

'A ship from that country docked in the harbour yesterday,' McLevy appended to his constable's remark; the inspector's knowledge of shipping movement was not to be gainsaid, pigs or no pigs. 'We'll check it over in case the man might have been a passenger or even crew.'

Roach looked at the corpse again.

'The hands are not those of a tarry-breek.'

'Could be an officer. We'll find out.'

Again the knock, again McLevy did not move.

'Something on your mind, James?'

'I'm thinking,' said the inspector. 'That this is going to be a bloody business.'

'Speaking of which,' remarked Roach. 'The weapon?'

'Seems to have hooked up through the gut,' Mulholland observed cheerfully. 'A sharp blade for sure.'

'It's a rare wee strake right enough,' McLevy nodded. 'Never seen one such before.'

'You would think right-handed?' Mulholland surmised.

'*Uhuh*. From the angle, the killer below this man's height.'

'The corpse is above average. Five foot eight, maybe?'

'*Uhuh*. A deal of strength in that blow.'

McLevy suddenly jerked his hand up, aiming at Mulholland's midriff. The constable nodded judiciously.

They both then leant forward to look at the body again as if confirming their deductions, putting Roach in mind of another painting from that damned exhibition where a couple of medical men displayed a flayed dejected carcass to some watching students. What was the title? *Anatomy Lesson*. His wife had been enraptured. Unlike the kippers.

In the silence, a repeated knock at the door was more peremptory this time. Roach called permission to enter, and Constable Ballantyne popped his head in. The red birthmark down the side of his face was pulsing – evidence of excitement mounting in the breast.

'Inspector Dunsmore's in the station, sir, and he's got a great big smile on his face.'

McLevy's countenance showed the exact opposite.

'Dunsmore? Whit does that struntie want wi' us?'

'I forgot tae ask him,' replied Ballantyne who, at times, could resemble a simple soul.

'Go away, Ballantyne,' said Mulholland quietly.

'Aye. I'll tell him you're coming.'

'Sir!' commanded Roach sharply.

'Aye. Right. Sir.'

Ballantyne disappeared. Roach's long saurian face creased in a bleak smile; it was not often he had the edge on these two. Mind you, he wasn't any happier than they would be at the news to be broken, but orders were orders. A certain piquancy the edict had not allowed for was that McLevy and Dunsmore loathed the sight of each other.

Dunsmore hailed from Paisley and for some reason McLevy had a grudge against that city. The other reason was that Adam

Dunsmore had recently moved from Haymarket to the Edinburgh City Police, who considered themselves a cut above the such as the street riff-raff of Leith.

Man's inhumanity to man, eh?

'Oh, I forgot to mention, Inspector,' he announced with an expression that reminded McLevy of the monster from his dream. 'There are some changes on the way. And I doubt you're going to like them. Not one little bit.'

Chapter 10

Far off methinks I hear the beaten drum

A series of events happened during the rest of that day and night, that had you put them as parts of a circle and spun the wheel, would have meshed together and overlapped into a strange entity. Yet that entity would not be a fixed shape; it could change as quickly as a mutant cell, should the ripples from one collide with the other.

And so one might be left with a narrative that was not from moment to moment trustworthy, where innocence might conceal guilt, guilt innocence, and the smallest seeds of unspoken thought could sprout up to cause havoc and unimaginable murder.

One thing is connected to another by an invisible chain and what might seem coincidence or happenstance is rarely such a thing.

A deeper vein runs through it all; the deadly trinity of past, present and future.

In other words, life goes on as usual.

Jean Brash returned to the Just Land having refused Jack Burns's playful offer to be the naked prototype for his latest idea – a modern version of *Venus Rising from the Waves* – an offer, it must be said, galvanised by a hurried but passionate kiss they had exchanged in the privacy of her coach.

She had been annoyed by him trying to show her up in front of the company; when he protested that not to be his intention, she fired another cannon: and what about him eyeing up that actress?

What actress?

The one with the sleekit face.

Sleekit?

You know what sleekit means.

Sneaky?

Sleekit!

At this point Jean realised she was in danger of fitting into a category that the male delights to clamp around the female like a neck-brace.

The advent of the green-eyed monster, no matter how mistaken such masculine perception, gives rise to a smug self-congratulatory huddle of prejudices, passed from father to son throughout the generations.

Therefore she stopped. And smiled. She was a goddess after all, was she not? Above mere mortals.

Or below the waves. Either way, out of sight.

Jack grinned in return, not realising how close he had been to getting a smack in the teeth and his precious straw hat fed to the carriage horses.

However, behind the smile, her blood was still up and as the coach rattled down the streets from Leith Links, Jean Brash perceived that there was a choice here between warfare and osculation. She hooked her finger into Jack's collar and made the call where two curves meet.

Would that the world did the same when its blood was up, but sadly warfare too often wins the day.

And one other matter concerned Jean. She had an instinct that the emotion which unsettled her might have nothing to do with Mister Burns and his wandering eye – that girl Emilia; her smile had been rigid, a dagger in the heart.

Or was Jean getting too damned dramatic?

The carriage had jolted to a halt, Angus shouted at the horses in a voice that could never be mistaken for Cupid, son of Venus, and she informed the sculptor, osculation over, that she had work to do not unconnected with the goddess and he had an exhibition to prepare.

So no thanks to the offer of rising from a bathtub supported by an empty cockleshell strewn with seaweed, and off she galloped home to find Hannah Semple with an odd expression on her craggy features.

'That Sapphic wifey's in the wee side room.'

'What?'

'You heard.'

'She's not due here until tomorrow.'

'Jumped the gun, then.'

Hannah scratched her head worriedly.

'Not that alone, she wanted another keek at the octopus.'

For a moment Jean was nonplussed, then she recalled that Sarah Baines in the guise of an Arab prince – this is when the past starts tripping up the present – had once been in the main salon watching shenanigans that, had anyone but known it, were a prelude to murder.

The girl had been smuggled in by a rowdy group of young bohemian types, one of which was Mister Burns himself. In fact it had been the beginning of a spark between him and a certain Mistress of the House.

He had glanced at Jean's décolletage and she had wondered about the strength of his powerful hands. Both curiosities had by now been satisfied.

So, when these two were busy scrutinising each other, Sarah must have been looking at Jean's favourite painting of a baleful octopus, then lacking the bullet hole it now sported on the forehead, dragging a scantily clad female under the waves to a watery doom.

The precise opposite of *Venus Rising*. How would you name such: *Daphne Descending*?

Jean had carted that work of art from bawdy-hoose to bawdy-hoose; it got the juices flowing in the clients for some reason. Perhaps they saw themselves to be a creature of deep suction? For the magpies Jean had a simpler message: that's what can happen if you don't keep your wits about you.

Not being part of the original conception, the bullet hole in the creature had been supplied by Jean herself in an excess of high spirits while on the trail of two killers.

And not too long after that, she had put a bullet into the very forehead of a man with his thoughts bent on her demise. In her mind, he was still looking at her in disbelief as the life seeped out of his eyes.

Despite her shock and repugnance, Jean had put another bullet in his heart just to make sure. A lady can't be too careful.

The gun in question was a two-cylinder derringer and the witness as regards the octopus shooting was an astonished Hannah Semple.

Now the old woman was not so much surprised as, an emotion not seen often upon her features, embarrassed.

'The girls were round her lik' a flock o' pigeons, so I had tae stick her out the way.'

'I should think so.'

'She's in there wi' Nettie Dunn. Drawin' lines.'

'Explain yourself.'

'Nettie jist shoved tae the front and off they went.'

'And you let them?'

'It was your notion in the first place and I'm no' anything tae dae wi' that bliddy nonsense!'

Mistress Brash realised that Mistress Semple was in a rare bate because this was a situation outwith her experience and it was possibly unfair to expect a keeper of the keys of the Just Land to handle bawdy-hoose portraiture, Sapphic manifestations, and a bullet-holed octopus at one and the same time.

'And we hae a deal of business on hand!'

Jean nodded assent. Besides regular trade, there was this anatomical convention at the university and nothing stimulated sensual appetite like rattling bones.

A private reservation had been made, a large sum deposited, and such must be honoured.

'Business is business,' she replied.

The Mistress of the Just Land motioned Hannah aside, walked to the door, took a deep breath, turned the handle and entered therein.

Chapter 11

Have more than thou showest,
Speak less than thou knowest

In the stables Plookie Galbraith hummed contentedly to himself as he curried the coat of Peggy, a sweet-natured grey mare who, along with her brother Pepper, a black gelding but still, like his name, fiery tempered, drew the carriage of Jean Brash.

The gelding was getting a stone in one of his shoes hooked out by Angus Dalrymple the coachman, whose twin daughters, Maggie and Mary, also pulled in harness at the Just Land.

Plookie knew better than to ask Angus what he thought of that particular situation: the man was an ex-blacksmith and Aberdonian to boot, with brawny arms and huge hands that could snap the boy like a twig. Besides, best let folk be the way they are – unless they harbour evil towards you.

Niven Taggart harboured evil. But until he made his move Plookie could only wait and see. Maybe it was just a bluff. Just big words.

Maybe.

As he slipped Peggy a welcome carrot to munch while her coat got combed, there was a soft jealous growl at his feet. In his other poche were still some crumbs of biscuit so he offered down an open hand and the dog Raggie licked it clean.

The mongrel had made himself at home in the stables,

snuffling in the hay, keeping well clear of the horses' hooves plus the boots of Angus, while never venturing far from his master and fellow mortal.

It had found a small patch of bare earth in the garden to do its business and solemnly scraped the loose soil to cover up the results, all the time looking around to make sure no footpads were on hand.

A habit from the wynds, where to be too engrossed in any activity would invite all manner of pikers.

It was touching to see how the wee dog was perking up – better fed and fussed over by the magpies though Plookie took good care that his master and comrade kept well at distance.

His knowledge of women was slender to non-existent and the Mistress had warned him to keep it that way.

'Look but don't touch,' she told him.

'Is it not better,' Plookie had replied with some concern, 'if I don't even look?'

Jean Brash had laughed and for a moment gazed straight at him as if she could see through the front he presented to the world.

'Don't get smart,' said she, and walked away.

In the stable, Peggy had just this minute loosed her bowels but it was a sweet enough smell and easy cleaned up from the straw. They had a big manure pile outside, and when it accordingly rotted the roses bloomed.

And so did Plookie.

He was happy. First time he could remember. He had no memory of parents, just a street boy, skinny, and an easy mark, beaten tae hell, so he assumed a halfwit identity as if it were a mask.

There were many names for the person he gave himself out to be – daftie, gommerel, tattie heid. He played them all until it was difficult for him to tell exactly what he had been or had become. However, he survived.

Good fortune he was so ugly – no temptation for a certain brand of man in the wynds and surely no crooked finger for the nymphs of the pavé.

He slept on the floor of a wee room in Vinegar Close – an old woman had possession. Auntie Mary. She wasn't his aunt really but she let him sleep just in front of the door, and he paid her what he could. Sometimes she was a bit wandert in mind and then he would take care of her – like the horses. He liked taking care of things but no one had ever taken care of him – until now.

For no reason he could think of, tears began to run down his face.

Don't get smart.

Plookie had never met anyone like Jean Brash. It was said she had once been the Queen of Crime, but all he could see was someone who looked direct and played fair.

Tears or not, Plookie was happy.

'Is that cuddy fed and watered?'

The boy swiftly wiped a sleeve across his face and turned to see the giant form of Angus glowering over, having emerged from the next stall. The man had a big red face and quite small eyes: he often put the boy in mind of a bull looking over a farmer's wall.

'Aye,' Plookie answered. 'In top fettle.'

Angus grunted but the mare was groomed neat and tidy, seemingly content with her lot.

'Best be on your way, then, 'fore the evening shift starts. Top fettle, eh?' For a second his lips twisted in what might pass for humour in Aberdeen, then he glowered again. 'On your way!'

'Aye. Right, sir. See you on tomorrow?'

'If God doesnae strike us down.'

'Right enough.' Plookie grinned lopsidedly. 'The Big Man calls the tune.'

Then he was gone, the dog trotting proudly at his heels.

Angus scraped his boot on one of the stable posts – the mistress was right as usual – the boy had a gift wi' animals. Pity he was so half-witted.

Chapter 12

Let go thy hold when a great wheel runs down a hill,
Lest it break thy neck

In the tent Emilia drew Billy Musgrave into the shadows, kissed him fiercely and pressed her body hard into his. Billy was taken aback; she usually played a touch aloof when company was at hand.

He was further shaken when she scraped her nails over his groin, her eyes burning something fierce.

'Too many folk here, Emmy.' It was his pet name for her but she was more animal than indulgence at this moment.

'I don't care.'

'Too risky!'

'Cowardy, cowardy custard, eats his mother's mustard.'

In response he grabbed her by the collar and ground his face into hers.

'Later. I'll dunt ye till your back breaks.'

Her sharp little teeth bit into his lower lip and she smiled like a vixen.

'I'll hold you to that, Billy Musgrave.'

Then she was gone with a final scrape that left him like a standing sodger in a sentry box.

He dug a thumbnail into his gold tooth in frustration, tugged at his equally gold earring, turned, and walked with some difficulty towards where the workmen were yet in the process of erecting the changing rooms.

When Emilia returned to the stage her blood was still hot. The fear that she had always dreaded had sparked off a violent desire, but it would have to wait.

Alfred was in the middle of the arena, oblivious to noise or distraction, a large cigar in stylish fingers, puffing smoke up into the air like a train, eyes lidded with great thoughts.

The man was a fool – she could lead him as easily as one could a donkey.

Bridget shot her a sideways glance; a desiccated old prune but the woman was not easy to read – the brains of the family for sure but that would not be hard given the competition on offer.

John Wilde was suffering. The poor bastard hadn't had a chance to sneak off and gulp at his flask, so he'd be drying up like a fallen leaf. Barnaby just stood there like a spectre at the feast. He had once made a feeble overture towards Billy and been firmly rebuffed.

The two lovers had laughed themselves near sick at the event but it was always worth keeping in mind. Desire, no matter how weak, can always be exploited.

And Melissa? She was stuffing her face with a sandwich of sorts that Kenneth Powrie had brought in – cheese, by the look of it, to suit the slippery tart's rodent disposition. She looked up, caught Emilia's eyes upon her and elegantly popped an errant crumb back into the moist open mouth with a little finger.

Emilia envied her that mouth; it had a voluptuous quality that her own aperture lacked, being small and rounded as if she were forever taken by surprise.

However, that had its own advantages. Like Billy's gold tooth.

They had walked through the key scenes of the play. In fact did the adoring public but realise, not the whole mammoth piece would be undertaken. They did not run to invading armies. Alfred, however, would make sure that Lear thundered to great effect and the rest followed suit.

This was an accepted custom – the star shone bright and lesser lights twinkled accordingly.

Emilia had never been involved in a venture of this scale, even if a trifle truncated, but she had no fear of an audience.

Unlike when she saw that face.

Looking into the woman's eyes, eyes that reminded her of a ghost she once knew; a ghost she had betrayed and helped to destroy. That brought real fear.

But next time she would be prepared – armoured against feeling. Against guilt. Spit in its face.

From a distance Kenneth watched as the girl joined the rest of the company. Something about her attracted the eye. Cordelia was always played as a heroic fine creature such as Melissa Fortune would emit, all virtue and nobility; Miss Emilia would be more akin to a spitfire.

A woman of fierce independence. What fun.

He was almost on his beam-ends, all the money gone upon preparing the venue and if the audience didn't come to cough up at the table it would be another tragedy.

Not many tickets had been sold, all would be word of mouth. Madness. But Kenneth felt more alive than he ever had in his life.

What fun.

And the play?

A man loses his reason, another his eyes, three sisters also step off this mortal coil, whether good or evil it matters not they die on stage, so does Lear, and another two that expire out of sight, to say nothing of the poor innocent Fool who ends up dangling from a rope.

Almost as bloody as a night out in Leith.

What fun.

Chapter 13

I heard myself proclaimed
And by the happy hollow of a tree
Escaped the hunt

The *Jupiter* was a steam clipper that typified the Dutch desire to play both ends against the middle. She was powered by wind filling the sails as is right and proper for her given purpose – that of bringing the imports of Holland to the harbour of Leith – but in the advent of being becalmed there was an auxiliary steam engine that would do the trick.

Her cargo had already been unloaded so she lay light in the waters of Leith harbour and would be setting off back to Rotterdam with the tide in a few days.

All shipshape and Bristol fashion as two men walked alongside the harbour wall towards her, one with steam rising from his ears, sign of a boiler malfunction perhaps, the other more akin to a tall sailing mast.

Mulholland glanced uneasily at his companion as McLevy stared straight ahead, his mind churning with the exchange endured with Adam Dunsmore.

The man was a nyaff. A skittering, snottery nyaff.

Roach had brought them all into his office and then, as Dunsmore smirked like a rat upon a dunghill, announced that for the next week

Edinburgh City Police would take precedence of command in Leith harbour and the environs. A certain shipment was making its way from Amsterdam which was so important, so secret that Dunsmore could not reveal an exact date until the very last moment.

But it was worth a fortune. A king's ransom.

'It's not that we don't trust you, McLevy,' he said with barely concealed glee. 'But loose tongues, and loose relations – who can tell the consequence?'

He was seated at the other side of the desk from Roach, behind whom McLevy and Mulholand stood like pallbearers. 'Silence is golden,' Dunsmore added as if to clarify the message for addled minds.

'Whit the hell does that mean?'

To this choleric utterance, the man smiled annoyingly and tapped the side of his nose.

'A word to the wise. Leith Station has aye had the reputation of being a touch over-adjacent to the gutter.'

Roach's long jaw began to flex from side to side while McLevy's neck swelled like a bullfrog. Mulholland merely tapped at the side of his leg where the hickory stick that had felled more Philistines than the ass's jawbone of Samson had its pride of place.

'And if not the gutter,' the unwelcome visitor continued, 'other places of ill repute.'

A sly hint of McLevy's rumoured confidential connection to a certain bawdy-hoose keeper.

'No offence, Lieutenant Roach,' said Dunsmore, perfectly aware that he was causing just that. 'But my superiors have instructed me, as I have recently conveyed to you, that I will be in sole charge of the forces on the harbour when the shipment arrives.'

Roach said nothing. Were he on the golf course now, Dunsmore's head shrunk to the size of a ball and balanced on the tee, he would have smashed it clean out of sight.

'Under whose authority is all this?'

To McLevy's query, Dunsmore smiled annoyingly.

'Your own chief constable for one.'

'I have not been so informed.'

'You are now. In person.'

As far as McLevy was concerned the only thing worse than having this wee skiterunt in their presence was the prospect of Chief Constable Murray Craddock alongside as well. Two cocks on the midden.

Dunsmore rose from the chair. 'You, Inspector, will be part of the forces on the field – the foot soldiers if you prefer – who will take orders from me. And obey them. To the letter. That is the instruction from those above you.'

Silence. Not golden.

To a less thick-skinned creature than Dunsmore it might have been a little unnerving, but he had a small man's capacity for a sense of worth that was out of proportion to the actual reality.

'To the letter,' he repeated, nodded with the air of a man who had places to go, proclaimed goodbyes and then left.

After the door closed the silence grew. Queen Victoria certainly wasn't going to break it, so Roach had a try of sorts.

'Well, there you are,' said he.

One of the harbour seagulls waddled towards the policemen hopeful of a piece of stale bread but it received a swift kick that just passed by the yellow beak and took to the sky with the realisation that some objects were more rapid than you might suppose.

'Feeling better?' asked Mulholland.

'One thing we can rely on,' came a surprisingly measured response. 'Adam Dunsmore is stupid.'

'You're not wrong there.'

'He will therefore make a horse's backside of himself.'

'Right to the end of the tail.'

'With a bit of luck, we will be on hand.'

'To watch the catastrophe.'

But it was small comfort and they both knew it. Having to take Dunsmore's orders would be like chewing on lumps of beetle dung.

They had now reached the Dutch ship and seemed at once to have hit good fortune. One of the crew, an old salt, recognised the man's description and took them higher up the chain of command.

A young officer, Bernard Cuyper, who spoke impeccable English with great pride, nodded soberly at the description of the dead man. Of course the police did not yet tell the young fellow that they were discussing a corpse – they liked to keep such surprises in store.

Erik de Witte was the man's name. A passenger from Rotterdam. Never travelled with the boat till this time but polite, well-mannered and charming.

He had made great play of his surname, which meant 'white-haired' – this caused much hilarity, given the colour of his own crowning glory.

While McLevy and Mulholland reflected they had no idea the Dutch were so easily amused, Bernard confirmed under further questioning that Meneer de Witte seemed to know his way around the city and had obviously visited before this. He had left early last evening.

All well and good. Could they see his cabin?

Bernard frowned and looked concerned. 'Has Meneer de Witte been robbed?'

'Possibly,' was the cagey response.

'I regret I must demur,' said Bernard. 'He had yet to let us know if he was on the point of a return voyage to Rotterdam. His cabin has been kept. His belongings interred within. I would need his permission – the cabin is' – he searched for words in the formal file of his English – 'untouchable under maritime law.'

It was then they broke the news regarding the gruesome fate of Erik de Witte, who would no longer make jokes about his white hair due to the scalp below being on the dead side, and an ashen hue then settled on Bernard's face.

'How dreadful,' he murmured. 'How – unfair. He was such a nice man.'

Even then he still seemed oddly reluctant, but when McLevy suggested that he'd leave Mulholland here on guard, come back with an official search warrant from the station and then rip through the whole vessel top to bottom that seemed to do the trick.

The ship itself was thronged with folk, it being a habit of the many clippers to welcome all comers on deck in order to drum up trade and encourage those who might distrust a cargo ship as mode of human transport. Children darted everywhere while their parents gazed indulgently on. The crowd parted as the three men moved through.

This was Leith, and McLevy was a known presence.

The bogey man.

Bernard took them down narrow stairs to a lower deck where some cabins were situated and pointed at a door at the end of the corridor. He spoke softly as if afraid to wake the dead.

'I am afraid it will be secured fast and Meneer de Witte had the key.'

'Don't worry,' replied McLevy. 'I have a magic spell for locks. *Open Sesame.*'

'You'd be amazed how it works,' Mulholland added.

Both men expected the young officer to hang around but Bernard retreated swiftly back up the stairs, eyes anxiously upon them as if unwilling to be contaminated by a murder investigation.

The inspector walked to the door and pulled out some lock-picks that were most decidedly against the law.

The mechanism itself was simple.

Yet just as he was to insert the first thin implement, he suddenly tensed. Mulholland joined him and put a rather large ear against the door – he heard what the inspector had divined – a faint scraping noise on the other side as if something were moving around in there.

McLevy took out his service revolver and motioned the constable away a little. The inspector inserted the implement with one hand gun in the other, twiddled for a moment till he heard a click, then banged the door with his shoulder at the same time.

The portal sprang inwards with unexpected ease and McLevy hurtled into the room, sprawling to the floor of the cabin whilst a following Mulholland stumbled over him. Any elements of comicality were stifled by the sudden report of the gun going off in the enclosed space.

The noise was startling and in the moment of detonated shock, a small body jumped up from where it had been raking in a drawer and squirmed through the open porthole. A momentary flash of a pale face, then the body kicked through and was gone.

McLevy rushed to the porthole and stuck his head outside. For a weird moment Mulholland thought the inspector was going to try to force his inappropriate bulk through the aperture but even McLevy had his limits.

Besides it was a visual clue he sought. Looking down, below was a calm sea with nary a floating felon to be found. And above? Some ropes hung down the side of the ship; he saw only disappearing boot heels as they vanished over the rim of the deck above.

'You could have shot me,' observed an aggrieved Mulholland as McLevy wrenched back inside.

'The safety catch must have slipped.'

'That gun's a menace.'

'Never you mind – get back up on deck!'

The lanky figure turned and sped up the narrow passageway with McLevy lumbering after.

The inspector was most decidedly the wrong shape for a jolly jack tar and the confines of the constricted corridors increased his irritation as Mulholland went out of sight ahead.

By the time the inspector emerged on deck, his subordinate was by the harbour side of the ship looking vainly over the docks and piers.

Some woman let out a terrified yelp and Mulholland turned back to see the cause.

'Put that thing away!'

In answer to this stern command, McLevy looked down to see the smoking revolver still clutched in his hand. He clicked on the catch, slid it into in his pocket, and attempted a reassuring smile to the assembled crowd looking at him with varying degrees of consternation.

As he moved rapidly through them, McLevy could hear Bernard announcing in his clean-cut English: 'Don't be alarmed, ladies and gentlemen and little children. He is a police officer. He only harms bad criminals.'

The inspector joined his constable who was looking over the warren of warehouses and harbour lanes that led away further to the wynds.

'I don't see sign of a living soul.'

A voice at their elbow.

'What has occurred?'

Bernard had popped up again.

'Somebody was already in the cabin,' McLevy answered. 'A dirty wee thief. Could be the killer, even.'

'How terrible!' Bernard seemed in great distress. 'I should have been – on guard. To protect him!'

For a moment McLevy cocked his head to the one side then he replied with what he thought to be a heartening smile that would, however, put anyone else in mind of a wolf on the prowl.

'Never mind, sir. Jist you go and see tae the – little children, eh?'

The young officer nodded assent, his face white and strained, then he left to attend his duties as the police looked out over the harbour again.

Indeed it was eerily deserted in the early light of evening.

'I know who he is. We'll catch him up.'

'Who might that be?'

'Wee Richie Powers.'

McLevy had glimpsed just enough of the face. The constable nodded thoughtfully.

'He wouldn't be the killer.'

'No. Hasnae the nerve. But Richie was in that cabin, so he knows something.'

'Out of his league.'

'As he will soon discover.'

Both men spoke quietly now; it was as if the previous helter-skelter had been like a bad rehearsal and they were now ready to play their real parts.

'Let's get back to the cabin,' said McLevy. 'And find out what that wee mannie was searching out.'

Bernard Cuyper watched them go back below. He was also out of his league.

Chapter 14

Let it be so; thy truth, then, be thy dower

Jean Brash looked at her reflection in the mirror with a certain amount of dispassion.

To all and sundry she was the Mistress of the Just Land, a woman who did not blink easy, shot straight and who had everything money could buy, plus a deal more.

She thus addressed the image.

'Whit is it you want, eh?'

The image did not reply but stuck out its tongue.

She laughed at the childish gesture, picked up a glass of champagne from her boudoir dressing-table and took a genteel sip.

Quite the lady now. You'd never guess a childhood of being trawled through the treacherous wynds of Leith by two nymphs of the pavé. Well not exactly nymphs; one, Jessie Sheridan, had seen more men come and go than Sunday snowflakes, and the other – Nan Dunlop – once the first had sadly given best to a consumptive cough, had then bartered Jean like a calling card thus gaining entry to the roughest bawdy-hoose in Leith. Jean had later pardoned the woman for that action; there is so much to forgive in life, and a start must be made somewhere.

Begin with yourself and move on.

Jean had had no childhood or youth. A whoremaister named Henry Preger had laid pitiless hands upon the girl and her innocence had been riven in the blink of an eye. He had whipped her to his side but never broken her spirit. Luckily the monstrous swine had died; fought with a young constable named James McLevy and been battered to hell. No reason Henry should have lost. He was brutal, violent, a giant of a man, heavy-booted, in his own tavern, the young callan defenceless, but some female had winked at the policeman and then Preger bit the dust.

At least such was the legend.

Not long after, Henry expired in his sickbed, a tincture of arsenic in a wholesome soup deemed to be the cause, administered by the same woman who had winked at the young policeman.

That was the consequent legend, and like most fabulous tales, difficult to prove one way or the other.

The woman had by this time become his business partner and, Henry's rancid soul departed, inherited a rundown kingdom that was transformed and relocated through the years to become a Kubla Khan of elegant depravity – the Just Land – depravity of course being in the eye of the beholder.

Henry Preger died. Jean Brash came to life, a legend born.

That's the way of it.

Have another sip of champagne?

Her mind shifted back to the episode with that Sapphic wifie, as Hannah Semple would have it.

One look from Jean as she entered the room had sent Nettie Dunn scurrying for the exit, though she had enough cheek in hand to issue a promise that tomorrow would be fine for another wee go.

As Nettie closed the door on the other side, an impudent smile on her lips, she encountered the basilisk stare of Hannah Semple. 'On your way, girlie,' she said levelly. 'We have a shift coming on and you'd best be fit for purpose.'

Nettie slid past the old woman, remembering a story of two keelies who had tried to rob what they mistook for a helpless ancient crone and ended up cut to ribbons.

Hannah watched thoughtfully as Nettie disappeared into the main salon. This arty-crafty stuff was a bugger.

In the other room, the sketcher, Sarah Baines, sat before her improvised easel, a stiff piece of cardboard to which she had pinned a large sheet of paper. For some reason she did not move but looked at Jean, not so much in defiance, more as if interrupted in mid-stream. The girl was gamine, elfin by appearance, hair cropped short in a way that emphasised her boyish qualities, yet there was no mistaking the clear beauty of her features and the curves of her slim body.

Or the spark of serious intent in her eyes.

Jean made no attempt to break the silence – most folk talk too damned much in any case – and moved behind the seated figure to scrutinise the drawing. Rough lines, but Sarah had caught the glint of insolence and mischief that was never far from Nettie's eyes, also the physical invitation that served her so well in attracting attention from the questing male. Just head and shoulders but the collar of the dress was open and the neck bare. Tending to plumpness, fleshly and inviting, but Hannah was right – Nettie was putting on the beef right enough – at the moment she could carry it through but the passage of time is a different burden.

And business is business.

'How come you're a day early, Miss Baines?'

Sarah flushed slightly; perhaps she had been expecting a comment upon the work.

'I arrived to – confirm my appointment for tomorrow with yourself but then – I became – distracted.'

'Nettie is a dab hand at distraction,' remarked Jean dryly. 'And I'm afraid you have overstayed your welcome.'

This crisp reprimand shot Sarah out of her chair to gather her stuff together in a flurry that owed more to impulsive youth than a recently expressed talent. She rolled the drawing up, secured the paper and hurriedly donned her coat and bonnet.

'I apologise if I have affected the – stewardship of your establishment, Mistress Brash.'

'Stewardship?'

'Day-to-day business – commercial management.'

'Of a bawdy-hoose?'

'Yes. That very thing. State of affairs.'

To this somewhat disjointed response, Jean said nothing. Stewardship indeed.

By now Sarah had reached the door, crammed most of her belongings into a large carpet reticule and was about to depart when the young woman recalled the reason why she'd come in the first place.

'Ah yes. Tomorrow, Mistress Brash – at what time?'

'Ten of the morning. Had we not agreed to that?'

'Had we?'

'In my recollection.'

'I am sure you are correct, madam. Ten it is.'

Hand on door handle, bonnet stuck on at a slightly askew angle – Sarah for all the world could have been imaged as 'young artist leaves bawdy-hoose in confusion'.

'Goodbye Mistress Brash.'

'How is your father these days?' asked the Mistress.

This was not a remark upon which to take one's leave. Due to events not necessarily his fault, though like many a minister the Reverend William Baines may have paid too much attention to the *perceived authority of God and not enough to his own conscience, the good man had found himself on the wrong end of a killer's knife. A bullet from a derringer shot through the garden window had postponed his meeting with the Almighty and Sarah knew only too well that the flexed finger had been encased in a glove of the latest fashion.*

Jean, who had not yet divested her outdoor clothing, was in fact wearing a similar doeskin handsheath but the original had been relinquished due to severe staining of mud, slime and blood when she had traced the killers to their lair via Plookie Galbraith, and begat both their deaths on the very same night.

Some nights are busier than others.

'My father – is well. I intend to stay this evening with him,' Sarah answered eventually.

'I'm sure he will be happy to have you all to himself – unless you have company?'

Sarah flushed once more. The liaison with Louisa Lumsden, headmistress of an exclusive girls' school at St Andrews where Sarah was now employed as arts teacher, was not, per se, public knowledge but her father certainly knew since he had found them lovingly entwined and no doubt Mistress Brash did as well since the woman seemed to be acquainted with every crevice of sensuality in Leith.

After a near death experience where sin, in the form of a bawdyhoose keeper, had saved his bacon, William Baines had decided that he would leave the high moral ground to those who could rise above such human frailty and let his daughter's happiness be his beacon of everlasting light. The good man drew the line, however, at mutual exhilaration in the family home, so when Louisa came to lecture in Edinburgh upon the burgeoning freedom movement for female independence the headmistress bunked up with Sarah in the artist's small studio. William had kept it rented for her and the narrow bed merely drew Louisa and herself closer together.

Yet surely Jean Brash did not mean all that with just the one remark?

And even if she did, to hell with it.

Sarah drew herself up proudly to the full height of her five foot four inches. 'Tomorrow at ten,' she announced. 'Goodbye.'

The door closed, then shot open again.

'I can find my own way out, thank you.'

'Exit by the garden,' Jean replied demurely. 'It might be safer. In case you find yourself in a pickle.'

The girl blinked – then was gone.

Jean took another sip of the champagne as the mirror image did the same, and smiled at the memory. Yet she was also conscious of an emptiness inside.

Sarah Baines was in love, like a red, red rose.

What must it be like to have someone whose absence left you feeling like a lost ship, as if a part of yourself had been wrenched away? To have someone who was like your own flesh and blood?

Jack Burns was a fine carnal outpost but no more. He had passion and vigour, however that was the limit.

To feel something deep. To be moved for good or bad by emotions that might jolt you into elemental life. Not the social, not the clever, not the controlled. No: just Jean Brash, unadorned and fundamental.

Is that what the dream meant? That little mouth, opening and closing – the child forsaken and lost – what was it searching for?

And what about that moment in the tent which had provoked such a feeling of unease?

All were questions that left her with a sense there might be more to her existence than she was prepared to realise. As if there was another life within her more powerful than the one she led, waiting to explode.

She remembered once standing in front of Edinburgh Castle and imagining for some daft reason that it was a huge animal from prehistory – covered in grass and stone, built upon and buried – and then one day someone would dig in too deep and disturb the behemoth within. And the moment this beast began to move, those on the surface would feel great unease as ground shifted and cracks split the earth under their very feet. What would happen when the beastie threw back its head and roared anguish at having slept so long?

A sharp rap on the door and Hannah poked her head inside – for some obscure reason holding a pink paper rose in stubby fingers.

'Some o' thae medical men are here already.'

Indeed Jean could now distinguish the tenor of voices from below. She had been so deep in thought that only now was it audible. Yet something about the voices was unusual – a musicality of sorts. A lightness and lilting quality of tone that was most unlike the lustful Celtic rumble.

'One o' them gave me this,' muttered Hannah, the paper rose twirling as if alive in her hand. To be true, the old woman had been feeling oddly disconcerted all of the day and this just put the tin lid upon things. Too much going on. And when was the last time, paper or not, a man had given her a flower?

Too long ago. And that was a gambling man, Donald McIver: he had made her laugh like no other and, now and again, when his luck was in, brought her a single red rose. Then his luck ran out.

He was at a big table, money mounting. Two young killers tried to rob it. A stray bullet. Queen of Spades.

Long ago.

'A paper rose, that's nice,' said Jean. 'Was there any reason?'

'He wis French,' Hannah answered. 'They dae such things like that. Gallant as buggery.'

'French?'

'The whole bliddy lot are the same.' Mistress Semple was both alarmed and allured. 'Lik' an invasion!'

Chapter 15

Such smiling rogues as these,
Like rats, oft bite the holy cords a-twain

The Pigs of Docherty tavern had once been the ruling kingdom of Leith harbour. Tucked away in a side alley, it looked from afar like a shebeen that had outgrown its purpose, the windows dirty, some sheets draped across to shield within from an enquiring gaze, the tavern sign itself a large porker with a whisky bottle balanced precariously on its back, mottled and weather-beaten like an old tub at sea.

However, the small door, with a sill to duck under unless bowed down by a hard life or rickets, led into a surprisingly large drinking den with low lighting of sorts, candle stubs and oil lamps that threw jagged flickering shadows resembling unruly spirits on the walls.

The illumination in the immediate environs of Docherty's was provided by a few unbroken street lamps and a gleam from the eyes of a vagrant scuttling rat that reflected a stray house light.

Inside, the tavern itself was often muffled in sound but it was not a peaceful quietness, more like an uneasy feeling in the air before a storm might break. The odd burst of laughter from the odd straggie Betty resting her bones before going back out on to the cold streets leavened the low mutter of voices.

At one time Henry Preger had ruled the tavern but he was long gone, body according to rumour having fed the fishes of the deep.

This was now the domain of the keelies; the young men of Leith who dressed in flashy scarves and bright colours, bunnets to the side of the head in the approved fashion. These bold fellows lived by their wits, outside the law, with their street kitties also decked in vivid hues never far from their side.

Youth has its own dangerous energy and both barmen of the place had seen enough faces ripped to shreds and blood spilled to last a lifetime. Brothers Frank and Eddie Strang. Old gadgies. Both sparing with words. They kept two pieces of lead piping behind the bar but rarely had to use them since the day that Niven Taggart and his gang had taken up residence.

They were known as the Bonny Boys, a pleasant enough appellation for a reckless bunch of wild hempies who had garnered a reputation for vicious action. However, this occurred out in the streets. Gang-to-gang warfare in the dead of night that left broken limbs and faces that would never be the same. Inside the tavern these nights, good order was kept through command issued by the leader of the pack.

Niven Taggart had bigger plans than street fights; though the rush of violence was a feeling like no other, it brought not a penny and he loved money as a babe did its mother's milk. He had always known that his destiny would be to sit upon the throne of crime, to be king of them all – it was in his blood. Born to rule.

And he was now looking into the face of a man who might well spoil what he had in mind.

Emilia Fleming sat beside the man in question, dressed vulgar, careless, showing flesh, saucy clothing, a gash of scarlet lipstick, eyes deeply shadowed; for all the world like a dirty wee trallop and she was thrilled to the marrow by the company kept.

He had fulfilled his promise and bent her near out of shape in their wild dunting. As she lay sated in the lodging room bed with his blue kerchief stuffed into her mouth to stifle cries of spasmodic pleasure lest it alert fellow lodgers of the cast, he slid out a long slim knife always kept strapped close to his wrist and traced its point down her cheek from just below the eye to the glistening mouth.

'You betray me, little girl – I'll cut your heart tae pieces and feed it to the hoodie crows.'

She had licked at the blade and smiled.

Now Billy Musgrave did the same, his gold tooth shining in the candlelight. He and Niven sat opposite at table, untouched whiskies before them, like two gamblers on the point of making a heavy wager.

Bob Golspie stood directly behind Niven, his massive frame near blocking out the light; most of the other gang members were scattered around some tables near at hand.

'A long time past, eh, Niven? And ye havenae grown an inch.'

Billy laughed easily, as if to take the sting out of what he had just delivered.

Niven smiled thin. For a moment his eyes rested on Emilia, who met the gaze boldly.

'Who's the wee whore?'

'I found her on the streets.'

The young man laughed again. Niven smiled in turn. Emilia clenched her knees together; a palpable tension was in the air and also a sense the two were feeling each other out, a skirmish searching at the weak points as one animal would another.

Billy looked round the tavern. Both barmen nodded over but no one else met his gaze. Some to avoid, some to disguise the fact that they might be on his side.

'Ye've got a nice wee nook here. Classy.'

'You should know,' replied Niven. 'It used tae be your hidey-hole.'

Bob Golspie scratched unworriedly at the nape of his neck. Nothing would happen now. Not yet.

Everyone knew the history. Billy Musgrave had run the show, led the Bonny Boys, but then a murder had taken place. Rival gang leader plunged deep, a cowardly attack from behind – the keelies had their own strange rules and backstabbers were considered beyond the pale.

What the intruder was doing wandering the Leith wynds was another matter for it was far from his own patch, but Billy had been seen in the vicinity and the stab wound was from a thin knife such as he would carry. He had always insisted that it was not his doing and in truth he was never known to be craven. However, it was deemed healthier for him to leave until things calmed down.

A truce had eventually been made but by then Billy was long gone and in the meantime Niven took over and made a good job of it. Niven was crafty. He thought deep. Billy had been more reckless, foolhardy; he would charge them into battles that cost dear in broken bones. Niven never made that kind of mistake. Cold-blooded and not all that popular but never made a foolish move.

However, now Billy was back. And he was no longer apt to charge in ramstam like a bullock. Learnt different – travel broadens the mind, they say.

There were some that Niven had thrown out for being too loyal to the banished king – and there might even be some of his followers remaining still members of the gang, but Bob wasn't one of them. He stood behind his chief in all senses.

'Ye're welcome to throw in with us, Billy, but it would be – under my command,' said Niven, almond eyes unblinking in the small face.

'Oh, I'm jist passing through,' replied the other with an easy smile. 'Jist passing through.'

The little whore suddenly let out a yelp of laughter and then lowered her eyes in what might seem like embarrassment.

Seemed a dirty wee type; hot as a fox probably knowing Billy but Niven had no time for women. His needs were otherwise – supremacy and the money that it brought.

'Passing through?'

'I work for a theatre company on the Leith Links,' Billy informed the listeners with a straight face. 'In charge of the arti-facts – that's whit they call them.'

Another snort from his wee kittie; her eyes were glittering like a hashish hound.

'I'm a respectable man now,' he continued. 'I only came by tae pay my compliments.'

'Consider them paid.'

The two men stared at each other: Billy seemingly relaxed and at ease, Niven like a coiled spring.

The thin knife still lay strapped to Billy's wrist and the hooked cutter remained in its harness. There would come a time when both were loosed and that would not be to share a picnic.

'Anyway,' Billy remarked as if they had so far been chewing the cud together, 'how're things?'

'Things?'

'Business. How is business?'

'Quiet.'

'That's not whit I hear.'

Niven said nothing and Bob spoke up.

'Whit do you hear?'

Niven's mind was racing. No doubt Billy had been making old acquaintances and despite Niven's best efforts, word of some kind was spreading through the streets. He had warned Bob and some of his closest men to keep their noses clean – no rammies, no pikery that might lead to reported incidents, something big might be on the way. Someone must have spoken out of turn. Or maybe the Dutchman had approached other folk?

Nothing of this showed in his face.

Billy grinned. His hand slid round the back of the wee whore, then reappeared over her shoulder to sneak inside the loose neck of her dress and quite deliberately squeeze the rounded breast. The woman let out a low moan. Bob's eyes popped, and for some reason the action stung Niven into a loss of composure as if someone had spat in his face.

'Whit did you hear?' he near hissed, one hand dropping under the table.

'That's my secret,' said Billy.

The wee whore laughed again, either daft on drugs or pig ignorant of impending violence, but then the tavern door opened with a rusty creak and every inhabitant at once became busy with matters of pressing importance.

James McLevy stood in that doorway, Mulholland looming at his back in the darkness. The inspector's eyes swept the place, perhaps searching someone out, and then alighted on the table.

'Niven Taggart,' he called jovially as if not sensing the tangible dissension in the room, 'just the man. I have a wee message for you.'

Billy kept his back to the door and his head well lowered; with a bit of good fortune the bastard would not see his face. But his hopes were in vain. McLevy, seeming to take Niven's silence for an invitation to deliver the message up close, walked through the other tables towards them, Mulholland never far from his back.

Other than their movement the whole place was frozen rigid – as if Medusa had made statues of them all – and it lasted till the moment McLevy reached his destination. Then the inspector saw a face he had not expected to view.

'Billy Musgrave,' said he. 'Well, well. The clans are gathering, eh? What brings you back here?'

'Jist a wee visit,' replied the young man. He wasn't grinning now – nobody grinned at McLevy.

The constable had meanwhile taken the opportunity to duck off quickly into the back room of the tavern. He came out again, shook his head at the inspector and then engaged Frank and Eddie in conversation.

'A wee visit, eh?' remarked McLevy. 'And where are you biding these days?'

'He's wi' a theatre company. Leith Links. Wi' the artifacts.' Niven volunteered the information with a sly smile. 'Ye should pay him a call, Inspector.'

McLevy's eyes had rested on Emilia. She made her face look slack and stupid. The eyes passed on.

'Maybe I will,' said the policeman.

'You've nothing on me, McLevy,' Billy offered hotly. 'Nothing!'

'Except maybe a stab in the back, eh?'

'Nothing proved, nothing seen, not a thing. Ye have nothing!'

'Not yet. But it won't take long.'

Then, as if remembering his mission, the inspector turned back to Niven Taggart as Mulholland loped back to rejoin the party.

'Oh that message? Not for you so much – pass it to a friend of yours – Richie Powers.'

Niven kept his face blank. The stupid wee bastard must have called attention to himself. He had been told to sneak on to the ship, search out the cabin and bring back any kind of writing or paper. Richie couldn't read so there was no danger of him making out a damn thing but the worry was someone else might.

A thing that might lead back to Niven, or even worse, might point indication to the plan ahead.

Pushing that body over the side of the pier was an action that Niven now regretted, but there had been danger of discovery and he had deep enjoyed watching it smash down into the water. Of course he had emptied the man's poche and his pocket book before throwing away the wallet separate, so who could glean anything from the corpse?

Even if it was found – for it might just sink deep.

But just to make sure he had sent Richie to cover all eventualities, given him the cabin key with the name of the ship and the number – a present from the dead man.

Yet now this swine of a policeman had turned up.

How much did McLevy know?

'No friend o' mine. Jist drinks in the place.'

'Not often. Jist sometimes,' added Bob to his leader's answer – he didn't have a blind notion what was going on but backed up Niven every time.

'Whit's the message anyhow?' asked Taggart.

'Tell him I'd like a wee word.'

McLevy and Niven stared at each other and the younger man could not resist pushing it further.

'Any particular reason – for the wee word?'

'Murder.'

McLevy laid the word like a card on the table and watched the results. Blank faces save for one. No matter how much you try to conceal, knowledge seeps out.

Niven's eyes tightened the merest fraction. Not much. Not much at all. But enough.

The evil wee snaffler *knew* something.

'Well – best be on our way, eh, Constable?'

A nod from Mulholland.

'Crime waits for no man.'

With that all-embracing generality, McLevy turned as if to go but then, having had the last word, stuck another in for luck, as his eye alighted once more upon Emilia.

'You should scrape that muck off your face, my wee chookie birdie. Who knows what ye may find underneath?'

She flinched a little under his scrutiny, but he wasn't quite finished. McLevy was beginning to enjoy himself and, like many an actor, hated to leave the stage.

'I was sorry tae hear about your mother, Niven.'

'So was I.'

'Dead and buried. Dearie me. Ye didnae invite me to the funeral.'

'Is that right?'

'It must have escaped your notice. What a pity. Nice wee woman.'

Mae Taggart, the diminutive departed, would in no way answer that description. The wonder of it all was that she had survived this long. The woman had worked Henry Preger's bawdy-hoose the Holy Land for a while, then right after he died went back on the streets – somewhere along the line on the instant, from some stray assignation she had fallen pregnant.

Oddly enough, Mae had refused the usual route of a backstreet gin bath, had the child and had it brought up by her older sister Maureen, who was unmarried and followed the more respectable trade of fencing shoplifted goods, mostly on a small scale. So while his mother plied her trade and then, when past it, ran two younger versions of herself, Niven grew up to be the shining light of Vinegar Close dressed neat from some fine department stores.

Maureen died and then not long after the mother followed suit. Sisters to the end.

In stature he took after his mother, the father's name never mentioned until, on her deathbed, exactly one month ago, Mae had told her loving son a secret that curdled his insides. Niven swore hard vengeance, she smiled at her bonny boy, and then walked the streets to pastures new.

'Oh well,' said the inspector. 'Death awaits us all, eh? The old man wi' the scythe.'

He leant down, a mirthless smile on the white face. 'Jist think. All of you sitting at this table. Not long now. Mouldering in the grave. Worms at your flesh.'

'Whit about you?' asked Billy, nettled at the far from rosy prospect.

'Me? I am immortal!'

McLevy suddenly let out a harsh roar of laughter, turned abruptly and headed away from them.

Yet the game was not quite over. As the policeman passed a table, one of the keelies stuck out his foot to trip the invader. No harm done, he could apologise, a wee accident but think of the glory.

Without pausing motion McLevy hit the man straight in the jaw and laid him sprawling on to the dirty floor. As his companion's hand made an unwise move towards a hidden weapon

Mulholland whipped out the hornbeam stick and cracked it down.

A howl of pain. A fractured bone. McLevy frowned.

'What for did you do that, Constable?'

Mulholland spoke his first words since entering. 'There was an insect on his hand, sir. I worried he might get bitten.'

'Aye. Right enough. An insect bite is a terrible thing.'

In the silence that was broken only by the groans of the two men, he looked back once more to the table.

'Don't forget the message,' he said, and then both were gone.

Emilia's mouth was dry. This was not a play, not a game where she and Billy could have fun.

Billy's eyes were locked on to Niven Taggart's, as if little had happened in the meantime. 'Ye must have a lot on your mind, Niven. We should talk about it sometime. Break bread thegither.'

Then he hauled her up and off they went in turn.

Niven watched them go, his fingers tapping lightly on the heft of the cutting tool.

'Whit's going on?' asked Bob.

It was a good question, but his leader failed to answer. Tonight he would have to lay out plans to his men and trust that they could keep their mouths shut. Tomorrow darkness would see his name made forever.

Outside the tavern, had a seagull soaring high above in the late night looked down to the harbour below, it would have seen figures of two younger characters heading off towards their lodging house near to the Links, and the policemen bound in quite another direction.

Billy was silent. He'd probably have to kill the wee bastard right enough. Was it worth it? Better wait – see what his spies could discover. He had enjoyed the cut and thrust – let the blood come later.

Emilia was trembling. This was not a show. If someone died, there could be no repeat performance. And yet she felt with the fear a rising excitement that would translate into a later desire. She might have to run off into the wynds for a widdle – been near wetting herself since sitting down. Or, to be more accurate, since that policeman had looked at her with those slate-grey eyes.

And one other person came into her mind; in fact had never really left it.

'That woman who arrived at the tent – Jean Brash – who is she?' she asked out of the blue. 'Alfred says she keeps a bawdy-hose.'

'She's a Queen Bee,' answered Billy not breaking stride, 'don't cross her. Friends in high places.'

Emilia licked her lips. After the manner of the French poet Baudelaire, she had taken to imbibing hashish in coffee. Her little pipe was also on hand and she looked forward to some calm reflection following tonight's events.

Coffee and hashish. Just the ticket. Not too often, but often enough and getting more so. Ran in the blood.

Billy was her supplier, though he never touched the stuff – might slow him down in the vital moment – she near laughed aloud at that thought.

A Queen Bee. But what if a bolt of lightning struck the hive?

McLevy and Mulholland were on the saunter, apparently aimless but nothing of the sort. They had found one object in the cabin to provide a final destination for this night but nothing else of note; either Richie Powers had scooped it all up or little had been there in the first place.

Time would tell.

'Did Frank and Eddie have anything to relate?'

'Richie was in the place last night, sir.'

'With?'

'The barmen wouldn't say but – their eyes shifted past me.'

'To the table?'

'Near enough.'

They walked on in silence, and then the constable spoke once more. 'The keelies. There's something on the go.'

'You're not wrong. And we'll be waiting.'

A saying of his Aunt Katie's came into Mulholland's mind and he recited it solemnly: ' "Can I walk you to church?" said the fox to the hen.'

'That's us,' replied McLevy. 'On our way tae church. And one thing more – that rip in the body.'

'The Dutchman?'

'Uhuh. Word has it that Niven Taggart carries a deep cutter. Sharp as a diamond. Low to high.'

'But what would be the reason?'

'I don't know. But if he sent Richie Powers tae snoop, that could be another link.'

'A long shot.'

'That's just how I like them.'

They passed on into the darkness while the seagull wheeled off in a seaward direction.

Each to his own.

Chapter 16

This is a brave night to cool a courtesan

Jean Brash had never been so happy and breathless in a month of Sundays. Perhaps a warning angel or Hannah Semple, though a man may rarely mistake one for the other, might whisper in an ear that she was dancing on the edge of fate, trying to deny the dark forces from a darker past that were slavering on her trail.

To hell with such mealy-mouthed caveats, the feet were free and her blood was racing.

In fact the selfsame Mistress Semple, while not exactly having her head turned, most certainly held it at an unaccustomed angle as she watched proceedings that combined classic formality with a riotous opposite.

It had fallen out as follows.

The *medical men* transpired to be six young students from Paris who had come visiting at Edinburgh University to sit at the feet of the surgical masters of bone amputation and kidney stone removal without – and this was the important part – killing off the patient.

Not in itself an ode to springtime but they were young vibrant men full of the joys of life and hungry to let loose – the professor in charge was Maurice Bergier, a shepherd by name over the flock, and it was he who had presented Hannah with the paper rose.

Monsieur Bergier was completely bald with a neat turned-up moustache, a sly twinkle in the eye, short and round as a butterball, however, according to the one magpie that landed upon his lap, disproportionately endowed: 'Like sittin' on one of thae castle cannons' was the somewhat startled verdict.

He had promised his *petits garçons* a night to remember, and was good as his word.

Maurice looked on benignly as the young men disappeared upstairs with their chosen *belle de nuit* and had winked across at Hannah. 'Love – *l'amour* – is such a gift,' he murmured.

'I wouldnae know,' she answered, but had stuck the paper rose through a buttonhole just beside where she kept the cut-throat razor concealed upon her person. One could look after the other.

However, none of this had caused Jean's dancing feet or racing blood. The cause of such celerity was the other professor, Gabriel Bonnard. In his late thirties, a tall, elegant and sardonic figure; his suit the colour of a raven's wing with a pure white shirt that set off his olive skin and contrasted the coal-black eyes. In truth, a handsome devil.

As the rest set the place alight with their verve and laughter he watched on with a measure of amused detachment that almost matched her own.

Of course they had been introduced by the ebullient shepherd, nodded politely, and then gone their separate ways, but, like circling planets or amorous sticklebacks, were acutely aware of each other's rippling emanations.

Gabriel, with a faint smile that intrigued Jean to the point of seeing if she might wipe it off his face, sat at the piano and played a classical piece, soft and low, very much at odds with the hectic laughter and badinage as the magpies, nostrils flared, scented flesh that was not yet yoked to the cart of domesticity.

Or, put more bluntly, once pressed in, the beast sprang out again. No help needed.

As regards the young bucks, they had never met women of such panache; they were well brought up young Catholic lads and whatever sexual adventures may or may not have been experienced, had never crossed swords with women that not only did not shy away but were headfirst and headlong, Nettie Dunn in the vanguard.

It was not exactly a meeting of minds but the mind is a much overlauded function in any case, best used for cataloguing dusty tomes or organising railway timetables and too damned bossy for its own good.

No – this was a collision of vibrant polarities where sparks of attraction flew into the air and then danced around in the upstairs bedrooms like so many splinters of fire.

Maurice, who seemed to have money to burn, had reserved, through an Edinburgh colleague, the Just Land for the whole evening. So as the young men returned downstairs, entwined in the arms of the magpies, spent and content, the limpid notes of Frederic Chopin accompanied them.

A curious peace descended.

Big Annie Drummond looked on, wrapped in the beauty of the ballade, fingers poised over an untouched cream bun; Maurice raised a champagne glass in Hannah's direction and she was struck by memory of a card. Her gambling lover had been the Jack of Hearts, but buried at the bottom of the pack for this long time.

Shuffle and deal them out once more?

Hope springs eternal.

The Dalrymple twins rested upon a chaise longue with two fresh-faced brothers from Montmartre and Nettie Dunn had found herself a boon companion in the form of a hefty cheerful fellow whose father ran a high-class *boucherie* in La Pigalle. The lad, Gaston, was slow of study but his cutting skills were unsurpassed and Nettie could vouch for an accompanying delicacy of touch. He also possessed a tongue not unlike that of an ox – useful if cavorting in the French style.

And still the music played shifting from the complex ballades to a less demanding piece where limpid romantic notes trickled over each other like a falling stream.

Was it a trick of the candlelight or did the octopus sway gently in the waves as it dragged the fraught damsel to a watery end?

In the cellars Maisie Powers bit hard at her lip because of a worry within, while Lily of course heard nothing as she regarded the untenanted Berkley Horse.

Young men, per se, do not desire punishment. It will arrive further down the line.

War or matrimony. *Faîtes vos jeux.*

As he played on with an easy grace, Monsieur Bonnard glanced up to find himself under the steady regard of a certain Jean Brash. She was wearing a gown of deep burgundy, a colour the mistress always worried might make her look like a tart but for some reason this night, felt it to match a coiled emotion.

'I admire Chopin,' she said simply.

Gabriel was not without his snobbish side – what medical man lacks a God-given sense of superior gifts? – so was unable to keep surprise from showing on his face.

'It is – quite beautiful, I thank you.'

His English was precise, but how would it fare in the wynds of Leith or the throes of love?

'A nocturne, of course,' he added, still playing softly with long deft fingers.

'E flat major. It's supposed to be one of the easiest to accomplish.'

There. Stick that in your pipe and smoke it.

'Mind you, Mister Bonnard, I don't suppose anything by Frederic Chopin is ever *that* simple.'

Throw the dog a bone.

'Do you play yourself?'

'Only the Jew's harp.' She favoured him with a charming smile, and the green eyes had a mocking light.

Gabriel brought the melody towards a calm completion and nodded acknowledgement of points scored.

'*Touché*, as one might say in Paris.'

'Might one?'

'One might.'

A level stare from one to the other, surgeon to bawdy-hoose keeper, before he brought his splayed fingers down to create a crashing chord that jolted everyone out of their post-coital torpor.

'See what the French have brought you? A basket full of sweet things – *la joie de l'amour* – now –'

He stood from the piano stool and struck a pose that was both parody and challenge.

'What have the Scots to offer?'

Maurice led the cheers; Jean was unperturbed.

'Finlay Craigie!'

Slowly from the shadows, in answer to the summons of his mistress, a crumpled one-eyed old man emerged from the corner where he had sat tucked away by the fire. The French looked at him in – what must be admitted to be – a puzzled disdain. What could this *clochard* bring to their immaculate gathering? Had they not proved themselves to be men of substance in the tilt of love?

Their professors, one a master of bacchanalian organisation, the other purveying the classical disciplines of musical genius?

From under his disreputable coat – a coat that had been trailed through many a low tavern and bore traces of a far from sober existence – Finlay produced a battered fiddle, ancient in appearance as the man himself. From another deep pocket he brought out a bow and scraped it once across the strings.

The French winced. This was not Chopin.

'Whit wad ye like, Mistress?' asked Finlay, swaying slightly for the shadows provide a fine nook for sneaking the odd whisky via the odd magpie and even Hannah Semple had been known to pass him a dram or two.

For he was the fiddler of the Just Land and on special nights was summoned from the dark wynds.

'Make your own choice, Finlay,' came the cool response. 'But make it fast.'

While he showed his two remaining fangs in a gap-toothed grin and tucked the fiddle under a chin that had rested when younger on many a welcoming bosom, big Annie Drummond sped to the piano, cream bun digested.

'We'll tak' it light for first,' announced the old man. ' "Johnnie Cope, Are Ye Waking Yet?" '

This Jacobite song that celebrated the Battle of Prestonpans where the Scots had got up far too early and keen for the English forces and their feeble commander Sir John Cope, was a melody Finlay could have and had played in his sleep. He banged his foot on the floorboards three times and then launched into a spirited version of the tune, yet not a note was out of place and as Annie began strong company on the piano, Jean Brash turned to Monsieur Bonnard.

'Let's see what you braw gallants have tae offer,' said she.

The magpies hauled the medicine men on to the floor while Maurice made for and bowed to a nonplussed Hannah.

'My dancin' days are over,' she muttered.

'Not so,' was the solemn reply. 'They just begin.'

Meanwhile Jean Brash laid it on the line.

'Dashing White Sergeant, assume your partners, form your sets and devil take the hindmost!'

While the octopus hauled for eternity at his writhing partner, perhaps hoping they might join in the revels, the boys were shoved into position and the dance took flight. It was a Dashing White Sergeant like no other, where instead of decorous exchange, a fierce meeting of pagan tribes erupted with the music as a go-between. Jean was in the middle of Gabriel and Maurice since Hannah made the excuse that she did not have her dancing shoes on and had left, apparently to fetch them.

As the fiddle bow near set the strings on fire, the magpies flew at it like the witches in 'Tam o' Shanter'.

The French at first were taken aback but then replied in kind, and as shirts, gowns and petticoats were unbuttoned then waist-coats plus any clothing that hinted constraint for male or female thrown to the side, it would have been a brave man who, like Canute, might have attempted to stop that particular tide.

The couples whirled each other round with such wild abandon that had they loosed their grip, someone would have hurtled through the air and only stopped as they hit the rose-embossed wallpaper of the hard bawdy-hoose wall.

When Nettie Dunn hooked arms with her mistress, the girl thought she had the chance to send Jean into such an orbit but found instead that she went careering off like a runaway carriage.

At last the dance came to a juddering halt. Finlay took pity upon the wrenched limbs and heaving lungs and switched to a slow waltz. It was at that moment Jean Brash realised she was happy.

Was it because she was in the arms of Gabriel Bonnard? He danced well, but so did she. Was it that for once, she had forgotten her identity and become just one more body at the dance?

We all strive for differentiation but it carries a heavy burden and sometimes it may be a blessed relief to merge into the rest of humanity. Like a pebble in a stream.

Who knows?

Yet Jean Brash danced, moved to the music as if in a dream and felt this lightness in her soul. Her lustrous hair caught the candle-light like a boy catches at a butterfly, and as Gabriel gazed down and met her eyes, did he not also lose himself in a dream?

Romance is such a daft but necessary delusion.

'Mistress – somebody waits on you outside,' Hannah Semple's voice cut through the music, bringing Jean back to earth.

The old woman had been on the way back with a pair of ancient dancing shoes she'd hooked out with the thought she might break the rule of a lifetime and hazard herself on the floor, when, as she looked in the room and saw her mistress alive with the fire of a dance, Hannah had heard the front door knocker sounding loud.

So she went there, consulted, came back and thus informed.

'The house is closed this night,' said Jean briskly. 'The clients informed. A private party.'

'Not tae this mannie.'

There was enough weight in Hannah's words for Jean to excuse herself to Monsieur Bonnard and leave.

Gabriel tried to disguise a miffed Gallic chagrin. 'It must be someone of a grand importance.'

He had stopped Hannah as she also turned to go, while others still danced around with varying degrees of grace to Finlay's fiddle.

'I'd introduce you, Mister Bonnard,' replied Hannah with a caustic smile. 'But ye might end up in jail.'

Chapter 17

I cannot draw a cart, nor eat dried oats;
If it be man's work, I'll do't.

James McLevy was seated in the kitchen of the Just Land at the long heavy table that served the magpies for their breakfast rendezvous.

Mulholland, as was his wont, stood in the far corner like an unattended lighthouse, while Jean sat contrary to the inspector on her second cup of coffee.

When she had emerged from the dancing, the exchange in the hall proceeded as follows.

It must be remembered here that Mistress Brash had seen a possible lightness of being nipped in the bud, and McLevy had been on his feet all day without so much as a herring tail upon which to chew.

Mulholland was silent except for the growling in a sympathetic stomach and Hannah, when she joined them in the hall, kept well out of the line of fire.

What do you want, McLevy?
Conversation.
This is a private party.
So?
So, you're not invited.
That colour doesnae suit you.
Oh?

Makes ye look cheap.

Is that your idea of conversation?

Next door the tune came to a halt and there was a confused babble of voices, then it went silent – perhaps they were all listening at the other side of the door?

A man lies dead. Cut up lik' a flesher's pig.

I'm sorry to hear so.

We found him on the sands.

On holiday maybe?

The tide brought him in.

Always possible.

You know him.

Do I?

According tae evidence.

What kind of evidence?

Discovered evidence.

A muffled shriek next door as Gaston lifted Nettie up into the air with his strong butcher's hands.

Well – are you going to tell me the name or is it a state secret?

Erik de Witte. Meneer Erik de Witte.

Another muffled shriek from Nettie – having been lifted up, she then slid slowly downwards.

You're a liar.

Silver hair. Cuts a handsome figure. Save for the spilled guts.

You are a bastard, McLevy.

Now – can we have that conversation?

Hannah had watched Jean turn white as the morning sheets on the line, then made an informed guess that the party might be over.

And so it proved.

She was given the task of herding the confused French from the premises – pacifying Maurice who was just getting into his stride, and assuring the icily indignant Gabriel that he would never be forgotten by her mistress. Allowing a few tender moments between students and magpies, and then shoving the Gallic horde out the door to be led through the streets by the inexhaustible Finlay, bribed for the purpose by his payment and a large hastily gulped dram.

He led them off like the Pied Piper and Hannah – the men dispatched – kept the women in hand – sent them all off to bed, turned out the lights on the octopus – and then rejoined her mistress.

Save for that one instruction to Hannah, Jean had not uttered a sound – face tight with shock. In the kitchen she brewed up coffee, slammed a mug in front of McLevy, ignored Mulholland who only imbibed water from the tap, drank one cup at a gulp, poured out another and then said her first words in a fair while.

'Tell me.'

And so he did. The story so far.

Mulholland watched the pair. Rumours at one time were rife that these two had shared more than a love of the best Lebanese brew but no one knew for sure. All that could be certain was that they had a history together.

On opposite sides. One as powerful as the other.

Jean was respectable now but that, like beauty, only runs skin deep – such would be McLevy's conclusion. The man himself, in her conclusion possessing no beauty skin deep or otherwise, looked back at the woman herself.

Both, despite outward appearance, were creatures of deep instinct and both were aware of a troubling aspect to all of this.

What it might be was not clear but it lurked below events as a troll under the earth.

However, on the surface of things, he ended the detailed recitation of the body on the sands, the mess that had been made of said corpus, and even threw in the fracas on the ship though he was careful yet, not to put a name to the intruder concerned.

Jean kept her face composed but the sick feeling remained from earlier.

'How did you find your way here?' she asked quietly.

McLevy then related how they had discovered a small travelling bag stuffed into a cupboard; there had not been much in the way of possessions, the man travelled light, but the searchers had come across a notebook in one of the side pockets of the bag.

'It was full of wee drawings, wi' a scratchy kind of writing, in Dutch no doubt, get it translated in case it has much relevance.'

He slurped at his coffee. She winced. The man sounded like a drainpipe.

'The drawings were fine crafted,' Mulholland contributed, leaning against the sink. 'Jewellery, necklaces and the like – earrings, bracelets, work of some merit, I'd say.'

'He made me this,' said Jean. 'Upon commission.'

She opened up the neck of her gown a little further to display an intricate silver necklace in the form of a plumed peacock. McLevy tried to ignore the swell of bosom that kept the bird in check.

'Very nice,' he muttered. 'But on the last page of that book was your name. In block capitals.'

'Underlined,' the constable added. 'Twice.'

McLevy leant over the table.

'Now why would that be?'

Jean decided to give him something to chew upon but not too much. It never does to overfeed the police.

'He visited last night.'

'Why?'

'Social for the most part. An old friend.'

'Is that so?'

'Why would it *not* be so?'

'For the most part?'

'That's what I said.'

McLevy sat back, picked up the coffee pot uninvited and poured himself another mugful.

'Ye'll sleep bugger all,' observed Hannah.

'I'm no' that bothered. Whit about you, Jean?'

'I sleep like a baby.'

They scanned each other's features.

'Tell me about Mister de Witte.'

She sighed. 'Like I say – an old friend.'

Images of the man's face from the previous night flooded into her mind. Smiling, teasing, easy provoked to sudden laughter, pale blue eyes creased in humour yet underneath she sensed the desperate hunger of a craftsman driven to extremes. And in extremity lies a careless move. She had tried to warn him against such but artists hear only the one voice: a siren song from the rocks.

'He visited. Last night. We had a meal – oysters if you must know.'

'Oysters – any left?'

'Not a chance.'

'I'm starvin' hungry.'

Hannah, wordlessly, emptied from a cupboard some sugar biscuits on to a plate and slid it across the table for McLevy to munch at speed. He waved one at Mulholland who shook his head – the constable had standards.

'So –' A stray crumb fell to the table and lay there like a lost soul. 'Whit did you and your old friend have tae talk about?'

'This and that. He had a proposition for me.'

'Such as?'

The lie came easy because it contained elements of the truth.

'To do with jewels. Wanted another commission.'

'And?'

'I told him I was well provided. Sorry – but no.'

'When did he leave this place?'

'Ten o'clock of the evening, I'd say.'

'He didnae last long after that.'

'From the state of the body, Mistress Brash,' the constable offered gravely, 'he'd been in the sea for some hours. Probably died the same night. The police surgeon will confirm. It tells us a great deal – decomposition.'

For some reason the dispassionate nature of that word brought the bile rising in Jean's throat. She took another slug of coffee to disguise that fact as McLevy ploughed onwards.

'And where did Meneer de Witte have his wee home, I wonder?'

'I believe he – had a workshop in Rotterdam.'

'Come all this way for nothing, eh?'

'I'm sure he had other people to see.'

'One of whom may have killed him.'

She made no answer to that. McLevy banged back the last of his coffee and stood up. Hannah hoped the bugger was about to leave but her mistress knew better.

The inspector began to wander round the kitchen, whistling through the gaps in his teeth. A good ear for music might identify another Jacobite air, 'Charlie is my Darlin', the Young Chevalier'.

'Ye know, Jeannie,' he remarked. 'Folk around you don't seem to live for very long.' He smiled at Hannah as if including her in the notion but the old woman did not rise to the bait.

'For instance, New Year past, did you not shoot a man dead?'

'To protect myself.'

'And before you shot him, incite that very man to kill his accomplice.'

'A girl has to look after herself.'

'And whit about the poor laddie that died in the church?'

'He was a madman!'

'One of God's creatures nevertheless,' was the sententious response. 'And all these years ago, your boon companion, Henry Preger – missing presumed dead.'

'He might still be kicking about, who knows?'

With that response Jean Brash came closer to the truth than might be realised.

'Ye're not far from a plague carrier,' McLevy continued remorselessly. 'And here's the latest casualty – all because he lacked a *commission*.' The twist given to the final word made it only too clear to one and all that McLevy might lack a certain belief in such explanation.

'And you have no idea why – after talking to you and setting off into the night – this man might be murdered?'

'No.'

Silence.

Jean pondered something.

'Ye said there was someone searching his cabin?'

'Aye. But he got away. Through a porthole. It being a ship.'

He added nothing more. She sensed he was waiting for another question and so decided not to ask it.

More silence.

'Thanks for the coffee.'

With that he was out the door followed by a slightly perplexed Mulholland.

The two women waited. After a moment the front door snapped shut as well.

Hannah let out a long breath. Quite often she revelled in the jousts between her mistress and McLevy but this exchange had uncovered a raw nerve.

'Mair tae this than meets the eye, eh?'

A sharp rap at the door and both women near jumped out of their skin for different reasons.

Maisie Powers poked her head inside, Lily hopping around behind.

'We've a' tidied up, Mistress. Lily polished the buckles and I greased the handles.'

This was not equine maintenance but the Berkley Horse, due to the various physical agitations of its clientele as Maisie laid on the lash, was subject to a certain amount of wear and tear. On quiet nights, therefore, it was expected that the pair, like any good wielder of leather strapping, would tend to this beast of burden.

'Go to bed then,' Jean replied. 'You'll be busy enough tomorrow.'

Indeed as part of the celebration of the arts in Edinburgh, the city would be flooded with all sorts of inquisitive visitors and some would no doubt desire more than just creative provocation.

Maisie nodded. She wondered whether to confide in her mistress what was disturbing her as regards her young and stupit glaikit wee nyaff of a brother but this was not the time or place.

So she closed the door and went up the stairs with heavy tread, followed by Lily who had observed Maisie's preoccupation but hoped her own inventive ministrations would lift the dark cloud.

In the kitchen, Jean stared into the empty coffee cup and spoke quietly, almost as if to herself. 'Erik de Witte had crime on his mind. He wanted revenge, he told me. He wanted me to help. A heavy lift.' The terminology was thief's cant for a big robbery and the very fact that Jean used the words was warning enough for Hannah.

'These days are long past for you, Mistress.'

'I told him so.' Jean's eyes were dark and troubled. 'I cut him short. He said no more. What kind of revenge, what crime – he said no more. I told him to go back to Rotterdam. He smiled, drank champagne, swallowed his oysters. And left.'

'Ye did right.'

'He went somewhere else. I fear – I may have sent him to his death.'

The dark apprehension begun this day had returned and the joy of the dance seemed long distant.

Outside in the street, a small precise figure made its way towards the door of the Just Land.

A busy night. As Hannah Semple was wont to remark, at times the place was like Waverly Station.

Kenneth Powrie hesitated for a moment; it was late, however the lights were on and needs must. When the devil drives.

Mulholland was puzzled as the policemen walked back down the hill.

'You didn't mention the name of Richie Powers, or want to speak with his sister?'

'No. I did not.'

Silence. Darkness.

Somewhere far in the night was the faint sound of fiddle music as Finlay, having led the French back to their fine hotel, made his own way to a less salubrious dwelling place.

'You mentioned his name in the tavern, though. Jean will find out. So will Maisie.'

'*Uhuh*. And they'll both wonder why I never asked.' A yellow lupine glint sparked in his eye. 'I like tae keep folk on the hop. That's when they make mistakes.'

Then he let out a roar of laughter. 'Besides – even if he was hiding up the leg of her drawers, Maisie Powers would tell me nothing.'

Mulholland sniffed. Sometimes the inspector's humour lacked a certain delicacy.

'You think Jean Brash connected to all this?'

'Already is.'

'I mean – *deep* connected.'

'Time will tell, Constable.'

They disappeared from view and the day ended.

Unbeknownst to any, the chain grew tighter.

Chapter 18

Her boat hath a leak.
And she must not speak.
Why she dares not come over to thee

Edinburgh, August 1844

The young woman's body was heavy now and the heat of summer, for it was a hot sweltering season unlike the usual city climes, clung round as if to squeeze all breath from out her body.

When a girl she had passed two old women in the park. They were sitting on a bench cackling like a pair of malicious broody hens about the fate of some unfortunate soul, and said one to the other, 'Forgot the sponge and vinegar and now there's a trout in the well!'

Margaret, the servant, who often accompanied her charge to make sure she was not contaminated by chance meetings with the common herd, sniffed and ushered the young girl past the pair but one shouted a gleeful farewell to speed them onwards.

'It'll happen tae you wan day my wee maiden – lik' humpin' a bag of coal!'

Eight months now she had carried the child within. No more walks in the park, only the four walls of her room, the frigid silence of the supper table, the visits from a family doctor sworn to secrecy, his humiliating examinations, and the growing knowledge that her body was becoming an unfamiliar – someone met on the road in a fairy tale – a stranger not known whether good or bad.

And like a kernel in that changing body, was another being. Moving sometimes and mirroring her moods as if aware and prescient.

When she was low in spirits, which was often, the baby would lie still, like a fish cleaning its gills in a stream letting the flow of blood pass through, but when her anger spurted into feeling, it would kick as if in sympathy, at times with a thud that she felt must echo through the silent house.

Of course the begetter was gone. Dermot. An employee of her father's who had employed himself to a different usage than the binding of books. Without a word, back to Ireland – perhaps to Dublin city – paid off no doubt, or threatened with legal proceedings?

More likely given enough money for the boat fare and dismissed like a dog that had fouled the carpet.

He had made no effort to communicate. Once, in desperation she had smuggled herself out of the house in the early evening and made her way to his lodgings in the squalid little wynd she had once thought so romantic.

The landlady had looked at her, gauged the condition and necessity, and then shook her head. 'Gone. Lock stock and barrel. Owes me the rent. Owes you a damn sight more, I'd say, lassie.'

Her eyes were not unkind but the woman had witnessed so many stories of men who did not stay the course.

When the girl had returned home and unlocked the door, her father was waiting behind it. He took the key from her hand and put it in his pocket without a word.

Then he spoke.

'Supper is ready. Boiled beef.'

Was he a cruel man? No. He lived by a rigid set of rules and she had broken the most sacred:

'Thou shalt honour thy father and thy mother that thy days may be long upon the land that the Lord thy God giveth thee.'

Thou shalt also, by the by, not commit fornication, especially with someone of a class below.

Her mother lived in the shadow of his rectitude and scarce could look at the errant offspring. A small woman who grew smaller by the day as her daughter multiplied.

In the last month the doctor had prescribed pills – an opiate of sorts to tranquillise the increasing hectic desperation, and she had grown so needy upon them. She hated that dependence but could not deny it. It kept her – removed. At a distance from anguish.

And the baby? For no one could dispute there was a baby – coming – into life – the baby was quiet now – as if also lulled into an ambiguous habituated state.

Only Margaret, it would seem, could bear to be near the mother-to-be; but it was not a warm loving presence, more like a sentry on duty.

And the young woman could sense that as well as a child, something else was being hatched. A conspiracy. To be kept from her. All of them – father, mother, and the servant – hiding it away. Was her mind playing tricks?

Removed.

Further and further from her true self. Who was she? What had she become?

At times she doubted her own sanity. Only the opiates kept her calm – the blessed opiates. Or were they a curse?

It was Margaret that gave them. Every morning, every twilight.

This will be good for you, Mistress. This will keep the boat on an even keel.

Am I a ship, for God's sake, you stupid woman?

Yet it was to Margaret she screamed when there was a sharp sound in her body like a knucklebone cracking and a huge gush of liquid spurted forth from inside – warm, like weak tea, soaking her undergarments and gown, spilling on to the floor, spreading in a stain on the carpet for all to see.

The mark of sin, the mark of guilt, see it spread like a reproachful tide; howl, and then howl again.

She had fallen to the floor with the sea all around her. Would the baby drown? Would they both sink deep in the fluid from her own secret parts?

Her eyes had been closed. She opened them to find Margaret looking down at her as a sudden contraction jackknifed the body.

'*Your waters have broken, Miss Jennet. Early doors.*'

'*Doors? What have doors to do with it?*'

These words, howled into the face above, produced a glint of compassion in the eyes, replaced almost at once by sworn obligation.

'*We need tae get you to bed.*'

'*I can't let them see me like this!*'

She struggled somehow to her feet dripping like a fountain, and Margaret with wiry strength wedged an arm round both shoulders and carted her to the bed.

Like a bag of coal, that's what the old witches had said and they were right.

She stretched out on the counterpane but then was jolted by another contraction.

'I'll send for the doctor, Mistress – lie still.'

With that, the servant was gone.

Above the bed where the young woman lay, was an ancestral portrait of her father's father looking down with grim disapproval.

'Go to hell,' she shouted up at him. 'And let me have my baby!'

Chapter 19

Then they for sudden joy did weep,
And I for sorrow sung,
That such a king should play bo-peep,
And go the fools among

Leith, 1883

Bridget Tyrone allowed a small bleak smile of satisfaction to exercise her thin mouth before asking of her brother, 'Alfred, I wonder if for once, my dear, you may have bitten off too large a portion for mastication?'

Below, behind and before them was chaos inside the billowing marquee that would soon house – in prospect at least – their performance of *King Lear*. A slightly truncated performance to an extent but one that would inhabit all the great speeches and grisly splendour of the tragedy. For what true follower of the Bard did not relish the eye gouging, then backstabbing, both literal and metaphoric, plus numerous deaths by poison and sword with the odd hanging thrown in?

Comedy would be in short supply, save for what apparently was happening upon the scene Bridget now surveyed.

The Tyrones had arrived, replenished by a fine hotel breakfast, at the appointed time for a last rehearsal, to meet the other three of the company who had made the best of their lumpy lodging-house porridge and now all stood upon the makeshift stage like shipwrecked sailors.

'Emilia is late,' muttered Alfred chewing on a cold cigar.

'Emilia Fleming is *always* late,' offered Melissa Fortune slyly. 'She prefers the comforts of her bed to the demands of professional rigour.'

She and Bridget had taken up positions of the malignant sisters on each side of the monarch; Melissa ready to pour poison into the hairy orifice, Bridget more concerned with what lay before them to which Emilia's presence would have made alteration by not one jot.

It would seem that the disordered madness in the play as it wound to a terrifying conclusion had flown the pages of Shakespeare and landed in Leith Links. Bits of rope hung down, hungry tendrils catching at the workers as they hammered and sawed at the benches where the theatrical *cognoscenti* were to park their discriminating behinds and marvel at the spectacle of imperial murder and mayhem.

The air was full of dirt and dust with both the company's more venerable actors, John Wilde and Barnaby Bunthorne, already wheezing fit to burst.

There was a mutinous sullen demeanour to the hoary-handed sons of toil who laboured below, and raised voices from the rear of the stage indicated that no succour was to be found in that direction either.

From behind the heavy drapery that stretched along the back of the stage, Billy Musgrave emerged to report that the thunder sheet, so essential for the storm scene, had a large dent stove into it by a passing plank of wood and might not thunder so much as clunk like rusty armour. The paddles of the wind machine were not in the greatest shape either but he could fix that, and the big wooden box where a turned handle activated the dried peas that simulated rain seemed to have rusted up and would most definitely need releasing oil.

Alfred waved a hand as if such problems were below his consideration – a mere bagatelle.

For his part, Billy had risen in the early hours, left Emilia like a satiated caterpillar in bed, and met up with the two keelies in Niven Taggart's gang still loyal to their old commander. One still nursed a fractured wrist and the other a swollen jaw from that bastard McLevy the night before, but what they had told him excited Billy and he had been calculating the odds ever since.

A scheme was forming in his mind and the more he determined, the more he liked it. The keelies had promised to come back in the afternoon and confirm their suspicions. A gang meeting would be held and they would be in attendance.

Meantime he still had a job to do and Billy prided himself on his practical abilities. Kill a rival, provoke Emilia to gouges that still stung love's lacerations down his back, fix a thunder sheet – it was all the same.

A man must do what lies in store.

Melissa gave Billy an appraising scrutiny. She had wondered whether to welcome that particular boat into harbour just to spite the little bitch if nothing else, and had not failed to notice the sinewy strength in that slim body of his but the idiot did not seem interested and besides, she had another target in mind.

Melissa was a stealer and loved to entice what did not belong to her.

Having delivered his unwelcome tidings, Billy looked at proceedings and delivered verdict. 'Not one bugger in charge,' he said and left.

The comment could be equally applied to those left perched on stage like parrots on a stand.

Bunthorne suddenly let out an explosive sneeze. There was a chill east wind blowing through the place and his fool's costume, now that he came to think of such, was skimpy and threadbare.

As this thought ran through the mind of the woebegone jester, Alfred struck a pose to indicate inner reflection but Bridget knew better. The man was incapable of attention beyond the span of a flea. Unless looking in the mirror.

'And pray – what is to be done, dear brother?'

To his sister's query, Alfred threw his arms aloft to declaim and align himself with tragic sovereignty:

Thou know'st, the first time that we smell the air,
We wawl and cry. I will preach to thee: mark.

Somewhat glumly recognising his cue, John Wilde responded as the loyal and mistreated Gloucester:

Alack, alack, the day.

The young boy who had so badly injured himself the previous occasion by distraction over such exotic creatures kept his head down and hammered in another nail.

'Alack the day indeed,' said Bridget wryly. 'And where – if I may ask – is Mister Powrie?'

Alfred clapped a hand to just above the eyebrows and stared into the melee below with keen and searching gaze. But he saw – as Billy Musgrave would have said – bugger all.

For Kenneth was at that moment being maltreated in the open air of springtime by two hefty specimens who had run out of patience. His collar had been twisted cruelly against the neck and the bright impish visage was contorted in pain as they pinned him up against the wall of the tent.

'Ye promised our money this day, Powrie – where the hell is it?'

'Ye see, sir,' said the more reasonable older man, 'we have tae pay the men. We have put out our own cash for materials. Payment is due.'

The younger suddenly rammed his hand between the fashionable trouser legs of the writhing entrepreneur and grasped hold of what in some circles were known by the appellation 'crown jewels'.

'Where is it or I'll pull these right frae the stalk lik' a sprout.'

'The money is on its way, my good fellow,' replied Kenneth, trying to be a man of the world but the voice a little tremulous and rising in pitch.

The younger man squeezed harder.

Kenneth yelped as tears of torment and humiliation formed in his eyes – the continuing problem with creative endeavour is that cruel moment when it meets the real world, or the harsh and bitter world, which calls itself reality. All his life he had ducked and dived but now there was nowhere to hide and a great deal to lose.

A great deal.

Plus, who is not to say the younger man was not relishing the role of revenger? Surely nothing lies more sweetly in the human breast than meting out violence in a justified cause?

'Last chance!'

Another anguished yelp.

'Easy there, son.'

'Shut up, Daddy.'

Of course they were father and son, as Kenneth knew well, surely that bespoke some compassion?

'Where's the damned money?'

'Right behind you,' said a voice.

The men turned to see a fashionably dressed woman, complete with parasol, facing them, outlined in a sudden shaft of bright sunlight that blinded both for a moment.

Beside her was a less finely attired old biddy whose hand was sliding inside the lining of her coat.

Perhaps it would be best to identify the two men – one was George Carter and the other his son Brownie. They ran a carpentry company that specialised in hurried construction and while George regarded himself as a reasonable man, Brownie had no such scruples.

Plus the fact that Kenneth had not paid them a penny since the start – charming George with promises that had failed to charm Brownie at all.

And now as the men blinked in the sudden sunlight, two women had appeared. Often maiden aunts come to the rescue of a favourite nephew in popular stories but neither woman looked remotely like a maiden aunt.

Then the sun dipped out of sight behind a cloud and George's jaw dropped.

'Mistress Brash – I beg your pardon – to be sure – I beg your pardon!'

Jean reached inside her reticule and brought out a sealed envelope that bore the insignia of the British Linen Bank.

'I understand you are owed deposit on your labour, the rest to be paid upon completion. Here it is.'

Brownie snatched the wrapping and tore it open. He had of course heard of this woman; however, he saw nothing to concern him – jist another fancy female. The money was there right enough. Forty pounds in notes.

The fancy female spoke with a certain authority. 'You better get inside and complete your work. The play opens this night.'

'Aye, right enough,' replied George hastily. 'C'mon, Brownie.'

The younger man ostentatiously put the envelope inside the pocket of a navy reefer jacket – bought from a smart shop – his pride and joy. It had bright enamel buttons and the old biddy reached out to finger one of them. She then did not exactly rip it from the stalk but her other hand flashed out with a cut-throat razor and chopped off the shiny trophy like a grape from the vine.

'Here you are,' said she. 'Compliments o' the house.'

Hannah had witnessed the bullyragging and while she held Kenneth in scant regard, a man was surely entitled to hold on to his most precious possessions.

Brownie's face flushed with anger but something in the level gaze of both women stilled any motion. The razor had not yet been sheathed and Jean's hand had slipped inside the reticule – something told the young lout that it wasn't another envelope she held.

George decided to exert paternal influence while he still had a son.

'Excuse the boy, Mistress,' he announced. 'He hasnae the sense God gave him.'

He hauled Brownie off into the tent whence his voice sailed back through the flap. 'Ye'll all be well paid this night so get tae work!'

Hannah Semple was not impressed by any of these events save the satisfaction of knowing that her hand had not lost its cunning and the blade still cut to order.

Kenneth had turned up on their doorstep in the dead of night like a waif from the storm with troubles galore and not only did the mistress admit to financing a damned tragedy but without a glimmer of remorse, proposed to throw good money after bad by saving the day. They had sped to the bank first thing and arrived none too soon.

But to what end?

'A bliddy load o' mountebanks,' she muttered.

The impresario meantime was only too aware of a lethal quality to Jean's gaze. He had deceived her as regards the expenditure and no amount of charm could compensate for that deception.

'You better get going Mister Powrie,' she said with a cool edge. 'I'll put my own people on the gate to count the takings this night. My trust in you has gone.'

A shamefaced nod then he and the trust departed.

'Am I supposed tae come to this damned piece o' nonsense?' asked Hannah looking askance at the large unwieldy tent, which was whipping up in the wind.

'Most certainly,' Jean replied. 'After all – you cut the button.'

Then she saw a figure hurriedly approaching far in the distance that brought a different feel to the game.

'Go back to the carriage,' she commanded Hannah. 'I'll be with you shortly.'

'Don't run away and join the circus,' grumbled Hannah as she left. 'Ye have an establishment tae run.'

And so as a slightly dishevelled Emilia Fleming, late risen and fogged by resinous extract, scrambled up the hill towards the tent, there waiting like a figure from a morality play – if a bawdy-hoose keeper could ever be said to represent such – was Jean Brash.

Elegant and poised. Unlike Miss Fleming.

And yet Miss Fleming had something up the sleeve – though it was a fairly ravelled one at this moment.

Emilia tried to pull herself up to a ladylike or even *young actress approaches the theatre where fame awaits* stature, but it was marred by her heel catching on a small mound of earth where a moudie-wort, if you were local which she was most certainly not, and mole by any other name, had left after a midnight excursion. She near sprawled but managed to right herself and ignored the glint of amusement in the other's eyes.

For a moment Emilia felt young, gauche, no longer a wild debauchee, no longer a witness to violent extremes, just an imma-ture – what was it that slate-eyed policeman had called her – *chookie birdie.* Hoping none of this confusion showed upon her face, she straightened further to meet the opposite regard.

'Miss Fleming, we meet again.'

'You must excuse me – I am late for rehearsal.'

'If I may be so bold?'

'Yes?'

'The buttons of your gown are – out of true. I am a great believer in buttons.'

Emilia's left hand went up to the collar of the gown where it showed above her coat – the damned woman was not mistaken. In her rush Emilia had done up the fastenings in maladjusted order.

A sudden rush of fury swept through. She could kill this bitch, yes one day she would kill the bitch, watch her crumble to pieces.

One day!

But behind the fury was a weakness and that was the worst – that was unbearable. As if her heart was being wrenched out of her body.

'I am late. You must excuse me!'

The girl almost threw herself through the opening in the tent to disappear from view.

Jean Brash was no longer amused.

The feeling that had haunted her from that dream – as if the ground was collapsing under her, as if she had stepped off the end of the known world – had returned from nowhere.

A call from below signalled that Hannah Semple was very much on the planet and waiting.

Jean unfurled the parasol to protect her fair visage from the biting wind and walked off into the day. She would set her people out to see if any trace could be found as regards the movements of Erik de Witte – a man surely must leave some trail behind – even if it's only blood.

A pity. He and Kenneth would have made great friends. They would have laughed together and she would have delighted in that.

She would make arrangements for Erik's funeral; as far as she knew he had no family. She would also make arrangements for vengeance. Once she found out who had killed him.

Death cuts both ways.

Chapter 20

The little dogs and all, Tray, Blanche and
Sweet-heart, see, they bark at me

It was rare that the dog annoyed his master but wee Raggie was chasing his tail as if plagued by fleas and then raising a head to let loose at something above.

Plookie Galbraith had been happily mucking out the stalls of both horses – the beasts about their lawful business of conveying the Mistress and Hannah to some decent destination, plus of course Angus the coachman, otherwise the carriage might career off in any direction – when the canine outburst occurred.

He emerged, pitchfork in hand, and attempted to shush the animal but it would not be consoled, crouching at the foot of a ladder that led upwards to the hayloft and barking fit to burst.

'There's nothing up there, Raggie – mebbye a big rat that would chew you up in toatie bits, eh?'

The dog barked again. It was working itself into a frenzy and before long one of the bawdy-hoose magpies would come out to complain about this hellish racket. That was to be avoided, especially if it happened to be Nettie Dunn; the girl had a habit of licking her lips when regarding Plookie, as if he were a mealie pudding.

Not only that. She was giving herself airs and graces, announcing to one and all that she was going to be an artist's model and who knows? She might quit the Just Land altogether to find fame and fortune in Paris posing without a stitch on while great painters fought duels over her.

Or words to that effect. Anyhow, she was a menace, because Plookie was not able to deny a certain attraction towards Nettie and the cheeky wee hizzie knew it.

Every time she breathed in deep, he blinked an eye.

If she arrived to find the cause of this clamjamfry and he had only a pitchfork with which to defend himself, anything might happen.

And had not Jean Brash warned him?

Look but don't touch.

The dog would not stop.

'All right, all right!'

Still holding the implement in case there was an onrush of rodents or ambush of magpies, Plookie clambered up the ladder to the top, shoved aside the big trapdoor in the hayloft floor, then stuck his head through the space, and saw – not a thing. Admittedly, it was a land of shadows in there but not a creature was stirring. A few wisps of straw blowing about in the draughts but nothing else.

'Ye happy now?'

This call downwards produced a low belly growl from Raggie but at least the beast was quietened.

Then Plookie heard quite another sound.

Like a broken reed. As if someone had stood upon a bird or such. Once in the wynds, he had witnessed a pack of feral dogs savagely attack something in their midst. He had shouted and kicked at them to scare the pack away – God knows where he'd got the courage but he managed to do it, and there was a pathetic scrap of wee scabby dog that had somehow wandered into the wrong terrain. It was bleeding from many nips and bites, and the noise it made near broke his heart.

A wounded cry, but not too loud in case it attracted more retribution.

This sound he heard was human, but it had the same bereft, abandoned feeling. 'Ye better come out,' said Plookie. 'I've got a big gun, pointing right at ye!'

A lie, of course, but just in case it was a devil out of hell in disguise, come to steal his soul.

Silence.

Then from behind a bale of straw a figure that bore resemblance to a cracked and broken insect crawled out sideways. It gasped out in a jagged, mewling sound that grated on his nerves.

'Better be quiet – or else!'

He wasn't sure how to proceed from here but the figure had at least stopped making that awful noise. Yet it did not move further.

Plookie hauled himself up on to the floor of the hayloft and crouched upright as straight as he could for it was a low-beamed wooden ceiling. With the pitchfork held before to demonstrate violent intent if assailed, he advanced on the inert form that was lying on its side, facing away.

There was something terrifying in its stillness, as if the thing were already dead, and Plookie tried to keep a primitive fear of demonic possession at bay.

He sighted and aimed the prongs.

'Name yourself!' he demanded like a man of mettle.

It turned over – a human face, bloody and battered, yet Plookie thought to find some recognition.

'Ye have tae help me – I'm bad hurted –' The words were hardly distinguishable but now the face was known.

In the wynds he had seen that face and it had connection to the Just Land.

The fear Plookie had felt was ignited like a flame and burnt through into his bones. No wonder Raggie had been howling to the heavens. This was trouble of the worst kind – and it was coming his way.

Chapter 21

Get thee glass eyes;
And like a scurvy politician, seem
To see the things thou dost not

Lieutenant Robert Roach was an unimaginative man, as befits a middle-ranked Mason; however, at this precise moment he might understand the incipient quiver of anger that could eventually lead to murder.

He glanced up backwards at James McLevy but his murderous missile of thought was directed elsewhere.

For his part, McLevy was more inclined towards instant strangulation or wringing of a scrawny neck, such as a farmer's wife might supply to a chosen chicken. Twist, pluck, boil.

The object of both these homicidal inclinations was one Inspector Adam Dunsmore, though not far behind in the pecking order as far as McLevy was concerned came Chief Constable Murray Craddock.

All five, if the non-committal form of Mulholland might be included in the mix, were grouped under the stern regard of Queen Victoria, who was immovable in portrait upon the wall of the lieutenant's office.

She had ruled there for many years and no such intemperate decisions as Lear inflicted upon his kingdom would have found favour in that weighty gaze. However, it did mean that she had now and then to listen in on some idiotic, egotistical statements such as were proceeding below.

'The Chief Constable was kind enough to honour me with his company to make certain that we all understand the' – Dunsmore rolled the word around in his mouth like a child would a winning marble – '*ramifications* of what is involved here.'

The chief constable inclined his head in agreement with this implication; it was no secret that he regarded Leith Station as an untidy blot upon his spotless career – especially a blemish in the shape of James McLevy who, despite all appearances to the contrary, managed to more or less continuously solve murder and foil criminality by some accidental fortune and certainly not by judgement or ability, in Craddock's infallible opinion.

McLevy spent so much time with the dirt and trash of Leith and further contamination lay in his cheek-by-jowl commune with Jean Brash – a creature that Craddock would love to view pleading piteously through the cell bars while he shook a stern head and then left her to stew in the steaming pot of sin. Sadly the woman was as slippery as a snake and also knew certain facts about those in civic control that rendered them susceptible to her blandishments.

Roach he deemed to be a weak link in the feeble chain of command of Leith, yet the station's success in keeping the lid on the lawless rabbit warrens of the wynds and harbours could not be denied.

Therefore the status quo endured but if Craddock had his way, he would raze the wynds to the ground, scour the harbour as one might disinfect a sink, and the parish would then be pristine, with no necessity for such enforcers of law.

However, until that lucky day the chief constable could take a deal of satisfaction from the look of suffused fury on McLevy's face and trust that Roach was developing an ulcer.

The lieutenant never outright defied his superior officer but Craddock could not rid himself of the feeling that, somewhere, somehow, Roach positioned on McLevy's side of the fence.

'Inspector Dunsmore will now reveal what has been confided to the Edinburgh City Police authorities and over which, as I believe has been more than clarified to all those present, he has complete command.'

In the silence that followed, Dunsmore took from his pocket a sealed envelope and made great show of prising aside the embossed waxed stamp, to then extract a single sheet of paper. He looked down importantly, pursed his lips, nodded like Moses on the mountain, and prepared to divulge.

In fact, Dunsmore had already been told and been planning this for weeks but it suited him to keep the thing unveiled till the very last minute.

The more he strung it out the more enjoyment.

'You will, I assume, gentlemen, have heard tell of the Tholberg necklace?'

He savoured the blank look on McLevy's face, while Roach answered on behalf of the ignorant.

'Worth a fortune, they say, and to be displayed at the Castle rooms as part of the civic celebration of culture. I read it in the paper.'

'Exactly, Lieutenant,' Craddock observed. 'Good that you keep abreast of present events.'

Roach rose above the condescending tone of his chief constable. 'I take it this is the valuable shipment you have mentioned, Inspector Dunsmore?'

'Indeed, Lieutenant. On the way from Amsterdam. And arrives in Leith harbour this very night by a chartered vessel – the *Deliverance*.'

Now all three faces were blank. With shock, no doubt – now he could lay it on with a trowel.

'My chosen men will be waiting with me to receive the necklace. A small picked band of excellent officers.'

This was his master plan as he outlined it to them.

Word had already been given to the papers that the necklace would arrive tomorrow morning by other means, on the train from London perhaps, under police guard, just to deflect any possible threats of robbery.

Meanwhile the jewellery would arrive by maritime subterfuge the night before, be transported to the Castle and then beneath the most severe security kept safe so that the public could file past to ogle at a unique combination of art and wealth.

However, the one fly in the ointment was that the delivery by ship would have to be in Leith harbour. This was McLevy's parish and to make sure that the inspector did not interfere with the plan, it was best that he be on the scene – to observe, to most definitely admire, but not to take part.

'And as regards myself?' asked Roach.

'You will be at the play of *King Lear* with your dear wife who never misses such events,' Craddock interposed briskly. 'As I shall be also. All of Edinburgh will be there. It is important that we do not alert any of those with criminal intent by our absence from the attendance.'

Roach failed to see how his lack of presence at a heavy-lunged Shakespearean tragedy would cause larcenous hordes of jewel thieves to descend on Leith, but frankly he was happy enough to avoid waiting in the cold harbour with an evil east wind blowing rain into his face – as, he shrewdly suspected, was the chief constable, who would rather marinate in genteel society.

'Do you have anything to say, McLevy?' asked Dunsmore, a trifle chagrined that his masterly recitation had produced so little reaction – the fellow was like a lump of cheese.

Finally, the lump spoke.

'How many comprise your chosen men?'

'Half a dozen. No more than that else we might attract attention.'

'Will they be armed?'

'Stout police sticks will be sufficient.'

'I concur absolutely, Inspector Dunsmore. Too often firearms have been used to ill effect in this parish.'

Craddock's snide reference touched upon a bone of contention. It was well known that McLevy's old service revolver had settled many a fracas between himself and the criminal fraternity, the only problem being that it was as much noted for noise as accuracy. Either McLevy's aim or the gun sight was at fault, but no murderous felon was left in any condition to lay blame on one or the other.

And what McLevy missed, Mulholland hit – with a hornbeam implement he had made and wielded like the great Cuchulain himself. The constable may have lacked the Irish hero's battle frenzy but his eye was unerring.

'And where will we be stationed, as it were?' he queried mildly. 'If we're not wanted on voyage, sir.'

Mulholland and McLevy flanked the seated Roach like defunct bookends as Craddock answered.

'You will remain at the side, Constable. You will – as I have emphasised – not take part. You will merely observe. From a distance. It will be' – Craddock stood up from where he had been sitting opposite the lieutenant at his desk – 'an opportunity for one and all to see how the expert conducts an operation with skill and certainty.'

A timid knock at the door sounded with neither skill nor certainty and at Roach's behest, Constable Ballantyne poked in a young and worried head. In truth should anyone typify the ramshackle nature of Leith Station, it was this particular entrant. If ever a man was born not to be a policeman, it was Ballantyne. His main focus in life seemed to be the protection of the station insects from the hobnailed boots of the other constables yet he possessed a curious innocence that somehow protected himself as well.

He also had a vivid scarlet birthmark that ran down the length of his face and disappeared into his collar.

'Em – sir?' he blurted to a stony-faced lieutenant.

'Yes, Constable?'

Ballantyne tried desperately not to catch anyone else's eye; the lieutenant's was bad enough.

'There's a hansom-cab driver, stuck outside for the, em—' Ballantyne coughed as if something had got stuck in his prominent windpipe. 'Chief Constable. He's gettin' dead impatient. Whit should I tell him?'

'Go away, Ballantyne,' replied Roach.

The constable's face registered confusion as to how he might convey that particular message.

'Go away,' Roach repeated, 'and tell the driver to wait – his hurry.'

That made better sense. Ballantyne left gratefully.

All this merely confirmed what Craddock had been suspecting for many years: the place was a dog's dinner. He shook his head and signalled to Dunsmore that it was time for the legitimate representatives of law and order to take their leave.

McLevy, during all of this, had remained uncommonly silent and Dunsmore addressed the mute inspector to drum sense into what he considered to be an obdurate skull.

'My men and I will be here at eight o'clock this night, McLevy. See that you're ready to take a secondary position according to rank. And – above all – above all, Inspector –' Like a character in an overwrought mime play, he raised forefinger to the lips and frowned, his eyes narrowed in warning. 'Not one word to a living person, McLevy. No matter how cosy the circumstance!'

This clear reference to caffeine liaisons with bawdy-hoose keepers caused McLevy's face to finally alter expression as he twitched up one side of a hirsute nostril.

Both Roach and Mulholland, assuming they were not included in this admonition, refrained from nasal reaction, though a muscle in the lieutenant's lantern jaw flexed to indicate some inner thought.

'Eight o'clock,' repeated Craddock as the invaders made for the door. 'The play will start at precisely the same time. Quite a coincidence, eh?'

Having issued his one *bon mot* of the decade, the chief constable left in state, with Dunsmore the lap dog at his heels.

Silence ensued.

Mulholland had been thinking.

'Half a dozen. That's not many. Not if that necklace is worth as much as they say.'

'It's worth more. And it brings bad luck.'

Finally – like the Delphic Oracle – the inspector had broken his self-imposed silence.

Roach sighed. Of course McLevy would know more about the approaching string of gems than he'd been prepared to let on, especially to an irritating fool such as Dunsmore.

'Enlighten us, James.'

The inspector raised finger to his lips in parody of the departed Dunsmore, then leant forward to whisper as if relating a dark secret.

'Thirty years ago in the country of Holland, Josef Tholberg is a very rich man but he's not a pleasant one. He wants to do something that will make his name live on forever. So he spends a king's ransom to assemble some of the most precious diamonds from the mines of such countries that forge them in the molten depths.'

'Molten depths? I hope you're not getting carried away here, McLevy.'

Roach glanced up uneasily at Victoria but Mulholland was gripped by the tale, large ears flapping.

'I'm with you, sir. Molten depths, it is.'

'He hires a group of craftsmen to create a thing of beauty. Priceless. But then a quarrel occurs, no one knows the cause but he dismisses them all. Without due payment. I did say he wasnae a nice man. So now Josef has his deepest desire. Three days later he dies in his sleep. A heart attack. The organ must have overflowed with joy. Too much money can do that. The necklace ends up in an Amsterdam museum and a legend grows that one of the largest diamonds was mined from a sacred mountain in South Africa – stolen from the gods – and is therefore cursed – bringing death wherever it goes. So they put it in a glass case where it cannot do harm.

And now it's on the way to Edinburgh. Bringing death.'

Dramatic recitation over, McLevy straightened up to speak in normal tones.

'That's the story anyway.'

'I remember some rumours of such in the papers,' observed Roach dryly. 'Figments of imagination.'

'What if it's already struck home?'

'How do you mean, Inspector?'

Mulholland was becoming unsettled. McLevy had that weird look on his face that signalled departure from the known universe. It usually meant he was communing with some buried instinct and it nearly always – for sure – ended up as a harbinger of violent murderous events.

Not unlike, if true, the necklace.

Connections were being made inside those neural pathways that might well be leading to catastrophe.

'Erik de Witte,' McLevy muttered almost to himself. 'A craftsman. In jewels. From Holland. He arrives here. He dies. Murdered.'

'A case you have yet to solve.'

McLevy paid no attention to this pertinent reminder and Mulholland was growing more uncomfortable by the second – the only person he knew that could divine the inspector's instincts was a certain female at the Just Land.

Peas in a pod, the pair of them.

'He couldn't have worked on the necklace all those years ago, sir, he'd be a babe in arms.'

'No. Correct.'

'And from what you have told me,' Roach said suspiciously, 'he also paid a visit to Jean Brash, who sent him on his way.'

'To die.'

More silence.

Roach had been sore stretched by his treatment at the hands of Dunsmore and Craddock and now his temper flared, jaw snapping like a crocodile.

'All I know is that when you and Mistress Brash get to grips, this station ends up in chaos and I become willy-nilly involved to the detriment of my reputation!'

McLevy pulled himself out of a labyrinth of thought where tangled recollection fought to make sense. De Witte had once fashioned her a necklace and Jean loved her jewellery but what had it to do with anything? Surely she would not be so foolish as to get immersed in any jewel-bound criminality? Or would she?

He remembered something Hannah Semple had recently muttered to him: *'The Mistress aye gets restless in spring. And when she gets restless – she wreaks bliddy havoc.'*

Ah well – the lieutenant may be right for once – get on with the case.

'We'll be out on the saunter, sir. Trawl the taverns and see if we can find a trace where de Witte went after the Just Land. No stone unturned!'

'On your way, then.'

As they moved to do so, raised voices were heard through the door coming from the main body of the station, one intonation identifiably an offended Ballantyne.

'Ye did that deliberate.'

'I did not!'

'Ye did so.'

'I cannae see whit I cannae see!'

'One of the constables must have stood upon a beetle,' deduced Mulholland. 'Ballantyne gets very aggrieved about such things.'

Roach closed his eyes. 'I thank God for the daily strength He sends me to endure the many vicissitudes visited upon my person.'

'I feel exactly the same, sir.'

To this platitudinous response of McLevy's, Roach snapped open his eyes once more. 'Get to hell out of my office,' he said, biting the words as a crocodile would a pygmy hog. 'And don't come back till you find something of use. Go away!'

They left, the door closed, and Roach cast a contrite glance up at Her Majesty for his lack of verbal grace and deportment.

She had survived seven assassination attempts, mostly by lunatics since murderous attempts upon the monarch by reason of political belief were frowned upon within her kingdom – nevertheless seven! One of them as recent as March of last year.

And you'd never guess it to look at her face.

Chapter 22

Some villain hath done me wrong

The cellars of the Just Land were normally used for two purposes. One, the laying on of leather to assuage the guilt that the rulers, not by birth but by dint of the capitalist system, might possibly feel at exploitation of those who slave below.

This guilt is hypothetical and may well be merely a naked desire for inflicted pain, but for some reason all this leads on to the second cellar usage. That of a cheese vault – the temperature being constant and never too warm, was perfect for the storing of the various dairy products. From Scotland crowdie, kebbock, Orkney, and from France – according to the taste of Mistress Brash – stronger specimens such as Camembert, Vieux Lille and the goaty Tomme de Chèvre which, in Hannah Semple's opinion, stank like the devil's backside.

Why capitalism should lead to a strong smell connected to Satan's hinder parts is another question entirely, but there was a third chamber – smaller, off to the side – and it was in this room on a hastily arranged pallet that the body lay.

The room itself was crowded.

Maisie Powers crouched near the straw mattress, Lily Baxter beside her.

Standing on the other side were Jean and Hannah.

A snuffling on the floor announced the presence of the dog

Raggie, chewing happily on a hard rind of hangman cheese that its master had come across on the floor.

Plookie would rather have been anywhere else on the planet but he was stuck in the place until dismissed.

Lying on the mattress, white as the ghost he had nearly become, was Richie Powers, Maisie's younger and stunted wee brother. Barely above five feet in height, childlike of body, innocent cheerful countenance like a choirboy – all useful for unauthorised entry but not for defending the possessor against brutal attack.

Jean and Hannah had returned to an unravelling story that may not have had the grandeur of *King Lear* on Leith Links but nonetheless possessed its own wounded elements.

In the hayloft, Plookie had recognised the battered face and run like a dervish headlong into the Just Land. Luckily, big Annie Drummond had at just that moment herded the magpies off for their monthly inspection by auld Doctor Fairbairn, an expert in matters of unwished-for manifestations such as *grandgore*, *glengorie*, *the ripples*, or any other malignant offshoot of unprotected congress.

Of course, the clients were supposedly sheathed up to the eyebrows but there was many a slip 'twixt cup and lip and no chances were to be taken by order of Jean Brash. Her damsels were to be, apart from the odd shenanigan, clean as a whistle. A man of venerable age, Douglas Fairbairn was trusted by the girls and had the manner somewhat of an irascible sheepdog rounding up the spring-heeled lambs; plus the fact that unlike most folk in Edinburgh, he was not prone to gossip, being teetotal and tight-mouthed.

Left alone in the kitchen were Maisie and Lily who had no truck with penetrative male incursion and thus no need to shed shanks for internal scrutiny. It was to them, therefore, that Plookie blurted news of the upsetting discovery in the stables.

Maisie was holding a cup of tea that fell to the flagstone floor and shattered into pieces; Lily, who had lip-read the evil tidings, grabbed her lover to hustle the woman out of there; Raggie licked at the spilt tea; and Plookie wiped up the mess, feeling it was all his fault.

Somehow they had transported the groaning heap of bones down the ladder and into the wee cellar room where a straw bed was installed from early days when Maisie had got occasionally got too carried away and the client needed to rest up before returning to the happy home.

The doctor had been summoned having ended the examinations and just about to leave, sworn to a secrecy he had never broken, and made cursory examination: ribcage heavy bruised, multiple contusions, possible inner complications yet to manifest, kidneys suffering a deal of rough usage; a sackful of sore bones. When Fairbairn stripped back Richie's shirt, the bruising on his back was extensive and could only have been caused by a severe kicking.

Strapping was improvised for the ribs from some torn stiff cloth and thick tape and then the doctor left promising to send by messenger ointment for the bruising and also to return the next day if advised to do so.

By the mercy of God – Fairbairn was a devout Good Templar, which made his attendance at a bawdy-hoose all the more striking – it would seem that the lungs were not punctured or damage inflicted upon the wall of the chest, so with rest might come recuperation.

With that he took his leave.

Richie had answered the doctor's questions with a mumble but was conscious enough to make sense. He would not say, however, who had done the deed and how it had happened; he merely lay there with his eyes closed.

The dog had accompanied Plookie all this time and now it whined – it was starving and the spilt tea had done little to alleviate that hunger.

At this point the door opened to admit Jean Brash and Hannah Semple.

And now they all looked at each other across the prone body of Richie Powers.

'What happened?' The speaker's face was cold, almost impersonal, eyes boring into his, and Plookie Galbraith realised at that moment exactly how you get to be the Mistress of the Just Land.

He explained as best he could the finding plus aftermath, but not the sick feeling in his gut that he *knew* who was behind all this, and his terrible fear of what might follow.

'Wake him up,' Jean demanded of Maisie.

'Mistress, he's bad hurted.'

'So the doctor told me. We met him on the hill. He was on the road. We were in the carriage. He told us. Now – wake your brother up.'

'Whit if he dies frae shock?'

'He brings trouble to my house. I need to know why.'

'We're no' a bliddy charity,' said Hannah. 'Your brother runs wi' a bad crowd. Rotten tae the core.'

Maisie's face set in stubborn line – Richie was her favourite. 'He's too kind hearted.'

'So was Jesus – see where it got him,' Hannah shot back.

Battle lines were being drawn and Plookie saw a chance to escape.

'Mistress, can I go now? Angus will be shouting. The horses 're steaming wi' that hill, and the dog's dead famished. I've tellt ye all that I know.'

'I hope so, Plookie.'

Her eyes were steady. Ice-green. He had to get out of there. It was like a nightmare. Once in the wynds, a bunch of boys had tracked him. An easy target. They had pulled him down, kicked him side to side, then one took out his weapon and aimed.

Urine is unmistakable. Warm, then cold, then stinks to high heaven.

They all did so. In turn. And it was then Plookie decided to be a daftie. Not worth pissing on. Who can get pleasure from pissing on something lower than a sewer?

One boy smaller than the rest. Runt of the litter. But he had a go. Good aim. Right between the eyes.

Richie Powers. Smiling like an angel.

And Niven Taggart was the devil.

Jean looked at the gangling frame. She could sense the fear but not the cause; however, she had enough to concern herself with at this moment. She nodded and Plookie left with the dog at his heels. After all, like it or not, according to Raggie he was leader of the pack.

Jean then turned back to Maisie Powers.

'Wake him up,' she said.

Chapter 23

Such smiling rogues as these,
Like rats, oft bite the holy cords a-twain
Which are too intrinse t' unloose.

He had thought himself to be safe.

After getting away from the ship, he was in a panic. Had McLevy seen him? Seen his face?

If the policeman had not done so, all would be well, and how could McLevy have seen? He was too quick out that porthole; too fast. Lik' a bolt o' lightning.

Just go back to Niven Taggart, tell him it was too difficult, too many people – aye – that would be best.

And that's what he did. In the tavern. Leaning over the table. Voice low, face honest.

Niven wasnae pleased but he nodded, took back the cabin key, mebbye use it some other time, slid a drink over by way of payment and Richie left in a hurry. He was safe, that was the main thing.

Except he was not safe.

That night. Late. Richie was in a card school – winning for a change, full of beans. He got a message someone wanted to see him outside.

He went out. Full of beans. It was Bob Golspie: Niven Taggart wanted his company. That should have rung alarms bells right away but Richie was winning. When you win you think your luck will never stop.

And never change.

He asked Bob the reason and the big man smiled.

'Another wee job – piece of cake,' said he.

But Bob did not say who would be doing the job and who would cut the cake.

They came in by the rear of the tavern and went to the back place where the Bonny Boys had their lair – it was a small room, thick walls and a heavy door.

Bob closed that door and leant back against it.

Niven smiled thin. Sitting at a table. Cards on it. Playing patience by candle.

He was winning as well, mebbye?

'Ye lied tae me,' said Niven.

'Eh?'

'McLevy was in this night. Looking for ye.'

'Whit did he say?'

'Enough.'

He turned over a card from the pack he held. It was the Four of Clubs.

'That's a bad-luck card,' remarked Niven. 'The Devil's Bedpost.'

He squared the pack up neatly.

'I gave ye that key tae get into the cabin. Ye were caught at it. McLevy saw you. Ye lied tae me.'

Then they battered hell out of him. Bob going easy though he did land some hard chops on the kidneys, but then Richie fell and Niven got to work with the boot.

Other than the big knife, this was his favourite.

He kicked in to the ribs and then carried on the previous diligence to the kidneys while Bob stood back in admiration.

Richie yelped and howled and when Niven stopped, spilled out what had occurred in the cabin.

'I thought he hadnae seen me!'

'Ye were wrong.'

Then while Richie whimpered in pain, in hellish pain on the dirty floor, Niven and Bob stood over and talked as if nothing had happened here.

'If he spills his guts tae McLevy, that's a lot of trouble for me.'

'He wouldnae dare, Niven.'

'If McLevy gets him in the cells. If he sticks that big gun of his under the wee skiter's nose.'

Richie squinted up through a rapidly closing eye; Bob looked worried.

'Murder.'

'Eh?'

'In the tavern. McLevy. He said "murder".'

'That's my business, Bob.'

Silence.

'Whit do we do with him?'

'Get rid.'

'But he's one of us, Niven. That's not good fortune.'

'He betrayed me.'

'He's a wee liar. Didnae know any better.'

Richie froze despite the pain. Killing one of your own was frowned on amongst the keelie gangs, unless there was strong reason. That was his only hope.

And Bob Golspie, despite the hammering he had meted out, was decent enough wi' Richie.

Niven sighed impatiently. 'I have too much on my mind. Tomorrow night is all that matters. Tie him up. I'll think about it later.'

'We cannae leave him here.'

'Stick him in the cubbyhole. Wi' the rats.'

Bob snickered in relief. The cubbyhole was a rodent-infested tiny alcove off the room. Under lock and key and where the Bonny Boys kept their cache of surplus weapons.

'That'll be funny. Bite him tae death.'

'Jist do it,' ordered Niven and left the room.

Bob knelt down and spat lightly into Richie's face.

'Ye're a lucky wee boy,' he grinned.

Chapter 24

The enemy's in view; draw up your powers.
Here is the guess of their true strength and forces
By diligent discovery

The lucky wee boy ended his recitation thus far and licked parched lips.

'I'm dead thirsty.'

Lily dipped a clean cloth into a basin of water that had been brought for the doctor and patted the material gently over Richie's cracked mouth – an oddly tender gesture that contrasted with the other faces in the room: Maisie's taut with worry; Hannah Semple's resembling a piece of rock that had fallen from a moonscape; and finally, the gaze of Jean Brash looking down at Richie, propped up on a pillow against the rough wall, as if he were an insect under a microscope.

'How did you get out of there?'

'Bob tied up the ropes careless. In a hurry mebbye.'

'Or he wanted you out of harm's way?' guessed Hannah.

'No. Bob kisses Niven Taggart's arse. He wouldnae cross him.'

'So – how did you get out?'

He wished the woman would stop looking at him like that. They said she had poisoned and killed people, set places on fire like a witch at Halloween; from that stare he could well believe it.

'I slipped the ropes anyhows. There was a wee window in the cubbyhole. I'm good wi' windows.'

He tried the semblance of a winning smile, but it just hurt his mouth and her face did not change.

'Why come here?'

'Nowhere else.'

Maisie spoke in the silence.

'You could have gone to – to my mother.'

Richie sniffed. 'She'd have killed me, Maisie.'

'What a pity.'

This acerbic comment from Hannah produced a faint grimace of humour from him but Richie was beginning to suffer from the aftershock of his beating. His mother had warned him that if he got into trouble with the keelies, he was on his own. She detested Niven Taggart and the like because they preyed on the poor. They were predators, leeches sucking the lifeblood from folk in the wynds.

Winifred Powers had brought up a family of decent shoplifters of mixed ability but at least they stole from ones who could afford the luxury of loss.

And she only warned the once.

His big sister Maisie aye had a soft spot for him, a respectable job in a bawdy-hoose, and so it was to her he fled. Through the back alleys in the dead of night, rats scuttling under his feet, squeezing his aching body through the tiniest gap in the railings by the big iron gate of the Just Land, into the garden. The peacocks had started squawking but then went back to sleep. The whole house was locked up tight so the only place was the stables – there was a wee chute for the straw bales that he climbed to get inside, and then somehow up that ladder.

He glossed over all this with the words: 'Well – here I am.' One of his teeth had been cut and he dribbled a bit of blood on to the damp cloth for effect.

It failed to impress either Jean or Hannah; they could see Richie Powers for what he was. Feral. Sly. Conniving wee bugger. Not without charm, not without appeal or even strength, because his survival instinct had driven him through an ordeal that would have sunk many another, but – not necessarily to be trusted.

His only loyalty would be to himself. He would manipulate his sister or anyone who loved him.

They had both met so many of this breed and though he was not beyond redemption, it would seem his path was set. In with a bad crowd.

Heading nowhere with both McLevy and Niven Taggart on his trail.

And now they were stuck with him, like a sheep with a tick.

Lily watched all the faces. She could sense the danger this person brought. Maisie, unconsciously, had placed her hand close to her brother's where it lay outside, upon the rough blanket that covered the bed.

He had always been the favourite of the family, the youngest, full of cheek like an imp of mischief, clever with his hands – he could fix anything that broke – but then he had slid into bad ways, especially after the arrival of his sister Jessie's baby – a little girl. Her mother had been in the Perth Penitentiary at the time, but other than that, the child seemed in fine fettle. She was the favoured one now, named after her grandmother who ruled the family, and Richie's nose had been put well and truly out of joint.

Jealous as hell.

Perhaps this would learn him a lesson?

The Mistress and Hannah had no such hope.

'You can stay here until recovered,' Jean addressed Richie in formal tones. 'There's a wee privy at the back you can use. Meals can be brought. I don't want you in the house. You are not to be seen. Once you are gone, it will be as if you have never existed.'

Richie bowed his head – either to hide a relieved smile, or to acknowledge a shaft of pain.

'Thank you, Mistress Brash,' Maisie blurted. 'You are very kind.'

Something, however, had just occurred to Lily and her fingers flew as this was communicated to Maisie. The mime was finished by Lily opening her mouth in a silent scream that was both comical and alarming.

'Whit the hell's a' this?' muttered Hannah. 'We're no' in a bliddy pantomime.'

Maisie interpreted: 'What about the cellar clientele, Mistress?'

'What?'

A matter of family etiquette had also been raised – did a big sister want her wee brother to audibly witness the way she made a living?

'They make a gey lot of noise, sometimes.'

For a moment there was a glint of humour in Jean's eyes before she answered in deadpan fashion: 'It will complete your brother's education.'

Hannah weighed in. 'And hey, Richie, ye badly need education, I've seen mair brains in a turnip.'

Being compared to a root vegetable nettled the wounded warrior. 'How come?'

'Ye thought tae give Jamie McLevy the slip? That he wouldnae catch sight of your face?'

'Uhuh.'

'Did it never occur? If you could see him, he could see you?'

Richie had no answer, except a hostile stare.

'You do not move from this room,' said Jean. 'Save when nature calls. Do you understand me?'

The damaged eye was slowly turning a shade of green and dark blue, giving Richie the look of a badly damaged cherub as he nodded slowly in response.

'He'll be as good as gold, Mistress.'

Maisie's hopeful words hung in the air as the two other women left.

Now all the aches and pains began to throb through Richie's body with a lot of worries to keep them company.

Niven Taggart would not take kindly to his escaping – how was he to get out of this? He might have to leave Edinburgh – that would take money.

He looked into his sister's anxious eyes. She was holding hands wi' the deaf and dumb girl.

Mebbye they were in love? That might be useful. All things are useful when your back is to the wall.

And so he smiled at his sister.

'I could strangle you,' said Maisie.

Chapter 25

Be govern'd by your knowledge, and proceed
I' the sway of your own will

The peacocks were strutting around the garden, males arranging tail feathers in such fashion as might tempt a credulous member of the opposite persuasion.

Jean had been silent since they emerged from the cellar door, up the stone steps and into the open air.

'Penny for your thoughts, Mistress?'

'Murder – and James McLevy.'

Jean Brash looked out over the grounds. It was only mid morning but it seemed as if time had been compressed into such an intense nugget that a year had passed since they had departed early that morning.

'Explain yourself,' Hannah replied.

'If we are to believe Richie, when the Inspector barged into the tavern he searched for young Mister Powers and cited as his reason "murder".'

'He didnae say a damned word when he was here about such murders and visits tae taverns.'

'No. That would be deliberate. He knows I'll find out, just wants to – stir the pot.'

'How come?'

'Because he suspects I may be involved in all this.'

'All what?'

'Who knows?'

'And are you?'

'I am *now*.'

One of the peacocks let out a mournful wail as if to underline her words.

'Niven Taggart had the key to Erik de Witte's cabin – he gave it to Richie. Looking for what, I wonder?'

'Ask the wee thief.'

'Richie would just be told to bring back anything he could get his hands on and also he maintains that he fled before being able to delve.'

This situation was full of misgivings, where trust was in short supply.

'I don't want to hazard over many questions. I don't want folk to know what I'm thinking.'

'Ye've let me know.'

'I can trust you.'

'Whit're you thinking in that case?'

'How could Niven have the key – unless he took it? And to take it – he might have to kill.'

Hannah nodded. 'That makes sense.'

The day had now become overcast to match the sombre tenor of Jean's thoughts. Her mind flashed back to when Erik de Witte had responded to her polite but firm refusal by elegantly sliding a last oyster down his throat, and following it with a final glass of champagne.

'I regret, Jean Brash, I cannot follow your good advice and go back home with my – how do you say – tail between my feet?'

'Legs.'

'Of course. Legs.'

He laughed but she was not so amused. His English was better than most of her native-born clients'. This was deflection.

'What will you do?' she queried.

'Always behind my plan, there is another plan. Like a magic trick. A mask behind a mask.'

More laughter. But not from her.

'What other plan, Erik?'

'Ah, but I am not allowed to tell. And you are not allowed to ask. This has been made clear by your very command. You are – so to say – hoist by your own petard.'

A mocking gleam in his eye to disguise the disappointment felt, then he stood, bent over to kiss her hand in a final farewell.

How final, neither knew at that moment.

'Goodnight, Jean Brash – till we meet again.'

With that he was out the door and into the darkness.

This she told to Hannah while the peacocks went back to their cages; it was near to feeding time and Plookie Galbraith would be appearing shortly. The exotic fish likewise were rippling the surface of the water. Jean would deal with their needs – there was always a danger of overfeeding the brutes.

Hannah absorbed all she had been told from now and before. Despite terse delivery, she had a tough logical mind that retained facts and came to conclusions.

'Ye said Mister de Witte intended tae rob?'

'Yes. A big robbery, he assured me.'

'For revenge?'

'His words.'

'Whit manner o' revenge?'

Unseen by both, a large ginger tomcat had leapt up upon the high wall that enclosed the garden as Jean paused a moment before answering.

'That – was his secret.'

Hannah grunted at this slightly ambiguous answer before returning to her pursuance. 'Big? That would need men. Whit he hoped tae get from you. Which he did not.'

'It would seem so.'

'So – should he fail – he had someone else in mind?'

'Uhuh. That would be his – other plan.'

'Niven Taggart has men. The Bonny Boys. A whole bliddy gang o' them.'

'Correct.'

Plookie emerged from the stable with a basin of birdseed, Raggie on a stringy lead, a thick home-made collar round his neck. As the birds eagerly pecked around, the dog stood its ground but made no aggressive move; it was not going to start a rammy over birdseed.

'Nice wee dug,' said Hannah out of the blue. 'No' too yappy.'

'Some things are nice in this world,' replied Jean.

Erik de Witte was dead. He had never been her lover or even offered so. She had often wondered if his taste lay in other channels, but no matter now. One thing was for sure: he had cherished his craft more than anything else. When he put the peacock necklace round her throat, all these years ago, it was as if adorning a queen.

'Beauty deserves beauty,' he had murmured.

As regards his last visit, things were happening at such a speed that she would keep certain matters he had confided that night to herself for the moment.

Hannah had quite enough information; the old woman would just worry herself to death if given any more.

'This robbery, Mistress – did he say when?'

'Soon. That's all.'

But he had said more than that. And it was aye useful to keep a card up the sleeve.

Somewhere in Leith, James McLevy would be putting things together in that brain of his – not for the first time, he and Jean would be on a collision course.

She had read in the newspaper that the Tholberg necklace would be arriving under guard at the train station. To attempt a robbery there would surely be foolish, yet Erik de Witte had hinted at grand theft and he was not stupid.

What did he have that gave him an edge?

So many questions, so few answers.

'Whit're ye going tae do, Mistress?'

'I do not entirely trust what Richie Powers has told us. Perhaps it is true. Perhaps not. Perhaps he is a spy.'

'Well, he suffered like buggery for that job.'

'If Niven Taggart killed my friend. Then there will be a reckoning.'

Hannah was not reassured by this remark. Reckonings, from her experience, could be a costly business.

'Ye don't know for sure.'

'I will put my people to watching Niven Taggart. For the moment that is all I *can* do.'

And then she had a further thought. 'We will also warn them not to get too close. Just – observation. In case of danger.'

'One thing puzzles me, Mistress.'

Jean watched Plookie return to the stables – the tall boy was hiding something from her but what was it? She felt she could trust him, but everyone has something to conceal.

'Speak your mind.'

'Niven Taggart has aye been a nothing. A keelie. With his gang. No' worth a spit. How come he's sprouted wings? How come he's such a big man now?'

Jean had only crossed paths with Taggart a few times, once in Vinegar Close when she and Hannah were walking through – it was an area of conduits Jean had known well as a child and on an impulse she had entered the wynd while passing by near the harbour.

Niven and Bob Golspie were hanging about on the corner. She had nodded coolly to both as a Queen Bee might. Bob had looked embarrassed – Jean had good acquaintance with his mother, Maggie Golspie, who was hard as nails, especially with her eldest-born. The mother had gone to Jean in debt to a lender and it had been sorted out. How, Bob did not know, but he knew there was a different kind of debt now owed. That of gratitude.

But Niven Taggart? There was something in his eyes that had disturbed her. A memory of something – someone – and a menace latent as a bad seed.

'Evil can grow. At a rate of knots.'

Hannah shook her head. 'This is a' too deep for me.'

The sound of agitated birds broke the mood. A pair of robins were flying furiously round a bush, chattering like castanets – spring brought forth fledglings, and a young and vulnerable bird brought out other beasts.

'That bliddy animal!'

At Hannah's shout, the ginger cat shot off from overhanging shrubbery and bolted back over the wall.

'Horace,' Jean identified.

'I know the bugger. Only too well.'

Horace was the cat of Jack Burns, who, like its master, had somehow found himself a calling place at the Just Land.

'Once these wee souls start falling out the nest it'll be carnage in this place.'

For some reason, an image from the dream, a dream that seemed in some way to have started all the events that followed, jumped into Jean's mind.

The baby.

For some reason, she had never looked it straight in the face. The eyes had always been hidden. Only the mouth – that questing, sucking mouth – was in her view. Always hungry. Seeking for the breast.

She brought herself out of the memory, yet had a realisation that the image had imprinted itself upon her, as would a boot-heel.

'We'd better get back,' she announced. 'I have many things to set in motion.'

'Aye – and one you've forgotten.'

'What?'

'That Sapphic wifie. Two o'clock this day. Are you not supposed tae be scratched on paper?'

'Oh my God.'

'Right enough.'

Sarah Baines had been promised an hour of Jean's time to begin a preliminary sketch for an eventual full-length painting of Mistress Brash in all her glory.

'A' this arty-crafty stuff creeps up on ye, eh?' commented Hannah Semple with a wicked smile.

Chapter 26

I will do such things.
What they are, yet I know not: but they shall be
The terrors of the earth

This was his safe haven. No one knew of it. No one could touch him here.

He had locked the door, curtained the window and stripped himself stark naked, save for the hook-knife that was strapped across him in its harness.

Now he could think clear without idiots like Bob Golspie fogging his mind with their mistakes, causing him untold complications.

This was the room where his mother had died. He had watched the life ebb from her eyes and remembered well her last words: 'Revenge me. Revenge us all.'

She had shrunk to the size of a shrewmouse, as if the marrow of her bones had been sucked dry by the greedy mouth of death. Only her eyes still lived. Not almond-shaped like his own but burning with a good and decent hatred.

Hatred is a fine fuel.

Then they closed. Then she was gone.

They say that when the man breathes his last, ancestral energy fires into the son. But the father's seed had shot like a spark into the mother, his mother Mae, so when she died was it not a double discharge?

He let out a strange choked laugh in the empty room.

Niven lay on the bed where his mother had died. It was kept clean, he made sure of that. The room itself, also kept clean as a winding sheet, was completely empty except for one three-legged stool.

He had sat upon that stool to watch her give up the ghost, holding her hand – like a withered leaf, a wormcast.

It was the room where Maureen, her sister, had raised him. Kept him neat and tidy. Shining. She had been a kind woman. But not clever.

Niven was clever. Born for something different. He had gone through the motions of being a keelie, but his heart wasn't in it.

What was he, though? Just a feeling of not belonging – he dressed and behaved different to the rest; they were wild, garish and flamboyant while he was *contained*.

And he smelled nice. He always liked to smell nice. And clean. Once a week he went to the barber. Once a week to the Turkish baths. Some men there looked at him but not for long – once he looked back.

Yet that was him. Complete. So – where did he belong? Where do you go from here?

When he asked after his father, Maureen shook her head. That was Mae's business.

Mae had promised that on his twenty-first birthday she would reveal a name. A lost name. For a dead man. But then death came to claim her before that happy day and he worried she would say nothing. And he would be left just Niven Taggart. Nothing more.

All this had disappeared when Mae, with what was near her last breath, told him the secret. Then the fire had burned.

So – vengeance it would be. Blood vengeance.

But not yet.

Now he had to plan. Or rather, *go over* the plan, make it simple as sin so that his men could understand: he could not afford any mistakes.

A pity Richie Powers had escaped. He should have killed the little vermin there and then.

How many *had* he killed?

Only three. So far.

One in defence, you might say. A lascar seaman crazed with opium who came at him one night, thinking he was an easy mark, thinking he was less than a man. He had wrested the man's huge curved knife from a trembling hand and made his first cut upwards. Some of the gore had spattered on his nice new coat. He would never be that careless again.

Second by reason of conquest. A different knife for a different reason, laying a trail to another door. A cold killing. Cold as the moon.

And the third? That was in a way the best because of it being a deep necessity and part of the present plan. Of course this did not preclude a certain satisfaction from the look of terrible pain on the face of the man before him as life departed. He had made a bad mistake thinking Niven to be something else. He had put out a hand. And he had told too much, thinking he could trust what might be touched.

The moral of the third death.

Billy Musgrave might be next. Even if he left when the play left the city, the once leader of the Bonny Boys would want to push his luck.

Just for badness.

And perhaps Billy would not even leave. Hold his ground. Perhaps he would wish Niven's crown. With that stupid little slut as queen.

But that was not important.

What was *necessary* would happen tonight and Niven knew exactly how it should be done. His gang would meet with him shortly and he would lay down the plan – yet he had a doubt of trust and would take good precautions over that doubt.

Back to Billy Musgrave again. Were there some who preferred the old days, holding on to old loyalties? If they did, they would pay the price.

He had outsmarted Billy long ago, stitched him up like a Jerusalem haddock.

This was what he loved best. By himself. Naked.

The ceiling above was mottled. That would not do. Not clean. Not tidy. He also sometimes heard scratching below the floorboards. Mice perhaps. Poison them.

Poison. Yes. Arsenic.

And after he had made his name, there would be blood and vengeance.

He was his father's son, after all.

Chapter 27

Give me an ounce of civet,
Good apothecary, to sweeten my imagination

Art is, to all intents and purposes, chaotic, whether rendered upon a canvas – as when Van Gogh's brushstrokes ran like wild horses across his fields – or who knows the madness of Mozart or Ludwig van in the throes of creation? Or say Nikolay Vasilyevich Gogol, a writer of such genius that his own nose ran away from him to lead another life? And last but not least, in the theatre itself – where such havoc is not confined to one person but spreads out like the plague.

Like a kiss of death.

Kenneth Powrie was experiencing the feeling of being slowly but surely separated from his senses, an army of poltergeists seemingly having found a home in the big tent. An evil wind that locals in the know named 'Scuddering Nancy' had suddenly whipped in from the sea – it was odd why explosive bursts of inclement weather were so often given female appellations, but such niceties were far from Kenneth's consideration.

When he had picked out Leith Links for the location, it had been calm as a convent, but anyone who lived there might have told him this was one chance in a hundred.

And a blast from the sea makes up its own rules.

These howling squalls, making the morning winds earlier seem like zephyrs, now came lancing in, finding gaps in the canvas where no gaps existed before, threatening to uproot the tent pegs, shrieking like banshees in and out of every crevice, and turning the whole place into an extempore storm scene from the looming tragedy.

Had Alfred Tyrone been of a mind, he might have launched into some lines from that particular passage such as

> And thou, all-shaking thunder,
> Smite flat the thick rotundity o' the world!
> Crack nature's moulds, all germens spill at once,
> That make ingrateful man!

But Alfred, if not exactly cowering, was holding fast to what he hoped was a firm thick tent pole, while the remnants of the *King Lear* cast huddled together behind him, trusting to the maxim of safety in numbers.

John Wilde, marooned alone at the rear, took a furtive slug from his brandy flask, not for the first time that day, and wished he had never crossed the border into this God-forsaken heathen land. He had been married once to a Scotchwoman who could drink him under the table, but thank God she had left the Great Wen, returning to the wilderness of Greenock.

Barnaby Bunthorne had already donned his jester's moth-eaten traditional hat, myriad cloth fronds sprouting like star-fish. The material had once been brightly coloured but had now faded to a dull acceptance of its role, not unlike the man himself. At the end of each frond was a cloth ball with a small bell inside. They tinkled as the wind blew up the back of his neck. Barnaby had been an Adonis in his youth, but even gods must fall to earth. Now he was a podgy, middle-aged fellow who – tinkled.

To the side and rearwards of the stage the partitions which made do for their makeshift dressing rooms buckled under the strain and one lurched at an intimate angle to provoke a shriek from Melissa Fortune. She had been comporting herself on the equally makeshift improvised privy and feared the incident might transport her into a different tale altogether. *The Fall of the House of Usher*, perhaps?

Like a threatened heroine, Melissa hastily pulled up her drawers and emerged to demand an explanation for such indignity. Mother Nature, however, was not interested and the few workmen still clearing away the debris of sawdust and shavings sniggered as she realised her petticoat was showing where hurriedly tucked into her skirt. She hastened to fix the fault.

This rectified, an icy stare silencing the unwanted observers, she stalked through the blasts to confront, if not Eurus, Greek god of the unlucky East Wind, then his nearest representative on earth, Kenneth Powrie.

The impresario was trying to organise some local young women who had been brought in to show folk to their seats and sell the programmes – if indeed they ever arrived, as the printers were slow as treacle in winter – and so did not appreciate being addressed as follows.

'This, Mister Powrie, is below contempt!'

'I cannot be held responsible for the vagaries of Edinburgh wind and weather,' retorted Kenneth somewhat waspishly, for he had been stretched thin by a hard day already and, let it not be forgotten, threatened with removal of his means of procreation; not that he had any great interest in that particular direction.

Procreation, in Kenneth's opinion, was an idiot's pastime. Fools rush in where angels fear to tread.

'How are we supposed to perform under these conditions, if you please, sir?'

This was meant to be delivered in magisterial tones that would shrivel the recipient but came out more like a screech, such as a macaw might make in the Amazon basin.

Then another voice cut in.

'We have no option *but* to perform, Miss Fortune. That is the nature of our profession.' Bridget Tyrone then turned to her brother. 'Is that not so, Alfred?'

A moment's hesitation, then his voice took issue with the wind: 'Exactly so. We shall prevail, Miss Fortune!'

Melissa shot Bridget a venomous Regan-like glare and was even more angered to see that, behind the Tyrones, that little slut Emilia Fleming had a sly, satisfied look on her face. It provoked her to further protest.

'This is surely beneath our dignity!'

Bridget's answering tenor made Melissa's previously frigid delivery seem like a melting sweetmeat on a puppy dog's nose.

'This is our job. We are paid. We perform.'

Kenneth sent up a silent prayer that the receipts from a so far unseen audience might cover the aforesaid payment and responded in kind.

'Well said, Mistress Tyrone, and see before you – we are almost at the mark!' He spread his arms wide after the manner of Alfred and indicated the vista before them.

Indeed there had been some improvement. The benches were now fixed and in position, long red cushions draped the length of each one, and old velvet drapes, supplied by Jean Brash, for what bawdy-hoose is without a plethora of velvet wrapping, hung round each side of the arena to enclose the spectators in warming welcome?

Admittedly they were billowing like the sails of a wind-scudded ship, and if stray tendrils of rough rope swayed hither and thither, would that not also add to the metaphor of a kingdom in turmoil? Perhaps a whole new form of cultural experience was being invented – the Theatre of Wind and Rope?

Emilia, sly look or not, was wondering if she might be sick in a bucket. The hashish-enhanced sensual excess of the previous night plus lack of breakfast porridge due to a late rising had left her bilious and nausea-prone. She had arrived behindhand and then worked like a dog as the company rehearsed the selected scenes that would be presented. No one expected the play of *Lear* to be performed in its entirety, but she had more than enough to do with what was proposed.

It had been a small relief to arrive at the last scene where Alfred as king – at the end of his tether – enters with Cordelia's dead body in his arms to berate all and sundry for what seems an interminable time before turning up his royal toes. By this time both Goneril and Regan were dead and there was no decent competition left on the stage, so Alfred could indulge himself to the limit while Bridget and Melissa lay there trusting to a lack of splinters on the bare boards.

A blessing for his spindly legs might be that, though physically voluptuous, Emilia was on the small side and so could be carried lightly while declaiming.

This lack of density plus the fact that when she auditioned for Alfred in a dingy room near Paddington Station, she dropped to her knees at the end before him, had secured Emilia the position – the action was not a part of the play but to plead for the role. It afforded him a splendid view of her bosom and of course appealed to the sense of superiority that he would consider the natural right of all great actors. To kneel is to recognise true genius.

'There is so much you can teach me,' she had averred, eyes moist with creative longing, 'and so much that I want to learn at your feet.'

Not from his mouth, however, for the combination of cigar fumes and somewhat rancid breath could be discerned whence she genuflected.

All in all, bosom and breath apart, for Alfred's libido was firmly entrenched in the folios of the Bard, she had a shrewd idea it was an absence of weight that had done the trick as the other actress in the audition room was more heifer than delicate fawn.

A sudden monstrous noise cracked through the air to bring Emilia out of these thoughts and jolt everyone into a demanding reality.

Billy Musgrave emerged from backstage with a big grin on his face. 'Fixed the thunder sheet, sir,' he shouted above the reverberations. 'Ready for duty!'

Alfred nodded solemnly. Bridget allowed herself a small tight smile. She liked Billy. Did not trust him one inch, but she liked him. He looked at her in a different way to most men, whose gaze slid past en route to other flesh on the bone. Billy met her eye.

'You may not need a wind machine, Mister Musgrave,' she observed wryly. 'Given present conditions.'

'Oh, this will pass, Mistress Tyrone,' he assured her with a straight face. 'Jist a wee breeze. About an hour, it'll die down. But soon as it gets dark back she comes again – Scuddering Nancy!'

Emilia noted that he had been in a heightened manic taking all of this day. Something had charged him like an electric current. Settle.

'Jist a wee joke,' he announced to the cast.

Another grin failed to totally alleviate the dismayed look on the faces before him, save for Bridget, who drooped one eyelash in what might have been a wink. He liked Bridget. Shame she was so bony. But the woman was sharp as a tack.

'I'll see tae the other effects, Sir Alfred.'

Billy disappeared backstage again. Of course the man was nothing of the sort but it suited Billy to make that mistake as if knighthood was only a matter of time.

That clap of thunder had somehow dissipated the tension. While Kenneth marshalled the local lassies to start tidying up the place instead of the cleaners he should have been employing and paying, Alfred led the company back on to the stage for a last proper run-though of the play before – before – yes – tonight was the performance. He paused, lit a cigar, surveyed the motley gathering before him and announced, 'This, my dears, is the moment of truth!'

Actors are a strange crew. With the exception of Melissa Fortune, who might regard herself as a princess twenty mattresses above a pea, they, when reality bites, would rather die than not perform.

The Tyrone company was no exception to this rule. Alfred shot out his sleeves, Bridget shut down that considerable intelligence and prepared, as far as possible, to do what she was told, Barnaby sucked in his belly and John Wilde patted his brandy flask.

Emilia was left behind. She had a blinding headache and had wondered about sneaking a slug of brandy from John's flask. If she had pressed her body in hard enough, he would have granted her a swig, the lecherous old devil.

But it was too late now.

As she started to move a hand pulled her back into the shadows. For a moment she was hidden from view – the hand lightly round her throat she knew well, her ear pressed against a mouth with which she had even better acquaintance.

Billy had doubled back to come round the other side.

'You and I are going to pay a wee visit.'

'Where?'

He laughed softly. 'Where treasure lies. Been thinkin' it tae bits all this day.'

'Will it be – perilous?'

'Enough tae wet your knickers.'

He pulled her in tight with his other hand so that her buttocks were jammed up against his groin. There was no doubt that Billy was primed for action.

'When?' she managed to utter, for his hand had tightened round her neck.

'This night.'

'But the play. And afterwards.'

There was to be a reception in one of the civic halls; the city had laid it on, not Kenneth Powrie, otherwise the sherry would be barley water and the canapés pastry scraps from the back bakery.

'Well after that. In the dead of night. A nice wee visit. A surprise party.' There was an edge to his voice that both thrilled and threatened.

Once in a low dive at the Bristol docks, a local tough had shoved his hand right up her skirts. She'd yelped and Billy cut the man's face with his knife as if slicing a piece of cheese. Then he'd grinned, gold tooth shining in the dingy candlelight.

'This wee bouncer is mine. Mine alone.'

It was a rough tavern filled with the detritus of ships that had sailed the Seven Seas. Yet few would meet his eye and those that did nodded ingratiation.

He crooked his arm for her to slide a hand through the offered space; they stepped delicately over the groaning man on the floor and walked out like royalty.

That was the thrill. The sliced flesh was the fear.

What if it was Emilia? What if she carried a scar for the rest of her life?

She could think of one other who would look well with a deserved impairment. Let it run, say, from the corner of an eye to the full mouth. We'd see who'd be smiling then at something out of true.

Hard to smile with teeth full of blood.

'Do I have to come?'

'You're my good-luck charm, Emmy. Besides —'

Billy bit softly into the lobe of her ear and she felt a shiver run through. 'When ye lean over, your bubbies pull the boys' eyes aside and that just might give me an edge.'

With such he shoved her out into the light, both aroused and unsettled.

His two keelies had come back not an hour earlier and had fleshed out what they told before. For sure it was tonight. A big lift, they said. Niven had taken Billy's rightful place. Only room for the one king.

Alfred had beckoned Emilia to join them onstage and the company prepared to run the first scene, which from the altered version would open with the words of Lear: 'Meantime we shall express our darker purpose'.

This by-play had escaped the notice of all the company concerned save one. As Jean Brash had walked him alone to the door last night, an instruction had been given: keep a close watch on Emilia Fleming; everything she does, says, and where she hangs her head.

No reason given. No questions asked. A nod and then he was out in the street.

Kenneth like a good boy had done what he was told and now had something to relate. Billy Musgrave, by the hidden looks of such, was a tight fit. Of course youth calls to youth, that's all it might signify, but Kenneth was desperate to get back into Jean's good books and this could be of interest to her.

Mister Musgrave, stage manager or not, was a keelie with rough companions. If Emilia Fleming was cheek-by-jowl with him, who knows what complications might ensue?

One thing was for sure. The girl had a curious combination of vulnerability and lethal mischief. If she enflamed an audience she way she roused men – wind or no wind, it could be a hot night.

He let out an optimistic and totally unfounded jink of laughter. The show must go on.

Meanwhile, the female cockroach that earlier on the day before scuttled to safety, had found herself a safe haven under the boards of the stage. It was damp, which suited the ootheca or sac where she carried her eggs. It was not long now till they hatched and joined the rest of a crawling universe.

Tonight it would all be happening. The King would die. But what about the Queen?

Chapter 28

I pray you: frame the
Business after your own wisdom

Jean Brash had assumed many strange positions in the Just Land but this present one took the sugar biscuit.

She had been given the choice to sit or stand and had chosen to be upright in full regalia.

Now, she wasn't so sure; the fashionable French concoction of a hat with imitation berries dangling like grapes above a pouting cherub was already beginning to irritate her. Like having a swarm of midgies after you.

The pale light of early afternoon was filtering through the windows of the small room that had been put aside for creative pursuits, and through the panes she could see the hoodie crows and seagulls circling in the grey sky, swooping and shrieking in the swirling wind.

None of them were wearing a French hat.

The portrait artist had already set up residence and previously warmed up with a swift sketch of Nettie Dunn, who dreamt that the curves of her body might find fame and fortune.

A rumour in the bawdy-hoose started by a muttered aside from Hannah Semple nosed it around that the wielder of pencil and brush might prefer different fusion. Nymph to nymph.

Nettie herself leant more to thrust and parry but curiosity had led her into a few encounters, one of which, with Francine, the French girl who used to run the cellar dungeon before Maisie Powers, had certainly opened her eyes to a radically different satisfaction.

If Lily Baxter, Francine's wee rub-a-dub, had found out, she would have drowned Nettie in the breakfast porridge, but the elegant Frenchwoman had returned to Paris, Maisie had taken the whip hand, Lily fell in love all over again and everything went back to normal.

If normal was quite the word.

However, before Nettie's seductive charms might hold sway, the Mistress sent word that she was arriving and the erstwhile model was told by Hannah the get to hell out of it and stay out until requested otherwise.

Nettie shot off, Hannah looked bleakly at the artist, shook her head, held the door open and in walked Mistress Brash, dressed in the height of fashion and supporter of all things cultural. She wore a lavender outdoor gown to set off her hair and eyes, Italian boots that as it were knocked her up by two more inches, and the afore-mentioned French chapeau.

Jean would have preferred the elements of this *mise en scène* to have occurred in her boudoir, but had been assured that, preliminary sketches made, there might be a change of location later were that her desire.

In truth she was, a rarity for her, undecided. The advantage of the boudoir was that no one save Hannah Semple would dare approach the place; whereas this small room a little off the hall felt – *exposed* – as if she were a public monument. The disadvantage was that of *intrusion* – artists, no matter how they wrap it up, are voyeurs of infinite capacity and their beady little eyes store up all sorts of information that would be unwelcome if aired abroad.

A woman's boudoir is a dark secret like the centre of a spider's web – entanglement rules.

And as regards the artist already in situ? Sarah Baines might as a rule have been covertly amused by Jean's indecision but could not rid herself of a chill feeling in her gut.

'I'm going to America. The New World. To carry the fight. This country is too small. Too mean at heart. You can come with me. If you have the sinews for warfare!'

Louisa Lumsden leant over and playfully brushed the sweat-tousled hair of her lover. Their passion had been both fierce and tender but then a moment of release when Sarah let out a low wrenching moan had, for some reason, provoked both into a fit of giggles.

'Don't die on me,' said Louisa, raising her head from a delicious engrossment. 'How could I explain it to your father?'

They both exploded into full-blown laughter; it echoed round the tiny studio that the Reverend William Baines had retained for his rebellious daughter. Yet behind Louisa's laughter was a secret. And after the fond gesture came the words that Sarah had been dreading.

She had been happy at St Leonard's – the fine academy for girls in St Andrews, herself as art teacher, Louisa the headmistress – happy for the first time in her life. In Edinburgh, she had felt herself forever out of step with a patriarchal Presbyterian society, not holy enough, not ladylike, attracted to her own kind – a duck out of water.

'Quack, quack,' said Sarah out of the blue.

'I beg your pardon?' asked the standing subject.

'Nothing,' came reply. 'Don't move please.'

She had felt this change coming, but despite her rebellion, her rejection of kirkbound pomposity, her refusal to bow down to authority – despite all this, and here's the rub – Sarah Baines was a homebody. She loved the certainty of recognised affection plus being cradled by the known. A regular life.

And Louisa was getting restless. She had come to the city to meet up with various women of the Edinburgh Suffrage Society to discuss the big meeting in Glasgow in November at the St Andrew's Hall.

Curious how the patron saint of Scotland seemed to have aligned himself to the cause of such protestation.

Cady Stanton from America, who had started it all at Seneca Falls, was coming over. She and Louisa had been in fervent correspondence. Many thousands were expected and many politicians – male, of course, since the idea of a female Member of Parliament would have given most of them what would be expressed in local parlance as the sulphur jaundies – would be noticeable by their absence. Municipal franchise was one thing but a political equivalent was beyond the pale. That's the way God had planned it forth.

She did not incline to big gatherings. Her sphere was small. Intense, not the macrocosm. Her voyage was always inwards. As Louisa spread her energy and folk bathed in her charisma, Sarah dug deep – like a well.

But the idea of losing her lover was chilling – we are not all born to fly like an eagle. And if she did not fly, where would she nest?

While all these doubts had been whirling through her mind, the other part of her – the recording angel– had been at work.

An image had formed. Only approximate lines as of yet but – a woman stood at a window. Fashionable gown, pert chapeau, and yet there was a sense of mystery.

What was she looking out towards? What was behind her?

Sarah had roughly filled in a dark background round the figure and the jagged sketch had a curious forbidding quality, as if – as if what?

While Sarah studied what she had drawn with a weird sense that it had not emerged from her but from another source, she became aware that someone lurked at her back. Time had passed. A good hour. And that was quite long enough for a Queen Bee to hold still.

Now the Mistress looked at herself in mutation. The face was not clear, the lines and a few smudges of colour formed a fleeting impression but there was an unmistakable feeling of fragility; in fact the whole impression was that of – an impending menace.

'Not very cheery, is it?' Jean observed.

'It is what I see before me,' replied Sarah.

'And what is that?'

'Power, strength, a solitary life.'

'I just want a painting, not a lecture,' retorted Jean, for some reason a little nettled by the answer.

'I shall endeavour to restrain my insights,' was the demure response.

The two women gazed at each other and there was a smile of sorts between them.

'My father sends you his best wishes.'

'So he should. I saved him from getting his throat cut.'

That was another story and indirectly the reason Jean had allowed this cheeky wee devil into the Just Land.

'Shall I proceed, Mistress Brash?'

'No. That will do for the day. I have a long haul ahead of me.'

She had killed the man who held the knife to the Reverend Baines's neck. Perhaps McLevy was correct. She left a trail of bodies. Not as many as him, though – the man was a walking massacre.

And what of the reverend's daughter? Jean's glance fell on the other sketch. Nettie Dunn's malapert face looked up. Another imp of mischief.

Jean sighed. All these young hussies jumping out at her. Is that what the baby in the dream meant?

Thank God for Hannah Semple. Old as the hills, grumpy as hell, but a fellow traveller who shared the same road.

Mind you – where did it lead?

She became aware that these thoughts were not necessarily worthy of the premier madame of Edinburgh and also that Sarah Baines was regarding her with a curious, almost dispassionate air.

Jack Burns – her lover – was younger by at least ten years. She enjoyed his physicality, rough-edged challenge and there was no doubting the talent. But what else lay between them? Real love or affection. How deep did it go?

Ding dong bell, Pussy's in the well.

Chapter 29

These late eclipses in the sun and moon portend
No good to us

The cat's eyes had narrowed to slits. Robin redbreasts had made a nest in one of the tall lilac bushes that grew up beside the garden wall of the Just Land.

Much activity and shrill cheeps that were music to a hungry feline's ears.

Horace had somewhat despaired of his master, Jack Burns. The man forever chipped away at blocks of stone and forgot about feeding time. He also was a poor specimen of a hunter.

The cat had tried bringing in dead mice or the occasional rat and laying it on the mat outside the door or by the fireplace, in order to provide a hint to the man within of a more productive pastime, yet this had been met with muttered curses and a thrown mallet in his direction.

But Horace did not despair. He was a proper predator and life divides into those who kill and those who die as a result.

In the room, while Jean had fallen silent at some inner preoccupation, Sarah Baines had begun to carefully pack away her painterly accoutrements. Her partly finished drawing of Jean was set up on an easel.

'I would like in time,' she remarked with the gravity of dedication, 'to lay down sketches of all the girls.'

Jean came out of her reverie at the statement. A hint of challenge behind the solemnity. Did this girl think she ruled the roost?

Artists are like that. Don't give them an inch.

'At work or at leisure?'

'I think best – at leisure.'

A wicked question met with a poker-faced response.

'Perhaps we can open a gallery? After all, everything here can be bought. You can sell your wares along with everyone else.'

This turn was leading to uncomfortable moral territory for the young Miss Baines. The girls in the Just Land had a certain independence that might be envied by many but their profession was – unmistakable.

'For if truth be told,' Jean continued remorselessly for she had sensed an element of condescension in the earlier part of their conversation and she would put this young whippersnapper to the sword, 'are we all – not just playthings?'

'Playthings?'

'Uhuh.'

'For men?'

'Forces beyond us. Above and afar.'

Sarah blinked. She had been prepared to be offended but now she was wandering in a circle.

'What is it that Shakespeare says, I wonder?' Jean had been close reading the play for she did not wish to risk ignorance on the first night. ' "The gods – they kill us for their sport" – something along those lines. To do with flies.'

'I'm not sure what you mean?'

'Are you not? What a pity.'

For a moment the clear eyes fixed on Sarah and the young woman revised any previous conception of bawdy-hoose keepers.

'I mean you have to fight tooth and nail just to have one wee moment that you can call your own.'

This emerged from Jean with such force that she herself was taken aback. Truth can have that effect. What was it Hannah Semple had said? *This is a' too deep for me.*

The Mistress laughed aloud all of a sudden. After all, what did she have to worry about?

A wounded tricky keelie in the cellars with an indulgent sister who might not be trusted to keep him in line; the vicious murder of a good friend that Jean had sworn to avenge; Niven Taggart, a killer, born to become her enemy; a play of shreds and tatters that might lose her a wheen o' money; a series of young women led by that damned actress to disturb her peace of mind. And above it all, like a hovering vulture, James McLevy, who suspected her of the past poisoning of former partner Henry Preger and a present involvement in robbery.

Add to such, a feeling of impending menace that had somehow found its way into her portrait, plus a brooding French pianist.

'The drawing,' Jean ordered. 'Put it in a frame.'

'But it is not finished or even close.'

'I want to look at it. Framed.'

'You can see it as it stands, surely?'

'Do what I say, if you don't mind.'

A dangerous glint in the eye. Sarah was once more wrong-footed by the change in tone and atmosphere. Was a bawdy-hoose always like this? The young woman scrabbled amongst bits and pieces stacked into a corner of the room, found a smallish solid enough wooden frame with a thin backing, pinned the drawing inside and balanced it again on the easel.

Jean nodded. There was no face yet to the figure. Just a blank. But it was herself.

'You may go now.'

Sarah flushed slightly at the peremptory tone, but she also knew, like many an artist, upon which side her bread was buttered.

'Might I come tomorrow?'

'Same time. Same place. Nothing changes.'

No more than that. No sweet goodbyes.

Sarah walked to the door but on a sudden thought turned back; she and Louisa would be going out with her father this evening.

'Will you be at the play tonight, Mistress Brash?'

'If God spares me. He will not of course spare the King, nor his daughters, virtuous or otherwise. Life is a bloody business, is it not?'

On that ironic and veiled utterance from Jean, Sarah Baines left the room.

Jean studied the portrait as the door opened and Hannah stuck her head in.

'Whit are your intentions for this night?'

'Survival.'

Hannah's face did not alter by much. 'Other than that?'

'Big Annie Drummond can run the house until I get back. She's done so before.'

'I'll make sure she keeps the faith.'

'You're coming with me.'

'Whit?'

'You heard.'

'I'm no' goin' tae a bliddy play!'

'You can keep me company.'

'Whit about your fancy boy? The chiseller.'

'Mister Burns may well be there. And so – will you.'

Hannah chewed at her lip. 'Do I have tae dress up?'

'You most certainly will.'

The old woman had a shrewd idea what lay behind this obdurate front. There would be more than the play on show tonight. Mistress Brash would also be exhibited. No doubt Kenneth Powrie would make a fuss and it would be clear to one and all Jean had a certain stake in the performance.

'So we'll be hobnobbing wi' the Unco Guid, eh?'

As usual, Hannah had stuck her finger through the facade. The great and righteous of Edinburgh society would be there, hoaching with hypocrisy as usual. And as much as Jean loathed them, she also desired their acceptance. She had no history of which to speak – no mother, no father, all lost in the mists of time. Raised in the wynds by an old woman who drank herself to death and left Jean to fare for herself in the jungle. Taken in hand by two women of the streets, she had fought her way up through violence and death to hold her head high.

That much was known but nothing else.

Jean despised this need to be held in respect for what she was. A fighter. An upright woman.

Who just happened to be a bawdy-hoose keeper.

The Unco Guid, eh? How had Scotland's greatest poet called them out?

> O ye wha are sae guid yoursel'
> Sae pious and sae holy
> Ye've nought to do but mark and tell
> Your neibor's fauts and folly!

199

A shout from the garden cut in and Jean hauled open the window of the room to look out over the lawn.

Plookie Galbraith was trying to pull something out of his dog's mouth. Finally he succeeded and looked up at them as the beast ran away. In his hand was a small lifeless bird. A fledgling – the feathers soaked and inert.

The young man's eyes were full of tears.

'It wasnae my dog, Mistress, that bastard cat did it. Raggie chased the thing away but then – chewed at the poor wee bird. Animals are like that.'

Jean sighed. 'Just find a place to bury it, Plookie. Where the wee scrap can find some peace. That's all we can hope for.'

As he shambled off to do so, Jean turned back in to see Hannah looking at the portrait.

'This arty-crafty stuff's a menace,' the Keeper of the Keys of the Just Land pronounced in considered judgement.

Chapter 30

O, look upon me, sir,
And hold your hands in benediction o'er me

Edinburgh, August 1844

The pain had been as if in death, not birth. The old servant one side of the bed, the doctor on the other.

She had screamed and bucked until it felt that nothing was real. Only the persecution – her body, her cervix stretching into agony as it dilated, the shuddering cracking of her very bones and always the pain.

The opiates, her beloved friends, her devious enemies, that took the young woman into a hazy sweet confinement where everything seemed not quite to touch her, had scattered like so many grains of sand and fled her consciousness.

Now the spasms of her body were almost continuous, one after another they came, like some kind of whiplash, her flesh a glove that was being turned inside out. She bit down hard into the pillow and tried not to thrash her limbs. That might harm the baby. But where was the baby? Given what waited outside, perhaps it preferred the womb, the amniotic universe.

But the womb had turned treacherous, the walls had buckled and the process of expulsion – a savage torturous rejection – had begun.

Like it or not. Here I come. Ready or not.

Adam and Eve were expelled from the Garden of Eden: is that what it meant?

The young woman lay on her side, facing away from the doctor so that he did not have to witness her private parts until absolutely necessary – that would be shameful, surely, and had she not caused sufficient shame and disgraced the family name?

Another brittle spasm, another stifled cry.

A hand appeared from behind holding a cloth. It had a cloying sweet odour.

'Chloroform,' said the doctor's voice, 'if you might inhale? It will help.'

If it was so helpful, why the hell hadn't he given it before? Was that part of the punishment? No. Just breathe in. Ah. Better. Oh yes. If opium falters then dear old chloroform will do the trick – aggh!

Knees up to the belly. Shift tucked up under the arms. Little short petticoat about the hips.

And after the blood and mess have been cleared away, then the soaking slimy petticoat is pulled off, the dry shift pulled down, and madam is as if nothing has ever happened. A maiden once more.

More cloth. More breath. More of the sweet oblivion.

Agghhh!

The old servant bent over and peered under the petticoat. 'The baby's head. I can see it, Doctor.'

Through the expanded cervix, the little stranger was finally taking a bow. Bringing as a present some of the undeserved pain it had suffered, an innocent whose world had turned upon it and squashed the tiny body through a tunnel of endless agony. Now emerging at the mercy of the lunatic planet.

And as the man finally moved round, the servant's lips twisted in bitter compassion as she looked into the glazed haunted eyes of the young woman. That deep auburn hair so admired and envied, dank with sweat and clumped like twisted roots.

'First the head, Miss Jennet,' she announced. 'The rest tae follow.'

And follow it did.

No one had ever spoken to the girl about matters of the body. Even her menses was never mentioned, passed by in silence except for some hemmed thick pads of cloth left by the bedside, then washed and returned – waste not, want not. A young woman who had never known her body, except for the fact she had let pleasure in, and see the rewards of pleasure!

Her mind was near unhinged by birth pangs as the poor haunted creature emerged, like an animal chased by hounds into the underbrush and coming out the other side with hot breath on its back. She could not see the baby, only feel the torture of the dilation. Lying on her side. How could this be right? Part of her would surely be pressing down; the head would be squeezed like an oatcake, like a dropped scone!

She suddenly pulled herself upright, clutching with each hand at the thick hanging curtain behind the bed.

Hauled herself straight, opened up her legs. Yes, no modesty, no maidenly virtue, and if she stained, if she let loose the bowels, so be it. Push and be damned!

A loud grunt, head back, eyes wide, that old bugger above was still glaring down at her, stern and grim, painted forever, dead as a doornail. Did he ever come out of a womb? Surely not.

Aghh! She could feel it now. Hers. Her baby. Now. One – more – push. Let there be light!

Then. Like a little blue fish, the child emerged. The young woman could hardly see, eyes full of tears and sweat running down her face to blind her all the more. The old woman was swift and sure, wrapped the baby up in a blanket, wiped at the face with a white cloth. 'A girl child,' she announced. 'Nothing amiss.'

The doctor had also been busy. Like a scaffie man clearing up the mess. The young woman laughed wildly at that notion and held out her arms.

Give me!

But the old servant did not move.

The doctor stood up, then shifted over to a basin to wash his hands. Then he dried them. Like Pontius Pilate.

The girl's arms were still outstretched.

The doctor took the blanket bundle and held it in his hands as if weighing a parcel to send in the post. A small choked cry came from the small tangled heap.

'I shall inform your father, of course, Miss Shields, and rest assured, the child will be cared for as befits a decent household.' He turned as if to leave.

'Give me my baby,' replied the young woman. 'Or I swear to you, the first chance I get I will cut my throat and you can have that on your saintly conscience.'

For a moment he hesitated.

'You need a stronger medication, young lady.'

Her arms had not trembled.

'Give me my baby.'

In truth the doctor was not a cruel man, merely following instructions. More cruelty is done under these words than any other.

'You will promise to take the medication?'

Although already near addicted, the young woman at times had tried to wean herself away from the opiates. If she agreed, she would be at their mercy, her will leached dry by the drugs.

Another choked cry.

She nodded and signed her soul away.

He stepped forward and put the bundle into her arms.

'I shall inform your father.'

As the doctor left the room, the old servant slipped a small pewter flask from her pocket and took a delicate sly sip of the cheap whisky within.

The baby mewled a little. The eyes were blue but that can change, the sea is blue then green according to the colour of the sky and the disposition of water. The young woman held the child against her breast. It seemed a quiet wee soul. Bonny.

'I will give you my name, my Christian name. For what it's worth. Poor wee lamb.'

For a moment it was as if a chasm opened under her very being as a future darkness waited to prevail, then she shook her head and held the baby in a tight embrace. They sat up together. Her eyes closed. The baby unmoving as the old servant swallowed a violet lozenge to disguise the whisky fumes.

The dead man in the portrait had not moved a muscle.

The young woman slid her forefinger into the baby's tiny hand, which then closed around it. Mother and daughter.

Joined together for a moment in time.

Chapter 31

When we are sick in fortune – often the surfeit
Of our own behaviour – we make guilty of our
Disasters the sun, the moon, and the stars

Leith, 1883

A crescent moon shone down on the deserted harbour as night began to draw a merciful veil over the stupidity of human beings, especially those hailing from Paisley.

Such as Inspector Adam Dunsmore, who was no doubt strutting importantly towards this rendezvous or riding in the comfort of a fine carriage, heroic as Hercules.

Mulholland and McLevy were huddled together on some damp stone steps, fenced in by an iron railing that led downwards to where a small boat might well have been anchored, however the berth was empty for the moment.

It had been a long day of some frustration. They had trawled the lower depths of Leith without success – nowhere in any of the taverns or dives could they find a trace of Erik de Witte's movements. No one remembered seeing a man of that description; his white hair and sartorial elegance surely hard to miss in the grime of Leith.

Nor was there a trace of Richie Powers. Folk knew him of course but not of late. Of late, he had disappeared from sight. He had been at a card school, gone outside to see someone but none of the players witnessed this meeting; unseen, outside, unwelcome as far as they were concerned – the wee bugger had been winning and he never came back.

So, nothing. Richie had gone to earth and Erik was heading that way via the gravedigger. Yet both policemen had sensed something in the streets. A tension. As if shadows were stalking each other and a game was being played out.

'A few of Jean Brash's people in and out the wynds, I notice,' the constable had murmured as they passed on the saunter, an apparently aimless stroll through Leith that fooled no one.

'I see such. Why is that, I wonder?'

'We could always ask them.'

'Jist as well talk tae the stone walls at the Castle.'

Jean's people were fiercely loyal, most of them owed her favours with money rarely mentioned.

As is well known in this world, where money lays a head corruption is the bedfellow, and lack of the filthy lucre promotes a close-mouthed cohesion that is anathema to the practising policeman.

'But it tells us one wee thing,' muttered McLevy. 'She has a hand in all this somewhere.'

'You've said so before.'

'As sure as the Sphinx.'

'We could pay a visit to the Just Land?'

'The best time tae catch Jean is when she least expects. She'll jist be waiting for us this time – laugh in our face. Armour-plated wi' subterfuge.'

An unexpected poetic turn of phrase from McLevy. Perhaps all this culture was catching.

'What about the Powers family? They're thick as thieves.'

'I have some of my people watching the place. Any sign of Richie – I'll be told.'

McLevy had his own unofficial folk on the street – he was also owed some favours but whereas Jean's were based on support for those in need, his were based on not throwing them into jail or the threat of exactly such a measure should they fail his instructions. A nice difference between the police and a bawdy-hoose keeper.

Before Mulholland could ask his next question, McLevy beat him to it.

'As regards Maisie Powers, I have wee Danny Summers on the qui vive at the Just Land. If she goes anywhere, she'll be well tracked.'

Danny Summers was a small unassuming man who could follow like a shadow. Once a pocket delver, he had dipped his digits in the wrong pouch and had the misfortune to be caught by McLevy. His *good* fortune was that the inspector handed the pocket book back to a careless citizen and informed Danny that next time it would be the Perth Penitentiary so best, at his age, to give up this life of crime and spy for the thief-catcher instead. Danny had agreed, took up with a wee widow in the Haymarket and had never looked back. He still kept his hand in – that is as regards lawful surveillance.

'You seem to have it all covered, then,' Mulholland remarked with a certain asperity.

'Not quite.'

And then the inspector had taken them on an unexpected course that provided an opening in this closed affair. They had returned to the *Jupiter*.

Why McLevy made the call was perhaps a mystery to even him but they were getting nowhere and something about a certain person's behaviour had niggled at him. So back they went to find themselves once more outside the cabin of Erik de Witte.

The door was slightly ajar, a strange choking noise coming from inside. Mulholland gripped his stick; McLevy eased his hand into a revolver pocket. This time they did not rush the portal since the inspector had no wish to trip over his own feet and again see someone disappear through the porthole.

They eased the door open to disclose the tearful disconsolate form of Bernard Cuyper. The young officer was sitting on a narrow bunk bed that had no doubt once borne the form of the dead man.

'A shipboard romance, eh?' said McLevy with a curious expression on his face that might even have teetered towards compassion.

Bernard nodded mutely and Mulholland was lost. Now and then the inspector would pull something like this and it forever defied definition.

The young officer had in some way reached a similar desire for clarification.

'How did you know?' he asked the brooding presence.

'When we went towards that cabin for the first time, anyone else would have been at our back, nosy, but you couldn't get away quick enough as soon as you knew about the death. At first I thought that might be because you had let the fellow in, been slipped a few pound coins, but that didnae fit with your character.'

'Thank you,' Bernard said simply.

'And then the words you used about de Witte's death, "I should have been on guard" – "to protect him". Of course it could have been merely your feelings of duty or even guilt. But when I thought about it after, I felt it might have been more.'

'I agree with the Inspector,' added Mulholland, trying to get in on the act. 'You seemed – more horror struck than guilty, if I may say so.'

McLevy gave the constable a withering sidelong glance but held his fire.

'I was,' replied Bernard, 'struck. With horror.'

McLevy took off his low-brimmed bowler, sat on a nearby chair, and smiled like a defrocked priest. 'So – why don't you jist – tell me the story?'

And a melancholy story it was. On the voyage over from Rotterdam, Bernard had found in Meneer de Witte someone of sensitivity and humour, which had encouraged the shy young officer to, as it were, unburden himself. It was at first psychological but then some clothing took part and they became lovers. Bernard was an innocent abroad and Erik was delighted to help shift such innocence to a more joyful, if less virtuous, passageway at sea. For the premier time in a rather dented Calvinist upbringing, Bernard was happy.

But then, that fateful night, Erik announced he had business to attend, left with a smile and promised that he would return full of the joys of spring. Sad to relate, his optimism had been – unfounded.

The tears had begun to flow again and a somewhat discomfited McLevy produced a well-worn handkerchief and stuck it under the young man's nose.

'Here,' he said. 'Pull your socks up, for God's sake. Worse things happen in the Indian Ocean.'

This brusque admonishment did the trick. Bernard blew his nose vigorously and blinked his eyes.

'Ye can keep the hankie,' muttered the inspector.

Mulholland had held to the side but now he leant in like a stork over a goldfish pool. 'If it's not too much trouble, sir. Might you be telling us, if – your friend gave any details of this – particular business?' The constable was playing the friendly card.

McLevy's craggy exterior was not fashioned for such overtures so he merely sat there and watched his hankie being tied into knots as Bernard answered.

'He said it was – a matter of wraak.'

'Rack? Like torture, you mean?'

'Sorry. On my tongue. Revenge in yours.'

'Revenge?' probed Mulholland. This was more promising. 'How would he go about that?'

'An old friend, Erik said, he might see, and hoped she might – give a hand. Over—'

Bernard's syntax was scrambling under pressure as McLevy broke into this cosy conversing.

'The old friend, we may know. But why the revenge?'

'He said – he was his father's son.'

'And?'

Bernard sighed. 'Erik liked to make a joke.'

'I didnae get tae know him that well,' muttered McLevy. 'Clarify.'

'Clarify?'

Bernard blew his nose. McLevy suppressed a sudden desire to throw him and the hankie out of a porthole. Mulholland recognised the danger signals and slid in before ejection, 'Revenge. What was the reason, sir?'

'His father was cheated, he said.'

'Cheated?'

'Yes.'

'Anything else?'

'He said it was a proverb. What is sauce for the goose – is sauce for the gander.'

'Gander?' asked McLevy.

'It is a big bird.'

Silence fell. The inspector had turned a strange puce colour. Mulholland nodded as if something he had heard made sense.

'Anything further, sir?'

'He said –"Bernard, *mijn lieverd*" – my darling – "for once I am on the inside, looking out." And laughed.'

'What do you think he meant?'

'I don't know. It might have been a joke.' Bernard smiled through tears. 'Erik liked to make a joke.'

Chapter 32

Yours in the ranks of death

The two keelies looked mortality in the face, their bowels turning to water – what they thought to be a clever enterprise revealed to be a pit full of scorpions.

They had turned up for the final gang meeting cock-a-hoop from their recent rendezvous with the man they considered the true leader only to find themselves held fast, stripped of weapons, hands tied behind and facing a devil's doom in the shape of Niven Taggart.

A man they had considered the false leader, but such consideration was a mistake. The leader in this case was the one who held all the cards.

'Ye met with Billy Musgrave this day. Not long ago. Talked. Shook hands. All friends together.'

How did he know? With a sickening jolt they remembered a young boy who had been trailing along behind them. They thought admiration to be the cause – a lot of the wynds children followed the keelies – their flashy-dan clothes, bright neckerchiefs and bunnets tae the side a great attraction.

So, they had ignored the boy as a scabby wee nyaff and he had slunk off. But not too far, it would seem.

Niven smiled as if he could read their scattered wits. Fear excited him. Worth its weight in gold.

'Bob's wee cousin followed ye. Saw whit he saw. So?' The hook-knife came out of its sheath and glittered in the dull candlelight of the small room at the back of the tavern. 'So,' Niven continued, the point of the weapon weaving circles in the air like a snake, 'whit did ye have to tell Billy Musgrave?'

The unwritten law that no one broke in the strange twisted world they all inhabited was that of betrayal. Of course, it was a fine point, and one that might have been argued by my learned counsellor, that their loyalty to the past was commendable – but this was no court of law. It was a ring of hostile faces, Bob Golspie to the fore, plus the unwavering icy stare from the operator of that knife.

'I don't like repeating myself,' said Niven.

He did not, in fact, repeat himself; he just waited.

The two keelies were near lost for words. All they could do was lie. The truth might kill them. One's wrist was still in severe pain whence a certain Constable Mulholland had cracked down a hornbeam stick; the other's jaw was yet sore bruised from a police inspector's fist. But that was nothing compared to what lay in store.

'It was jist – a wee visit –' A mumble from the bruised jaw. 'Jist tae say hello.'

'Ye could have said that before. Many times. Why this day? Why not before?'

'We didnae – think – before. We forgot.'

Disbelief has its own silence.

'Whit did ye tell him?' asked Bob, to save his leader repetition.

'Nothing. Jist – a wee visit –'

The knife moved so quick it might well have been a snake, cutting the flesh from the hip up to under the oxter. Niven had refined that sweep in the butcher's shop where he had helped to slice open many a carcass in return for the blade being sharpened, but this was not a cow on the hook.

The keelie howled and looked down in dismayed agony at the blood already seeping through his clothes.

'Didnae cut deep,' said Niven. 'Next time, though.'

In his pain the bruised man blurted out what could not be ignored. 'If we tell ye, you'll kill us!'

'Kill you anyway' was the reply, and Niven laughed at such wit. No one else did.

Then Niven stepped forwards once more and put the tip of the blade as he had rehearsed once before with Plookie Galbraith, into the crotch of the other keelie. 'Your turn.'

The man fell backward in sheer terror but was held upright by those behind.

If any present had been students of the Bard, they might have instanced Macbeth splitting a certain opponent, Macdonwald of the Western Isles, 'from the nave to th'chops' – that is, from the navel to the jawbone.

But of course the greatest fear is that of the watcher, knowing that he'll be next, so the bruised keelie let out an anguished howl.

'I'll tell ye, I'll tell ye!'

To be honest, he only beat his threatened comrade by the whisker of a heartbeat.

A look of disappointment came over Niven's face. It may have been an evil joke on his part, because he did not lack a wicked sense of humour, or it may in fact have been reality, but the point of the knife did not budge. 'Spit it out,' he said. 'Or we'll see how his guts look on the floor before yours do the same.'

The bruised man told all, his comrade stiff at attention, nodding now and then to show willing.

They had informed Billy Musgrave of as much as they knew about a planned robbery for this night but not the whereabouts or the target because that was yet a secret.

And what did Billy think?

Billy did not say.

Another dig with the point. Another frightened yelp.

Come to think of it, Billy seemed to have some plan in mind but he would not divulge. All he *did* say was that he would just wait and see.

Niven nodded as if that made sense and then casually drew back the knife to batter the heft into the keelie's face, splitting his lip and knocking out a front tooth. After all, it was only fair: his companion had been ripped up the side. Share and share alike.

There was an acrid smell of urine as the sliced accomplice finally lost control of his bladder and fell forward on to the floor.

'Too bad,' came the observation. 'Ye're going tae stink in that wee cubby hole.'

Niven shot Bob Golspie a cold glance. 'When you tie them up this occasion, do it well. I don't have time tae deal wi' this now.'

Bob nodded contritely. 'Whit'll we do with them after?'

'Whit ye do wi' rats. Drown such.'

No one knew how serious Niven was when he made this statement, but nothing in his face suggested it to be a joke. The cut keelie on the floor whimpered as Bob hauled him roughly to his feet, then nodded at one other of the gang who had experience of knots – his father had been a tarry-breeks who had sadly fallen into the sea during a wild storm inside his head caused by speel-the-wa whisky and therefore passed on no further maritime wisdom, but enough that the son could tightly bind a rope.

While the victims were being hauled away, blood and urine dripping at the stern, Niven pondered. Billy Musgrave was not a fool: he would wait to see successful outcome of the robbery, not of course knowing any more than what he had been told. Which was not very much, except that it was a heavy lift. Just *how* heavy was Niven's secret, but a little of that secret was about to be divulged.

He would not tell his gang about the *absolute* value, just that it was a big haul. If his plan worked, no one would see them, no one would know, and the best bit was no one would think it to be a wee band of keelies – they would be looking for high-end robbers. That was the best bit. Who would suspect them?

Billy would no doubt think to cut in. Let someone else do the dirty work then scoop the pot. Yet to do so he would have to kill Niven.

What Billy did *not* know was that he was now on his own, no one on the inside. He would be slashed to pieces because Niven was now forewarned. He was – after all – his father's son.

Everything was working out just fine. Everything was well. Niven in command.

And after he had won the battle, after he had engineered the lift that would make his name, after he had watched Billy spew up his life and maybe that wee slut could keep him company – however, after all that – after all that – would be the final vengeance.

Jean Brash. He had not yet decided how to kill her, except it should be slow.

He had heard about the death of a thousand cuts, but that was Chinese and might end up in a mess. Niven did not like things in a mess, even for someone who deserved to suffer; besides, it might spoil the clean lines – he'd want to see every moment. No, not the thousand cuts.

What about poison? Haul open her mouth and pour it in; watch her wriggle and die like an infected worm? There was some decent justice in that.

Or maybe one slice? Cut through the neck and watch her head bounce like the French Revolution? Not slow but – satisfying. Especially if the eyes were still open.

He became aware that everyone was waiting for him to speak. He was the leader. He was the king.

Bob came back in with his helper. 'Trussed up lik' bubbly jocks,' he announced.

This local word for turkey cocks caused a few smiles and lessened the tension. Niven was pleased enough; it would be a long night and let them laugh.

Now to business. Address the troops.

'Did ye bring as commanded?'

Solemn nods in answer.

'Show me.'

Equally solemnly each man reached into his pocket and laid an implement on the table. It was a weapon of sorts, but not of a deadly persuasion. A powerful catapult. Used more in warfare when they were growing up. Fitted with a sharp stone in the pouch, strong elastic pulled back and released, it shot a missile that could leave its mark and then some.

Niven nodded. Now he would tell them the plan.

Everything was fine.

Everything a marvel to behold.

Chapter 33

I have watched and travell'd hard;
Some time I shall sleep out, the rest I'll whistle.
A good man's fortune may grow out at heels

'Inspector McLevy – are you awake?'

Both men had fallen into a deep well of contemplation while the water lapped below. In McLevy's case, trying to make sense of what had been revealed so far and the feeling that all the fragments floating around in his brain must surely coalesce at some point; Mulholland, being a keen apiarist, worrying that a queen bee recently enticed with her swarm into one of his empty hives, would not stay put and prosper. You never knew with women. They can up sticks when you least expect.

These weighty considerations were interrupted by the voice of Constable Ballantyne and they snapped alert to see his earnest face, birthmark pulsating in the darkening gloom, peering down at them.

'Whit the hell are you doing here, Ballantyne?'

'Obeying orders, sir.'

'*Whose* orders?'

'Yours.'

'Eh? Oh – aye – right enough.'

While the inspector shook his overcoated self, like a post-hibernating bear, Mulholland had another query in mind.

'How did you know where to find us?'

'The Inspector told me.'

'That's useful. Why don't we just run up a flag and let everyone know?'

'No need for sarcasm,' McLevy remonstrated.

'I brought the message, sir. Soon as it arrived. As per orders.'

Ballantyne handed over a crumpled thin piece of paper – a telegram of sorts by the looks – and while McLevy scanned it, Mulholland took charge.

'You better get back to the station, Ballantyne. If Inspector Dunsmore sees you here, we're all up in smoke.'

'Can I no' help? I'm dead good at sentries.'

'If we have need, Ballantyne, don't you worry. We'll be calling out your name.'

'I'll be at the station. And I can call back later on my way home.'

'That's a blessing to know.'

The constable nodded gravely and then, with sprightly step, disappeared into the gathering dark while McLevy squinted with some satisfaction at the contents of the telegram.

'Mind letting me in on all this?' asked Mulholland, whose patience was beginning to wear thin. McLevy in this form made the Vatican look like an open book.

'I have a friend in Amsterdam,' replied the inspector. 'Used tae be a soldier, now a tobacco exporter. It's aye important, constable, to have a friend in all the big cities of Europe.'

As if you could tell one from the other was Mulholland's unkind thought. But he bit his tongue and waited for elucidation.

'I telegrammed him tae ask if he might find the names of the original craftsmen who worked on the Tholberg necklace. Here is the list. Read for yourself.'

The harbour was lit by a series of gas lamps, a pallid illumination but enough to make out the written designations. One stood out like a fox in a hen house, and the constable pronounced it aloud.

'Martin de Witte.'

'Now what's the betting,' breathed McLevy with a hunter's gleam in his eye, 'that this mannie is the father of our recently deceased Erik?'

'I won't give you odds.'

'So, here's whit I think. There was bad blood with the craftsmen who slaved to make that necklace. They were cheated. His father was cheated. That was what he said. Erik. When he wasnae making jokes.'

'Not often you're wrong but you're right this time,' observed Mulholland, coming over a little Irish in the rush of what might prove a breakthrough.

'So – if the father was bilked, his best work debased, his son – no doubt raised in the same tradition – wants to avenge the wrong.'

'How?'

'Eh?'

'How does he avenge it?'

'He steals the necklace.'

A simple enough statement, but Mulholland blinked as though hit over the head by Charles Darwin's 'Formation of vegetable mould through the action of worms'.

'That's why he would go tae Jean Brash. She'd have the organisation for such a venture.'

'But she told him to get lost.'

'That's whit she claims,' McLevy muttered. 'But she's in there somewhere.'

'Even if she is, which I hard doubt, or he went somewhere else for help and got himself chopped to bits, the poor soul was wasting his time.'

'How come?'

Mulholland sighed: the man was like a dog with a butcher's bone. 'Because – it's a mirage. Did you not read the paper this morning?'

The fake story that Dunsmore had concocted to mislead any potential jewel thief had been spread all over the *Leith Herald*. It made great play of the necklace arriving under heavy escort by train to Edinburgh, and the many extensive precautions that would be taken.

'Whoever, wherever, whatever, the wrong time, the wrong place, Waverly Station – even if he was there with reinforcements, a waste of time!'

'On the other hand?'

Mulholland was about to try losing his temper but then remembered that the energy given off doing so often alarmed his bees. It was a good way to get yourself stung. Moreover, just when you thought the inspector had dug himself a hole he'd pop up again like Hydra's teeth.

'I'm listening,' he offered quietly.

Something the young officer had related was stuck in McLevy's mind. It might be nothing but he had learned over the years that, like grit in the oyster, things that stick were not to be undervalued.

I'm on the inside looking out, said Meneer de Witte.

'What if Erik de Witte knew the *real* route of the necklace. No matter the rumours spread?'

'How would he know that?'

'A friend at the museum, in the trade, he moved in these circles no doubt.'

'Well, he's dead now.'

'But if he passed that information on – to someone he thought was going to help him – and in fact that might well be the reason for his death—'

'He was cut out of the deal?'

'Cut up and cut out,' said McLevy with grim humour.

'The other person decides to go it alone?'

'Why not? They have everything they need.'

'It's all conjecture.'

'Makes sense tae me.'

Solemnly, Mulholland took a sticky piece of honeycomb out of a greaseproof paper, broke off a part and handed it to McLevy. Both men climbed the steps so they could rest elbows on the flagstone harbour floor, and munched hungrily.

'Manna from heaven,' said the inspector.

The constable was in contemplation. 'All right. Accepting what you say, which I don't but if I was bereft enough to do so – you believe there might be some kind of attack this night?'

'Anything is possible.'

'But the only person remotely in the frame is Niven Taggart because I'm not having it that Jean Brash is waiting in the shadows with a cutlass in her teeth!'

Now Mulholland was getting poetic.

'All I'm saying is – she might have a finger in the pie,' was the stubborn response.

'Leave the pie alone. The only person in the frame is Niven Taggart. A keelie! He and his gang don't have the nerve or brains.'

'I'm not so sure,' said McLevy. 'The gang for certain. Keelies. But Taggart may have more to him. He pits me in mind of somebody.'

'Who?'

Before the inspector could answer, a recognised but unwelcome voice cut in on the exchange from distance.

'Well, McLevy. At least you're punctual. I suppose we must be grateful for small mercies.'

Figures had appeared further down the harbour, emerging from where the bonded warehouses provided cover; the crescent moon had vanished behind the clouds leaving only the murky lamplight to silhouette Adam Dunsmore and his six chosen sentinels. A faint sea haar was beginning to drift in but even through the mist and distance, the smirk on Dunsmore's face was unmistakable. He and his men had walked through what seemed deserted streets and then the alleys of the harbour to arrive in state.

It was at least two hours until the appointed time for delivery to be made but Dunsmore had insisted that they all meet well in advance so that he could admire himself for as long as possible.

'I expect you to keep out of sight, McLevy. My men and I will shelter in the lee of the nearest warehouse but when we walk forward to make contact with the ship, I command you to stay in position.'

'Whit a little snotter,' muttered the inspector.

'Do you understand all this, McLevy?'

A hand waved affirmative, or the gesture might also be construed as indicating hope that Dunsmore should fall off the edge of the harbour wall.

'Are you going to tell him?' whispered Mulholland.

'Tell him what?'

'What you think.'

'Conjecture, ye deemed it.'

'Even though. Are you?'

McLevy glanced to where Dunsmore tilted his head as if searching the sky for suspects, then turned back to address his constable.

'Whit do you think?'

Chapter 34

And pat he comes like the catastrophe of the old comedy

Kenneth Powrie was, in words that in no way reflected the grandeur of Shakespeare's language, up to high doh.

It was all very well for actors to skulk behind the arras, as it were, preen themselves before a mirror and then call themselves tragedians; what about those on the front line?

What about the terror of that situation?

At first it had seemed that no one would come. That not one footfall would be heard. That the performance would be enacted to Kenneth, the local lassies and the two sharp-featured, keen-eyed female bead-counters that Jean Brash had sent to keep an eye on where the money, if it ever came, went.

An empty theatre is a terrifying prospect.

Like a grave waiting for a tenant.

However, *mirabile dictu,* not only did God as in *King Lear* stand up for bastards, he must have had a soft spot for impresarios as well.

The first sign was the jingle of carriage horses as they arrived, then female voices and muttered oaths from the men as they followed their eager spouses up the rough path, lit on each side by outdoor lanterns, that led to the tented theatre. Mercifully the wind had died down, and through the mist of a gathering sea haar in came the first arrivals dressed up to the nines.

226

Like unto Noah's Ark, two by two, then more, then a great deal more and not only the high society of the city who regarded artistic appreciation their unalienable right, but also folk that had possibly never seen the inside of a theatre before – not that this was like the inside of any known theatre.

For a start there was no numbering of seats; the benches, cushioned though they were for the backsides of the culture-conscious, had an egalitarian bent in that how many sat alongside upon them depended greatly upon posterior size. Thus it was difficult to maintain social distance when buttock to buttock with those lesser financially gifted.

Lieutenant Roach and his wife had sadly been marooned towards the front with Chief Constable Craddock and some of his Masonic cronies. The lieutenant's wife was safely ensconced towards the middle of the bench flanked by two of her bridge club harpies, as Roach had privately named them having suffered a recent mauling at their hands when partnering his spouse – who had the card-playing concentration of an easily distracted ostrich. He, however, sat close to the aisle passage and had Craddock right beside him.

The chief constable took out his pocket watch, looked at the time, tapped the glass face meaningfully, and then leant over to impart some sotto voce words of great import. 'Our men will be in position by now. This is a proud moment for the policing of our great city.'

Roach nodded. He did not feel proud, more concerned over the proximity of his inspector's combustibility to Adam Dunsmore's inherent pomposity. He would have to rely on Mulholland and the misty evening to keep things tamped down; yet there was an uncomfortable rumbling in his stomach that was either the result of the herring at supper or an ominous premonition.

Meanwhile more folk flooded in, more money in the box, more reason for Kenneth Powrie to hop spasmodically into the air, caught between deep anxiety and promised joy. Was he for once going to succeed? The place was heaving – what could go wrong?

'You evil little bitch!'

This was not a paraphrase from the relationship in the present play, but issued from backstage. Melissa Fortune, in her Regan costume, had just had her hem stood upon by Emilia Fleming. The action had resulted in Melissa jerking somewhat comically backwards accompanied by the sound of rending material.

Barnaby, who doubled as Wardrobe Mistress, was on the scene in a shot, his jester's hat tinkling in sympathy as he bent over to look at the back of the dress. He was dressed for his first acting part, that of Kent – a man of great loyalty to a wilfully mistaken king – but always on performance nights wore his jester's cap for good luck.

He whipped it off before venturing on stage unless of course essaying the part of the fool – a role he found to be, as the years ground on, more and more his lot in life. As the fool loved Lear so Barnaby loved Alfred, but sadly such love was, by both rulers, unappreciated.

The nearest he came to contact was assisting Alfred into his royal costume, braving the bad breath and considering it a small price to pay as he eased the spindly legs into thick tights that both kept the king warm plus provided a more manly calf.

'It was an accident,' protested Emilia dressed in white for purity as Cordelia, Melissa being in malevolent livid green with Bridget, who kept her hems very much to herself, draped in an unflattering sable gown that made her look more like a black widow than a seductive sister.

Bridget doubted very much if it was in fact an accident, but nerves were apt to be shredded at this point in time pre performance, so keep the peace.

'Best to save such dramatics for the stage, Miss Fortune, I'm sure you can put them to good use. Can the dress be redeemed, Mister Bunthorne?'

'Oh yes, Miss Tyrone. Please do not move, Miss Fortune. I should be loath to prick you.'

While Melissa stood in a fury, Barnaby fetched over a little workbasket, deftly threaded a needle and then made swift repair. In truth he was a kindly soul and expressed his feminine side most comfortably in such matters.

John Wilde was not on hand, having, as usual, a bracer somewhere for the night ahead, and Alfred was in front of a full-length mirror, intoning one of Lear's speeches while smoking a cigar and admiring his elegance of gesture. A great bonus for the aforesaid bad of breath is that they cannot ever inflict it upon themselves. Unlike the passing of wind. God's little blessing.

And so Melissa stood while Barnaby sowed.

Emilia ghosted past her rival as if butter would not melt in such a sultry mouth but was arrested in motion by Bridget's hand on her arm.

> We are not the first
> Who, with best meaning, have incurr'd the worst.

The murmured lines were recognised by Emilia since they belonged to her own character and were addressed to Lear towards

229

the end of the play. While their import was not immediately clear in this context, the warning tone was unmistakable.

A nod of the head, slightly cocked to the side for comic effect, and Emilia moved to a gap in the curtain in order to spy out upon the audience.

'My God, it's approaching full,' she reported, 'scarce an empty seat. Not a night for the faint-hearted!'

'Or the hardly sober,' Bridget murmured as John Wilde approached, weaving a little as befits a man who would be blinded later on by a faintly squeamish Barnaby doubling further as the Duke of Cornwall.

Whether an audience could distinguish between these different roles is a moot point, but there were no more bodies to spare.

Alfred turned from the mirror and raised his hands upwards to the air in benediction. 'May the gods be with us!' he proclaimed.

Billy Musgrave appeared as if in answer to this call, in his mortal disguise as stage manager.

'Not long now, ladies and gentlemen,' he said. 'Look tae your laurels.'

A wicked gold-toothed grin, a tug at his earring and he was gone.

Emilia peeped out again and then froze. Three figures had appeared at the front entrance of the tent. One man, two women. The man she knew by sight. The old woman she had merely glimpsed earlier that morning. But the other woman, the one whose sight had frozen her to the bone, stood like a queen between them. She had a beautiful vivid emerald cloak around her shoulders with a dark-burgundy evening gown below, to contrast the green eyes and match the hair that, in the flickering lights of the lamps and candles, seemed deep copper as a new-fallen chestnut in autumn.

'Mistress Brash!'

If the entrance itself had not yet turned a few negligent heads, then Kenneth Powrie's fluting tones completed the effect. The buzz of the audience dropped a few notches, and Jean was conscious of as many eyes that might grace a muster of peacocks, trained upon her.

This was what she wanted.

This was what she dreaded.

Acceptance. Envy. Disdain. Downright hatred.

Many of them, resentful women and guilty men, might love to see Jean stopped in her tracks but they could not deny her entry. Especially after Kenneth's next words, not uttered in any craven desire to flatter, but from a deeper, more honourable part of himself, perhaps the part that Jean sensed and would wish to preserve.

All of us may have some kernel of decency that this rough world has not yet corrupted, and would we not welcome any hint of protective insulation, even if it came from a bawdy-hoose keeper?

'Mistress Brash. Without your angelic support, none of this would be possible. I commend and dedicate this performance and those following to your name and beauty!'

'God Almighty, will the man never shut up?' muttered a discombobulated Hannah, who had dressed up as best she could but did not relish being the target of all eyes.

Yet Jean would seem to glory in it. Head raised high, she moved forwards with one hand laid lightly in the manly crooked arm of Jack Burns, who revelled in this limelight for many different reasons. He loved to thumb his nose at respectable society; however, this would also make his name sing in various social and artistic circles and therefore when it came to his own sculpture exhibition, the ladies most especially would be curious to behold the naked figures.

Men may buy, but women do the choosing.

And Jack loved to be adored by ladies. It was a problem surfacing of late, that he had realised adoration to be uncharacteristic of the woman beside him. She neither asked for nor provided same.

For this moment, though, he would bask in her reflected light.

So the three walked to the seats Kenneth had carefully put aside for them – not in the very front row by Jean's request – too many chances of a stab in the back – but, as chance would have it, directly behind Lieutenant Roach and a now seething Murray Craddock.

A signal from Kenneth and the lamplighting was lowered, some candles snuffed, the lights on the stage brightened, a crash of the thunder sheet courtesy of Billy Musgrave – which was as much as the Tyrone Company could afford by way of musical effects – and Alfred Tyrone led his motley crew onstage.

Emilia's thoughts were in turmoil. Of course she should have known that the damned woman would be on hand, but somehow it had slipped her mind. Or she had deliberately shoved the possibility down into the depths to join the other hidden secrets.

She had automatically taken up position with the other two women grouped around Alfred – Barnaby and John Wilde on the outskirts of the gathering.

The audience had fallen silent. From their point of view, after the initial thunderclap that had startled those with sensitive eardrums, the five figures had walked slowly on to the stage and taken up positions.

All eyes were at first attracted to the tall imposing persona of Lear in a gold cloak as he spread his arms wide, but then they fastened on the small figure in white. Cordelia, surely – the virtuous virgin. Unlike the two taller women, she was dark-complexioned, almost a Romany quality to her skin, the hair not knotted tight and pulled behind but loose, tumbling in dark curls to her white shoulders. Chastity was not the word that came to mind.

Jean Brash narrowed her eyes. She had received a note from Kenneth Powrie informing her of a definite closeness between Emilia and Billy Musgrave.

The girl was dangerous. On or off stage. There was a reckless hunger, which came off her like a spoor.

As if she sensed that thought, Emilia turned her head for she had seen right well where Jean was seated. The two locked eyes, but then Alfred sawed the air with a commanding gesture, Emilia turned back, Melissa arched her back to thrust forth a heavy bosom at odds with her slim body – a movement that attracted a certain sculptor's notice – Bridget focused inner attention as she inevitably did, John Wilde stifled an inappropriate belch, Barnaby blinked expectantly, and Alfred shook the scroll of heavy paper that represented a map of his soon to be divided kingdom.

It attracted the eyes of the audience back where they belonged. To Alfred.

Meantime we shall express our darker purpose!

The words rolled out over the silent audience, echoed backstage to where Billy Musgrave might well have given them credence, and then disappeared into the ether, heading towards the harbour area where they were bound to find purchase and employment.

Chapter 35

All friends shall taste
The wages of their virtue, and all foes
The cup of their deservings

The sea haar had now settled in like a witch in front of her cauldron. Leith harbour was shrouded in a darkness that was profound and dank, the fog's clammy fingers hooking down many a police collar to arrest the blood.

Only the lamplight from the gas mantles above shone through the glass to provide any kind of illumination. It created strange forms in the mist, like so many goblins, warped and misshapen, up to no good, ready to wreak whatever mischief the devil might command.

Mulholland's honeycomb had run its course, and he and McLevy were now hunched grimly on the stairs like shipwrecked sailors. Very dimly in the distance, if they peeped over the harbour edge above, they could just about make out the equally disconsolate outlines of Dunsmore's men where they huddled against the warehouse walls.

It was small compensation but not much.

The fog also muffled all sounds, and it felt cold as the tomb.

'How long is all this going to be?'

Mulholland did not enjoy the arthritic clime; he was warmblooded by nature, unlike his inspector, who had the vital fluids of an Eskimo.

'We'll live till we die,' was the somewhat obscure response. In truth McLevy was perversely cheerful in the gloom at the thought of Dunsmore possibly suffering from hypothermia. The stupid gommerel had turned up in a smart overcoat to impress the arriving messengers, but it was thin-lined, unlike McLevy's own thick ursine covering.

Mulholland was in his usual police cape with a regulation helmet on his head like the proverbial pea on top of a mountain. The sight never failed to provide simple-minded amusement for the inspector.

'Well, I told him,' McLevy grunted.

'I know, I know!'

'And whit did he say?'

Mulholland groaned inwardly. He had prevailed upon the inspector to divulge his unverified suppositions to Dunsmore, in case by some wild chance they might have value, but this had been treated with complete disdain.

'He said you should stick to street crime.'

'The word he used was *gutter*.'

McLevy was quite enjoying the insult now that he came to think about it. The gutter was where everything started and ended, one way or the other.

What he had less enjoyed was the cold contempt in Dunsmore's eyes accompanied by a thin superior smile. The little struntie had followed up the *gutter* reference with the words: 'It has been already made clear to you, Inspector, that your presence is only here on sufferance. I would advise you to keep distance and learn a lesson.'

In truth Dunsmore had hit these new heights of superciliousness due to the maxim that sadly applies to so many of the human race: give a man power and he trumpets like an elephant – minus that beast's herbivorous policy.

As a spark can be fanned into flame, so the dented ego that has nursed a grievance against the rest of the world for not recognising its genius can rage into life and a man may leave fellow feeling in his wake in order to avenge all of the misfortunes and slights in his existence, most of which never happened.

Or as the Scots tongue would have it – *a heid bummer knows nae mercy.*

Having delivered the reprimand, Dunsmore's small trim figure marched off into the mist, master of it all.

That had been a few hours ago, and nothing had changed save that the crescent moon decided to take the night off under cover of the black clouds and the mist was, if anything, even thicker and oozing like ectoplasm.

'So there ye are, Mulholland,' McLevy murmured. 'Ye deliver me up tae insults and calumnies.'

The constable's indignant response was cut short when a ship's horn sounded three sharp blows in the dark. Both men became at once alert. This was the agreed signal. At least that much had been confided to them.

Dunsmore came immediately out from his lair, walking with purpose, face stern as befits a man with a mission, followed by his six chosen myrmidons, each with meaty hand upon a truncheon.

McLevy and Mulholland strained ears to hear the plashing of oars as a small boat approached the side of the pier.

The inspector was itching to get closer but Mulholland shook a warning head.

'Out of sight, out of mind,' he admonished softly.

'Whit the hell does that mean?' was the grumpy response from McLevy as he squinted into the fog.

A murmur of voices as three men got up on to the harbour side and a formal handover, once Dunsmore had properly identified himself, took place.

A small leather bag, the contents of which remained unperused due to the fact that it was tightly locked and buckled with the crust of a red seal, was passed over and without more ado the three visitors clambered back down to their rowing boat and sped off into the gloom.

The hairs on McLevy's neck were prickling with tension as if he sensed danger. But why should he worry?

Dunsmore turned, tucked the bag under his arm, and marched proudly at the head of his troops, walking past the two Leith policemen who peeped over, not unlike a pair of children watching a courting couple.

'He should be in the middle, not the forefront,' observed the constable, 'under deep protection.'

'A law unto himself.'

This sardonic remark was the last moment either man was to know stillness and silence for a long time.

For as Dunsmore and his men in the faint light from the high gas mantles that provided the only source of illumination in the night stepped into a narrow space between the warehouses, a sudden fusillade of missiles cracked accurately through the glass mantles and in what seemed an instant the place was plunged into pitch black.

The sound of running feet came next and then the yelps and yells of conflict.

'Holy Jaysus, you were right!' gasped Mulholland in a rare blasphemous exclamation.

'Much good it did me,' grumbled McLevy as he hiked himself up on to the harbour, scrabbling for his service revolver while Mulholland drew out his hornbeam stick.

'Well,' said the inspector, 'here we go, Constable.'

'How do we tell one from the other?'

'Knock them all down.'

It was going to plan and Niven Taggart had an unaccustomed rush of joy as he hammered down one of the city policemen and kicked the man full in the face to make sure he abdicated responsibility.

When that Dutch idiot had confided to him all the details about the plans for the shipment including the false trail at Waverly Station, the man had signed his death warrant. *A friend, he had said, had told him. He had a friend in the museum. A close friend.*

Another of his friends – not such a refined specimen, a rough piece of work the Dutchman had met on a previous visit to Edinburgh – had recommended Niven as a man of action. With a gang. Safety in numbers.

Erik de Witte had offered a decent amount for the undertaking but wanted the necklace for himself. Claimed it belonged to his father.

A sin to use your father's name in vain – a man deserved to die for that alone.

He had laid his hand on Niven's shoulder. It might have travelled elsewhere but for the righteous cut.

Niven had reconnoitred the harbour, noted the only source of light, and watched this night as his men fitted their catapults and let fly. Not one missed. He had made the gang dwell in the darkness, concealed behind one of the customs sheds – for tobacco judging by the smell – and sit there like owls till their eyes were accustomed to the dark and swirling mist. And now they reaped the benefit.

Another squeal of pain as Bob Golspie smashed his hefty fist into another defender. The man's nose broke and a huge gush of blood covered Bob's clothing. Niven had insisted they all wore dark and muffled up their faces but this was a coat Bob admired upon himself.

Now it was spoiled.

So he hit the man again, this time in the throat, and grinned like a berserk over at Niven, blood that was not his own dripping down his face and falling from the coat.

Down the fellow went. All was well.

Except for the stupid little bastard who held to the bag. He had tried to wriggle underneath a fallen comrade to escape and scrambled to his feet only to have Bob's forearm hooked round his windpipe.

Dunsmore's face was streaked with mist and the sweat of fear. Yet he would not let go the bag, he would surely die first. It was his duty.

Niven's knife gleamed in the dark. He gestured towards the bag.

Let it go.

Dunsmore clutched tighter. Think of the shame. Think of the laughter in Leith. Think of the scornful faces.

It had all been conducted in silence save for the muffled cries of the police as they went down like ninepins, but then there was a loud howl of pain from one of the keelies as a stick battered flesh.

Niven froze. This was not in the plan.

Another howl as a revolver barrel crashed into a skull and then a voice that was only too familiar in the Stygian darkness.

'I am James McLevy, Inspector of Police – you will surrender tae me or I'll blow your brains apart!'

To emphasise this, there was a sudden spurt of flame and a muffled crack in the fog as a revolver was fired into the air.

Dunsmore's eyes widened. He held the bag tighter and managed to choke out a name as Bob's forearm crushed at his throat.

'*McLevy!*'

'Kill him,' said Niven Taggart.

Bob's limb moved in reflex to command. Dunsmore's chin went up until he was staring at the vaults of a very murky heaven and then came a sickening snap of gristle and bone, as his neck was broken.

One moment there is life and the next there is death – only Satan knows the difference. Or the Almighty. *Faîtes vos jeux.*

The little man fell down like a broken doll. Niven did not hesitate. He swooped, knife in one hand, and picked up the leather bag.

'We divide company,' he ordered. 'Meet later.' He did not specify the meeting place, however, but was gone, heading back into the jungle of harbour wynds.

Bob let out an agonised animal growl before staggering off obediently in the opposite direction to Niven, heading for Salamander Street and the more open terrain beyond; telltale drops of blood at his heels following like a faithful dog.

The last of the keelies went down under Mulholland's hornbeam stick but Adam Dunsmore did not move. Had his eyes been able to see, he would have observed McLevy and the constable rushing in to stand over him.

And then a young constable with a large red birthmark running down his neck had appeared as well, Ballantyne as promised having come back on his way home just to see if he might lend a hand to his inspector.

Dunsmore was lying in the gutter of the alley, where a man of his calling surely did not belong.

But he had died on duty. What more could be desired from a practising policeman?

Chapter 36

You do me wrong to take me out o' the grave:
Thou art a soul in bliss; but I am bound
Upon a wheel of fire, that mine own tears
Do scald like molten lead

The theatre is a strange and contradictory beast. In all senses the performance of *Lear* should have been an irretrievable disaster.

A threadbare company, little in the way of props and effects, the play itself cut back to the bone, moving only from one impacted scene to another including all of the gory episodes: eyeball extractions, self-stabbing, painful plucking of beards, agonising demise by poison and various death wounds.

The whole performed with gusto, but somewhat mitigated when the odd corpse had to resurrect himself as unobtrusively as possible, to return in another guise.

From where Sarah Baines sat towards the back, she could see Jean Brash at the front – her artist's eye noticing that it was strange how the Mistress of the Just Land seemed to attract light, her emerald cloak glowing in the pale light of lantern and flickering candle. Even in that brief study she had made of Jean standing by the window, Sarah had noticed how the light of day seemed drawn towards her like a lover.

Sarah's thigh was nestling comfortably yet not too noticeably against that of her own lover, Louisa Lumsden. Her father, the

Reverend William Baines, sat on the other side – Sarah being in the middle. An odd threesome.

Louisa was a handsomely gifted tall woman of dark hair and clear complexion; like Lear himself, born to command, being the headmistress of a young ladies' academy. Her partner in crime as some folk might think, Sapphic practice being rated akin to witchcraft, was a small elfin creature with a fiery disposition that hid contradictory desires to remain at home. Add to this a man of God who still bore the faint marks of attempted strangulation on his neck – of course hidden by the clerical collar – and you have a mixture that might qualify for an enactment all of its own.

However, the three watched, enthralled like the rest of the audience, as somehow the genius of the play shone through the occasional lack of quality.

Or perhaps because of that very deficit, as if the Bard himself had thought he had better take a hand?

For who is to say what is good and what is bad in theatre? Dull is the worst, on that we may all agree.

Jean Brash turned her head for a moment to look at Kenneth Powrie as he stood by the side of the tent. She wasn't missing anything, as Lear had just finished railing against the storm with the Fool hanging round his knees, and been rewarded with a round of applause. Alfred struck a pose. Barnaby Bunthorne tinkled.

Kenneth clasped his hands together as if in prayer and grinned at Jean, then blew her a kiss. She closed one eye in a wink – he was as close as she could get to an unreliable little monster of a sibling.

Mind you, given Maisie Power's wee brother, who would want a blood relative?

Their erstwhile family bond reformed and Kenneth's dubious financial shenanigans forgiven, both turned back to the unfolding play.

And still somehow it shone. In truth, Alfred Tyrone took little or no notice of the other actors, viewing them as staging posts for his great speeches in a way that chimed strangely apposite with Lear himself in his demented grandeur. The empty and hollow quality of Alfred's own acting resonated as the king became a mere carapace; it created a weird self-inflicted pathos that touched the audience because of the latent realisation that madness is indeed the final port of call for everyone.

And as a king should, so Lear led his subjects.

Barnaby as the Fool, the intelligent but powerless observer, turned laughter into pain and then such agony back into laughter like an alchemist.

Most of John Wilde's attention was involved in remaining upright, yet the backwash of gravity involved allowed him a solemn air of probity. He pronounced each line as if he were walking over the nearest peat bog where a traveller must watch every step taken.

Bridget gave an incisive reading of a ruthless woman who craves power but is at last undone by lust. How the moment when she lost her virginity in Plymouth to a randy fellow thespian during a run of *Love's Labour's Lost* played into this might be hard to tell, but that one moment she had surrendered to an inner drive had its harsh reality. When she later heard the selfsame boastful man tell his cronies in their dressing room 'any port in a storm', something froze in her heart. Now it was all grist to the creative mill.

Melissa as Regan, equally as evil as her sister but far more competent at deception, did not have to fish far into the depths of her being to find such attributes.

And last but not least? Emilia Fleming. She gave the character a curious air. As if Cordelia herself were playing the part of virtue but under that, was a raw unhealed wound caused by familial rejection. A face forever turned away from her.

Billy Musgrave watched from the back of the stage – he could see the effect she had on the audience but he knew her better than that. He knew her to the bone. She was both addicted to and terrified by her delight in violence. And he could supply it.

It was an unsettling ambivalence that intrigued even Hannah Semple as she watched.

'Tricky wee bugger,' she muttered to Jean.

Her mistress said nothing. With the mounting excitement of this performance came an undercurrent of a strange unsettling tremor that was not quite dread but certainly not joy. Like standing blindfold at the edge of a cliff.

It is always a danger for women to feel that they are in a play or novel of their own making.

Jean Brash had been marked by fate before and that inexorable revelation had its own bitter taste.

Jack Burns had in no way noticed that Melissa Fortune's green dress was sewn up in the lower back.

Roach, who was directly in front, had found that as usual in matters of culture his mind had wandered; he hoped the Tholberg necklace was by now safe in the Castle and that McLevy had, for once, behaved himself.

Craddock had been puzzled from the very beginning; the notion of giving away anything was foreign to his nature and dividing a kingdom would be akin to subletting a position at the Masonic Lodge. Also, a waft of French cologne made him conscious of a certain bawdy-hoose keeper sitting behind and although the woman had been quiet so far, Craddock was reminded of the fact that every time he had crossed swords with her, Jean Brash had, as it were, run him through the gizzard.

Roach's wife and the bridge club harpies were biting at their fingernails. Towards the end, when Lear carried the small, crumpled figure in white across the stage to lay her down tenderly – in fact over the exact spot where the female cockroach crouched patiently under the boards with her sac of eggs – and intoned the last words

> Why should a dog, a horse, a rat, have life,
> And thou no breath at all? Thou'lt come no more,
> Never, never, never, never, never!
> Pray you, undo this button: thank you, sir.
> Do you see this? Look on her, look, her lips,
> Look there, look there!

the audience were transfixed as the king expired also and Emilia to her credit did not flinch as Alfred's breath swept over like an unwelcome miasma.

Melissa and Bridget were already decorously in place as the evil but deceased sisters, John Wilde was still upright and so all that was left was for Barnaby in his alter ego part of Albany to perform the last rites.

> The weight of this sad time we must obey;
> Speak what we feel, not what we ought to say.
> The oldest hath borne most: we that are young
> Shall never see so much, nor live so long.

According to stage direction it was then *exeunt, with a dead march* but lacking the numbers for such since most were recumbent upon the boards, the end was signalled by Barnaby bowing his head in sorrow as the lights dimmed and, at the very last, all that could be seen was the white dress where Cordelia lay like a broken butterfly.

For a moment the image glowed in the retina, then it faded like memory itself.

Silence.

Then the applause erupted and continued as the lights came up and the cast rose somewhat shakily to their feet.

Due to the aforementioned fact that they had in recent memory lost three of their main theatres to incendiary mishaps, the populace had been deprived of dramatic infusion and this tragic advent had been like a rush of blood; a galvanic attack of the poetic and irrational had exploded amongst them like a bomb.

Who knows but that deprivation had caused the idea of the Festival of Culture to take place in Edinburgh and of course there were critics who said it would never last, but for this moment there was an almost tribal primitive abandon as the audience put their hands together.

Primitive abandon, that is, as far as an Edinburgh audience was concerned.

Curtain call after curtain call, there not being a noticeable curtain adding to the fervour, took place as Alfred Tyrone finally received the adulation his great talent deserved. In his eyes, it was only right and about time, but he was generous enough to allow his fellow thespians some show in the light of glory as he beckoned one after another to bow low.

In Wilde's case, this meant restoring himself upright again – not in itself an easy task. Meanwhile, Barnaby in unaccustomed elation had donned his jester's hat – it sat most oddly with his

Albany costume – and performed a little hop into the air, clicking his heels together just for the mischief of it.

Bridget maintained a cool decorum, Melissa bowed deep to let her green gown décolletage divulge the bounteous gifts of Mother Nature, while Emilia did likewise in virginal disclosure stage left, kneeling like a humble female supplicant with a sting in her tail.

Alfred stood in the middle and spread his arms to include the whole cast, God Almighty, and anyone else who happened to be passing by.

And then the applause faltered.

Jean Brash sat bolt upright. Hannah clutched her cut-throat razor. Evening wear or not, the weapon was in place.

And then another silence.

And then the screams began.

Chapter 37

Were't my fitness
To let these hands obey my blood,
They are apt enough to dislocate and tear
Thy flesh and bones

He had run like a hunted animal through the wynds till he got to Salamander Street, at the top of which stood the slaughterhouse like a castle of skin and bone. The sea haar had lifted suddenly to expose bare streets and that did not work in his favour.

The bastards were still on his track. Every time he looked back he could sense them following like a pair of wolves, but now he had a better chance.

The hem of the coat had dripped blood and that was why they had been able to trace him – he had just that minute seen the guilty trail and ripped the thing off his body to hurl into the darkness. The blood on his face had dried by now. It did not drip. That was good.

He cut through the back streets to the edge of Leith Links, mind rigid with panic.

Bob Golspie always did what he was told. His mother Maggie had chastened him hard as a child and, despite a huge bulk, could still bring him to heel with one word or glance. Niven Taggart was the same – Bob did what Niven told him. The same fear coursed through him.

Bob smiled and seemed good-natured but he broke bodies to command.

Never a neck, though. The man had fallen. The man was police. He had not moved. So Bob had been a good boy – Niven had said 'kill him'.

An unbidden scream rose in his throat. No, wait. That was *not* good. To kill a policeman. Even a little one. No, that was *not* good.

Jesus, was that footsteps behind? He had caught an earlier glimpse of the pursuers and could swear it was that evil swine McLevy and the tall constable – the one wi' the stick – this was very bad.

He would escape them, though, for Bob was clever. See? He did not follow the path of light that lay up the hill; he would skirt it round the side.

At the top was a big tent. And lights. Lights were not good. But then outside the area of light, there was a dark place. It seemed to go on forever. Darkness.

Bob did not enjoy the dark. When he was a bad boy, a dirty wee rascal, caught maybe with his foot on a cat's face and it yowling blue murder, his mother aye locked him in the coal bunker to teach a lesson. He'd squatted there sookin' in the dust, choking, eyes gummed up with salty tears, and whimpered in bad fear till she turned the key to let him out.

Even now when he stood well above her, when he could break her in two, he was still afraid.

He had hated waiting in the harbour in the blackness that closed them all off but Niven said it must be done. And then the neck. It must be done.

Another sound behind him, the bastards were still at his back!

But Bob was clever. He would fool them. They would think of him running into the dark to escape but he would find a better place.

See? Here. Under the tent. Out of sight. But now it was dark again. Crawl. Under boards. Then – wait – was that Billy Musgrave he saw? By a big metal sheet. How was that possible? No – go the other way.

And there was a hellish loud noise, like rain battering down, or thunder, or horses' hooves maybe, and shouts. And he had to get out. Into the light!

Bob found himself in a big empty space with strange people in strange costumes all looking at him, and then loud screams and a man with a funny hat like a coxcomb shoved him down. Break them all in pieces!

But then he turned to see the faces, all of them, looking at him, mouths open and shut, pointing, and it was like an explosion in his ears, all that noise and the light, and one of them onstage, in white, it was that slut, that little slut of Billy's, grab her, crush her, round the neck – he was good at that!

The audience had seen a huge figure in a dark shirt lumber on to the stage. Could this be part of the play? Surely not. He was like a monster, a troll, face covered in dried blood as he knocked someone to the ground, trampled over the jester's hat and then clamped an arm around Cordelia's pretty white throat.

Then *another* uninvited performer appeared. A man with a gun. This was definitely not in period.

James McLevy looked across the stage to where Bob Golspie stood with his arm crooked round the neck of a young woman the inspector just about recognised as Billy Musgrave's wee whore.

An actress, eh? That would explain her in the tavern, looking for thrills. And Billy had appeared just behind them, hand sliding down his leg, for a sweetie, no doubt, to offer Bob.

Before Billy could make a move, however, Mulholland appeared adjacent to him: the constable had been sent round the other flank as soon as they saw the situation.

Billy therefore stayed his hand.

Mulholland's stick was by his side. The *Lear* cast were huddled together at the back of the stage, Bridget at the front like a ship's figurehead while the one who had been knocked down crawled towards them, holding doggedly on to his jester's hat.

McLevy raised the hand with the gun – not pointing at anyone, just brought up to view – and stretched out the other, palm downwards as if to give a blessing.

It had a magical effect on the audience, who subdued the noise to a fearful murmur.

'I didnae know ye for a histrionic, Bob,' said the inspector conversationally. 'Have you future plans in that direction?'

'You lee me alone, McLevy, or I'll kill this wee bitch!'

Bob wrenched Emilia round so that her body was between himself and the inspector, who walked forward slowly, smiling like a man out for a walk in the park.

'Is that part o' the play?' he asked. 'It's very good. You should take it up for a living.'

Roach meanwhile had slid from his seat and was moving down the aisle towards the front of the stage.

He caught Mulholland's eye – both knew that it was somehow vital to distract Bob so that the inspector got a clear shot, though his shooting would never have worried Buffalo Bill Cody.

That, however, was a chance they'd have to take.

Bob stood centre stage – traditionally the most powerful position – McLevy to his left, Roach further away, cast at the back, Mulholland to the right.

Emilia was choking as the arm, like an iron bar, cut into her windpipe.

Billy Musgrave tensed to make a move, but then another voice from directly in front of them all pierced through the thick silence.

'Bob Golspie – does your mother know you're out?'

Jean Brash stood sharp to the right where she had slipped round. Her eyes were blazing and she seemed the very epitome of outraged parental anger.

The big man's eyes widened in shock.

'You know fine well what she would think of this kind of behaviour. A disgrace to her good name!'

As Jean spoke she moved further to the side, taking Bob's eyeline with her and opening up his body slightly to McLevy, who seemed negligent and calm as if not really interested.

'I was talking to her the other day, and whit do you think she said to me?'

This sharp rebuke in form of question jolted Bob further. Indeed, what would his mother think?

'That boy. He better behave himself!'

In fact Jean was running out of maternal reprimands and McLevy had not yet made a move. Was the man a statue?

One more go. Move further to the side.

'Wait till I tell her, just you wait!'

'That's no' fair!' Bob protested.

That was the moment Emilia twisted out of his grip for a second to pull away and as Bob stretched to haul her back, James McLevy drew up his pistol.

Some of the audience had of course already seen onstage shots fired, mostly by dastardly villains in melodramas, but this noise was different. There was no flash of fake powder, no bluff crack; this was a louder menacing explosion that rung the ears, and the effect was also poles apart. The bullet smashed into the side of Bob's head and spun him round to fall in a heap on the boards.

Emilia staggered off to the safety of her fellow thespians and in the dreadful silence Jean Brash bit off the following words to James McLevy:

'Could you not have just aimed to wound?'

'I did,' he replied. 'But he must have moved. I cannae help it if somebody moves.'

Mulholland was already by the body. He looked up and shook his head. Roach flexed his jaw like an irritated crocodile – what in God's name was going on? He did not dare turn round to meet the eyes of his chief constable, who would no doubt be apoplectic.

Kenneth Powrie clasped his hands together once more but there was an element of calculation in his eyes.

McLevy still had not budged. A pity he had killed Bob. Now they had less chance of finding Niven Taggart's whereabouts.

Jean sighed in frustration though shaking inside – that had been touch and go. She thus addressed James McLevy: 'How come every time I try to do something nice, you have tae spoil it?'

Chapter 38

Let us deal justly.
Sleepest or wakest thou, jolly shepherd?

On the principle of waste not want not and despite a grisly insertion from the real world, it had been decided at Kenneth Powrie's urging that the post-performance event of civic reception might as well go ahead.

To tell truth the audience were in sore need of a strong drink and after all, the city was paying for it. Plus, it is not every night you witness the death of royalty and a murderous beast upon the same stage – one make believe, one the opposite – and who is to say which has made the greater impression?

Various theatregoers vied with each other in reliving the vivid happenings, Roach's wife to the fore with the bridge club harpies to back her up – their seats had a grandstand view as the gun exploded and the man's head did likewise.

As previously stated, it is often difficult to tell difference between the stage and real life, especially as regards the rarely witnessed event of a bullet through the skull. Usually there was more blood in the theatre and folk take a lot longer to die.

Bob Golspie had fallen like a stricken oak and landed face down so that only the constable had seen the damage done and he would no doubt be used to that sort of thing, therefore it was hard to make comparisons.

So Mrs Roach trilled like an agitated blackbird and the harpies played chorus.

The lieutenant of course was nowhere to be seen; he had remained behind to oversee an official investigation but rumours were already flying. A robbery. In the harbour. Injuries. Broken bones. Gunshots. How McLevy and Mulholland came to be involved was murky as a sea haar but there was the inspector bold as brass upon a legitimate stage.

The civic hall that housed this welter of voices was situated on Princes Street, but down at Leith harbour a very different exchange was occurring.

Craddock had somehow twisted events in his mind to the effect that McLevy's interference had in fact caused this disastrous occurrence. After being told about the attack and robbery, the chief constable insisted they return to the pierside and after a necessary but repugnant search of Bob's pockets to make sure he had not secreted the Tholberg necklace, there was little else of use to be gleaned.

They left the body onstage. Arrange for it to be picked up later. No rush. Not going anywhere. Performance over. No applause.

At the scene of the crime, Ballantyne had excelled himself, not in Roach's tetchy surmise a difficult task. The constable had alerted the harbour watch and then arranged for the bruised and battered city policemen to be patched up by volunteers from the nearest hospital, led by the matron who fortunately enough happened to be his mother and very proud of her aspiring son – her dream was the office of inspector, but she'd settle for sergeant at the desk.

The keelies had been thrown into a corner already handcuffed and tightly bound; their wounds could wait.

That was the positive.

On the negative side was the disappearance of a priceless necklace and the death of Adam Dunsmore, which overbalanced the scales somewhat.

McLevy and Mulholland had noted the distant passing over of a small leather bag but there was no sign of the object despite a minute search of the narrow alley where the ambush had taken place. To McLevy's mind there could be only one culprit: his gang and Golspie his right hand man.

'Niven Taggart,' he stated. 'Has tae be.'

'But he's just a – a keelie!'

To his lieutenant's expostulation, McLevy's lips twisted in a sardonic smile. 'Rose above himself, maybe.'

'He killed an officer of the law!'

Having delivered this righteous reprimand, Craddock looked down at the body of Dunsmore now covered chastely with a rough blanket until the carry wagon came to take him back to a station he detested. There to lie in the cold room until the police surgeon arrived to pronounce and dissect.

Not hard to find the cause of death, the inspector thought, *even for a claret-ridden specimen like Doctor Jarvis. The angle of the head gave it away in big lumps.*

'You find this scum of the earth, McLevy – this is your mess. Now clean it up!'

A cold lupine glint came into McLevy's eyes. He had never liked Dunsmore but he would find his killer. However, certain things must be clarified.

'I warned ye,' he answered the chief constable. 'I told you. There were not enough men. You paid no heed.'

'We did not expect – the diversion was in the papers. *How* did they get to know the opposite?'

'I've given explanation of that.'

McLevy had told both Roach and Craddock of what he had informed Dunsmore and the fact it had been ignored. He kept Jean Brash's name out of it for the moment; Craddock had enough prejudices in his basket.

The chief constable spat out one of them.

'I'm not sure I believe such. More likely someone has been bribed. And betrayed his sacred trust.'

The implication behind this somewhat florid remark was obvious. Roach's back stiffened, Mulholland pursed his lips as if finding a wasp in the beehive, yet McLevy, for such a choleric individual, was still as the night.

'It is *your* mess, not mine.'

Before Craddock could draw breath to contradict the inspector's flat statement, Roach beat him to it.

'Only three men knew the plan at our station. One is myself, and the other two I would stake my life upon.'

Now and again the lieutenant could nail it down, thought Mulholland. *Not often. But now and again.*

'I'll away and find this mannie,' said McLevy to Roach as if the chief constable did not exist. 'It will not be easy, he'll be hunkered down. But I'll find him – eventually. That's my job.'

With such he turned abruptly and walked off followed by the silent Mulholland, only stopping to tap Ballantyne on the shoulder. 'Ye did well, Constable. Don't give up the fight.'

McLevy left Ballantyne to wonder exactly what fight he was supposed to espouse and the two figures were lost in the night.

'Let us hope he is a man of his word.' Craddock found he was addressing these words into thin air as Roach had mysteriously moved position to talk with one of the bandaged policemen being tended to by Ballantyne's mother.

'Let us hope so,' Craddock repeated somewhat foolishly, as his eyes fixed on the crumpled form beneath the blanket.

Adam Dunsmore, but for the present state of his existence, would no doubt have agreed.

Chapter 39

I serve you, madam:
Your graces are right welcome

Another mysterious move signalled Jean Brash slipping back into the reception.

A note had been delivered that one of her people was waiting outside and while Jean conducted some pertinent business, she left Hannah to glower at a finger sandwich of crab paste augmented by some low-class champagne.

What she had learned was not good and Jean felt herself being inexorably drawn into a situation that would be fraught with danger. Again she was assailed by a feeling of a deep primal vengeance on her trail.

'Whit's the verdict?' asked Hannah.

Previously Jean had tried to prise some information from the inspector but all he would mutter was there had been a rammy at the harbour and that was the limit to be divulged.

Now she knew more.

'A big robbery, I'm told. A man dead at the harbour. A policeman. Niven Taggart's gang.'

'Whit kind of robbery?'

'That is not yet clear.'

'None of our business.'

No answer. Hannah tried again.

'A matter for McLevy then, Mistress.'

'Not entirely.'

It would be too much of a coincidence for this robbery not to tie in with Erik de Witte.

'My people were watching from far. I warned them to keep it that way. They saw Taggart running but – lost him in the fog.'

'As I say. McLevy's concern.'

Jean did not answer and Hannah had seen that look on her face before. A cold implacable anger; there was a core to the Mistress that could not be moved or shaken. It always meant trouble. Hopefully for someone else. And this crab paste concoction was hellish. Who in their right mind would want to make paste out of a crab?

'Mistress Brash?'

Jean came out of some very dark thoughts to find Kenneth Powrie beaming up at her.

'What a wonderful evening!'

The impresario would seem to have overlooked the shot and resultant dead body.

'In what way?' she asked.

'The publicity! Once word gets round, everyone will wish to wend their way towards Leith Links. Think of the excitement, it will be a sensation. Beyond measure!' Kenneth leant closer to speak softly. 'You will get your money back and more, Mistress Brash. I can guarantee you that.'

For some reason this made Jean feel like a grave robber.

She nodded nevertheless and Kenneth shot off to inform members of the audience that, should they wish, he could offer them a slightly reduced ticket price for the next visit. Who knows what might happen then?

Kenneth had now found his purpose in life. The buying and selling of culture. Poetry in motion.

Amongst the crowd Jean spotted the elfin figure of Sarah Baines, her father no longer on hand – gone back to pray for the soul of Bob Golspie, no doubt. Beside her was Louisa Lumsden. Tall, elegant, wearing a red cloak – just like little Red Riding Hood. The notion made Jean smile to herself as the woman caught her regard and looked boldly back. Headmistress to bawdy-hoose keeper.

Out of the blue, Jean winked at the woman and was rewarded with a startled glance. Sarah sensed something and turned to look over at her portraiture subject, who was innocence personified.

'Well, if a girl can't get up to mischief what else can she do?'

This remark from Jean puzzled Hannah but anything was better than that cold look and the crab paste.

'Speakin' o' mischief,' she muttered.

Jean followed her gaze to where the cast of *Lear* were holding court, Alfred cigar in hand, gesturing with bravado to a rapt gathering of admirers amongst whom were the lieutenant's wife and the bridge club harpies.

John Wilde had given best to gravity and leant against the wall with a large whisky in hand, a curiously seraphic look on his face as if he had reached nirvana.

Barnaby, nose a little swollen from his tumble, had stationed himself at Alfred's elbow, still to a certain extent playing the fool but an element of sadness in his eyes – he never would be the hero of the hour. Always the bridesmaid. By no means the bride.

Jack Burns, straw hat at an angle, was talking nineteen to the dozen with Bridget, Melissa Fortune and Emilia. He was obviously discussing his own metier, for as the sculptor waved his hands decisively in the air, Jean recognised the shape of a goddess. Bridget appeared interested, Melissa *very* interested and Emilia? Her face was strangely blank.

Part of that was a longing to get back to the lodgings and indulge herself with a pipeful of hashish: her nerves were jangling after an exchange with Billy Musgrave. The exchange was the other part: at the back of the dressing room before she came on to the reception. Billy had a wild look to his eyes like an animal scenting blood.

'I know where he bides. His secret wee den. I know it. A robbery, they say. A stash. I'll take it from him.'

'Why?'

'Bad blood. He took what's mine. I was king. I take whit's his. That's fair.'

'Fair?'

Billy laughed at the look on her face. 'He has nothing. No gang. Bob Golspie shot lik' a dog. I have two men at my back. The meet is arranged.'

'Surely you can wait?'

'Strike while the iron's hot, Emmy.'

'I don't feel any heat.'

He laughed again, pulled her in tight. 'I want ye with me. Ye'll like it. Warm ye up.'

'I can't. I have a reception. People. An audience.'

'Forget them.'

'No.'

'Ye said ye wanted tae watch.'

'That was before.'

'You're my good luck charm.'

'I'm not coming Billy!'

He looked into her face and saw that something had changed. 'Suit yerself.'

And he was gone.

Was she the only one who had felt such a shock when Bob Golspie had a bullet crash through his head? Perhaps the audience from a distance somehow saw it as part of the performance but she had been at close hand. Too close for comfort as the bullet struck home, the flesh parted and bone splintered blood.

The rest of the actors would turn it into another drama. That was their way. The real world was not their concern. It would be an anecdote in years to come. Is that what she wanted? Like a hashish dream?

She came out of these thoughts to find herself staring straight at Jean Brash.

Who was staring straight back with a mocking but not unfriendly smile on her countenance. As if to say, *well?*

On an impulse Emilia stuck her tongue full out at the woman, then turned away abruptly.

Hannah had been morosely wondering when the hell they could get out of this damned place but then she was astonished to hear Jean laugh like a market woman.

'Whit's going on?'

'Nothing for nosy folk.'

Hannah grunted. A'body full of jokes these days. She noticed that while most folk were pointed for some reason in their direction, one was not: she pointed at Emilia Fleming's back.

'Ye'd think she might thank ye for saving her bliddy life.'

'I believe she already has.'

Jean shivered suddenly. It felt as if the very air itself was unsafe, as if wheels had come off the carriage and its body was hurtling onwards like a blind beggar. A strange jittery excitement seemed to have possessed them all. However, she had things to do back in the Just Land – and dangers to be faced, even if she was not sure in what form they would come.

And another thought came into her head. Who would tell Maggie Golspie that her son had been shot dead on a stage in Leith Links?

She would send a note. The least Jean could do since she'd been part responsible for the killing.

'Get our coats,' she said urgently. 'Time to go.'

'Thank God for that,' said a relieved Hannah already on her way.

Jack Burns caught the movement and crossed over leaving his trio of Graces to commune with each other.

'Leaving?'

'Yes.'

Hannah returned and Jack helped Jean on with her emerald cloak. For a moment they looked at each other. He was a handsome specimen, for sure. Not a sinuous lover like Monsieur Bonnard would no doubt be, yet she would not have to swim the Channel to arrive in his arms.

Ready, willing and, for the most part, able.

'Would you admire my company, Mistress Brash?'

'Not tonight,' she answered. 'I have – too much on hand. But soon, my mannie. Best prepare yourself.'

He nodded with good grace and perhaps the slightest tinge of – what? Relief? Release? Regret?

'That champagne was near bad as the sandwich,' announced Hannah, also now accoutred for the open air but without the assistance of Mister Burns. 'Can we go and get some decent provender?'

Jack, in a farewell gesture, raised Jean's hand to his lips and kissed it. This did not go unnoticed.

'Mistress Brash, are you leaving us already?'

This fluted call from Kenneth brought a brief nod in response from Jean who cursed a little inside because she had hoped to slip out unseen. Now, it seemed, everyone was turned in her direction as Kenneth raised a glass of the mediocre bubbly.

'A toast!' he exclaimed. 'To a divine messenger who has rescued the day!' That covered both Jean's earlier support in saving his procreative bacon, and later diversionary tactics to achieve the opposite effect for Bob Golspie.

Glasses were raised and a confused murmur ensued.

It should have been a moment of triumph for Jean; however, she was aware of many different attitudes in many a different regard. The Unco Guid in all their glory. Envy, grudged admiration, downright hostility, a cold measure in respectable eyes. In contrast a warm thespian acknowledgement from Alfred and Barnaby, the distaff side of *Lear* being a mixed bag.

And had she been one of the audience looking back at herself? What would she have seen or sensed? A knowledge within that Jean Brash would never be accepted. Always an outsider. Never one of us.

Yet, this time, she felt as much in charge as she did in the Just Land. At this moment, something had changed. If you can't be yourself, you can't be anything.

An enigmatic smile, a nod of acknowledgement, a cool flicker of the eyelash to a grinning Jack Burns and Jean swept elegantly out of the door trailed by the slightly less graceful form of Hannah Semple.

In the confused hubbub that followed, Emilia had stubbornly kept her back to proceedings. When she turned round again, her tormentor had gone.

'You might at least, Miss Fleming,' said Bridget Tyrone with some asperity, 'recognise the departure of our esteemed patroness. Someone who not only has supported us financially but, unless I may misconstrue events, could well have saved your life.'

Melissa Fortune nodded agreement, always glad to sink the knife, but part of her attention was elsewhere – many things are worth stealing.

A jewel comes in many guises.

Emilia flushed, aware she had made a complete fool of herself. *I hate her*, she thought to herself. *One day, I'll kill the bitch. She deserves it.*

But Miss Fleming could not deny. Thanks to Jean Brash, she was still alive to enjoy such hatred.

Chapter 40

Despite thy victor sword and fire-new fortune,
Thy valour and thy heart, thou art a traitor

Niven Taggart had never witnessed beauty; it was not part of his existence. He held the necklace up to catch the flickering candle-light in the small room – his den – his lair – his secret haven – and was conscious of a feeling in his guts, like something twisting inside.

Pain and pleasure.

Something in his lost soul had been touched by the sight.

Beauty.

The diamonds sparkled like stars, or like sunlight on a wide stream.

Once when a little boy he had sat by Puddocky Burn as they all called the Waters of Leith, and a morning sun had hit the rippling surface to create a multitude of dancing lights. Niven had picked up the biggest rock he could find and thrown it into the water. Then he ran away, his almond eyes yellow with a disturbed fury, not looking back.

But now? He looked his fill. This beauty belonged to him. He had killed for it so that was only right.

Now, he was king.

One of the diamonds in particular, the main piece of the display, seemed to glow from deep inside as well as catching and reflecting light. It drew him like a magnet.

He hesitated, and then very slowly brought the chain of diamonds closer. The one he most desired spun just before his eyes and he slipped it into his mouth. It felt cold, slithered on his tongue, he closed his lips around, moved it to and fro, and felt an urge to swallow it whole.

He would never give up the treasure. Not for all the money in the world. It was *his*.

'Ye look stupit, Niven.'

Billy Musgrave's mocking words crashed through the beautiful dream as if a bucket of dirty water had been thrown into Niven's enraptured face.

In his trance, the king of the keelies had not heard the lock of the door snick open as Billy's greased knife slid in to spring the mechanism.

Niven had also in his haste forgotten to put the door chain in place. These mistakes can kill you.

He spat out the diamond, dropped the necklace behind and levered himself bolt upright.

Naked. As he liked to be in that room. Bare scuddie.

He had been lying on the bed as always but now he was standing, curved knife hooked up before his body.

Billy laughed, eyes focused on a certain part of the displayed anatomy. 'There's not much tae ye, is there, Niven?'

Niven Taggart flushed. But he had his knife. The necklace was safe on the bed sheets at his back.

'Looks like a nice wee stash you have there, eh?'

Billy's words were oddly comforting. So Niven's opponent did not know the priceless value of the necklace and he never would because he could never have it.

Billy moved easily into the centre of the room and grinned,

gold tooth glinting like a diamond. 'Ye wondering how come I know your hidey-hole?'

Niven nodded, eyes trained on Billy's own knife, held loosely by the side.

'I aye had two men in your gang. Good men. My boys. They followed you one night. Saw where ye bide. That was careless, Niven.'

Another nod. He knew what Billy was trying to do. Keep him off balance. But now it was his turn.

'Good boys, eh?'

'The best.'

'I left them battered tae bits inside a cupboard wi' the rats for company. Dead by now. Nothing tae breathe.'

This time it was Niven who laughed. A high-pitched noise like a fox on heat.

Billy thought fast. That would explain why they hadn't made the meet to back him up. In fact, though Billy and Niven did not know this, the only meet the keelies would achieve was when the door got kicked open and they looked into the white face of Inspector James McLevy, teeth bared like a wolf.

But one way or another Billy now needed an edge. Something to provoke. Often the man who made the first rash move in this sort of face-off near always ended up the dead one.

Both were skilled in knife fights, and as they spoke shifted round the bare floorboards of the room, searching out an opportunity to strike.

'Dead, eh?' ventured Billy.

'For sure.'

'Like Bob Golspie, then?'

'Whit?'

'McLevy blew his head apart. Jean Brash set him up. It was funny tae watch. Fat bastard. Shot tae buggery.'

'Ye're a liar!'

'I would have pissed on him but there were too many folk watching.'

Billy roared with laughter and Niven's eyes blazed with a cold fury: Jean Brash. She'd done it. He'd cut her guts out. Cut them deep!

Yet still he watched and still he circled. His skinny naked body should have been an easy target, easy meat. Billy made a feint with his knife hand, grinning, and then suddenly spat straight into Niven's face.

The naked man reeled back and Billy made his move. One cut, hard in, if not kill then wound, no need to do it right off, just slice the low belly, carve a smile in it, see the flesh part, the blood spurt, then as Niven looks down in dismay, another cut up the side to the oxter, that hurts like hell and cripples the arm, then it's just back low again, where the legs meet the body, tender like a sweetheart's kiss.

Then it's all over.

You can stand back then, admire the handy work. As if it was a painting. Red sunset.

Except it did not quite happen like that.

Not quite.

Billy made the cut well enough. In the belly, but not the intended depth. A good slice that drew claret yet not quite the shock of paralysing pain.

For as Billy plunged in, Niven drove up the hooked knife, his wiry naked body fusing the gesture with all its strength, to rip from just below the ribcage to butcher the heart, then pulled back down, out and away.

'You were good, Billy,' said Niven to the fallen adversary who sprawled at his feet, surprise and agony carving lines on his face. 'But not – good enough.'

No need for another gash. The life was fading from the eyes but there was still time. Kneel down.

'These years ago – when that stupit swine frae the other gang was knifed in the back? That was me. Arranged tae meet – tae talk peace, he thought.'

The naked man giggled. This was *dead* funny.

'I did him. Wi' a knife like yours. In the back. Bad as hell, eh? I knew you'd get the blame. And ye did.'

Niven looked deep into the eyes of a dying man. Still a shred of life yet. Good.

'You lost everything. I got it. I'm the king.'

The light went out. Billy was gone. His mouth fell open and the gold tooth gleamed its last.

Niven stood up shakily. Have to clean and bind the wound, get himself dressed. And then? He looked at the necklace where it lay on the bed. It was still beautiful.

He would have to leave Edinburgh but he would survive. No one could stop him.

But first? First, there was a matter of honour.

Chapter 41

Humanity must perforce prey on itself,
Like monsters of the deep

Danny Summers was about to pack it in. All very well for McLevy
to put him on a watch for Maisie Powers in case she went visiting
her wee brother Richie, a boy hidden away somewhere that the
inspector would dearly like to get his hands on.

Furthermore, for Danny to keep an eye on the Just Land
because McLevy was in suspicion that Jean Brash was up to something, though when was that woman *not* up to something?

Anyhow Maisie had not poked her nose outside the place,
Jean's carriage had returned not long before, and the house was
dormant.

It was also cold, dark and late. Spring was fine during the day
but at night, inhospitable as any other Edinburgh hour of
darkness.

Danny was anxious to get back to the Haymarket where his
merry wee widow waited. Not for much longer though would she
be a widow; they planned to marry later in the year. Mind you,
this kind of caper might be a casualty. Who'd want their man
hanging about outside a bawdy-hoose past midnight?

Time to go home, eh? Wave goodbye to a useless endeavour.

And then he saw the figures coming up the side street towards
the garden wall of the Just Land. Keeping to the shadows. For a

moment they stopped at a side door and in the silence Danny heard the click of a key in the lock and then as the door opened, in they slipped.

One of the figures was known to Danny; caught in a stray beam from the lamplight.

He'd need to get to McLevy quick, it could be worth a fine reward. But where to locate the inspector? At the station maybe? Go through the wynds first, on the way there. Jist in case.

McLevy had promised he'd look in on his watcher but Leith was in an uproar, Danny had heard some news. The inspector would be a busy man.

A big robbery. Keelies at the harbour.

And McLevy would therefore be very interested in Danny's information. The little man broke into a trot. He was fit as a fiddle and on the qui vive.

In the kitchen of the Just Land, Jean Brash took a slug of strong coffee, Lebanese with more than a dash of brandy, and then observed her portrait. She'd brought it in from the little study next door where Sarah Baines had toiled earlier this day. For the life of her Jean couldn't think of a reason why she'd done this, but events of this night had unsettled her and what would it grant? A chance to look at herself from a distance?

The small wooden-framed drawing was set up on its easel just beside the table where she sat.

A *woman gazes out of a window. Looking for better days,* as Hannah Semple might say. *A life that lacks nothing yet is curiously empty.*

Hannah came bustling in to disturb the reverie. 'The girls are a' pit tae bed. A busy enough night Big Annie Drummond said, but nothing untoward. Nane o' they mad Frenchmen. Mair's the pity.'

'That wee man with the moustache had his eye on you,' Jean teased.

'Well, he's gone now.'

Indeed the French brigade had left that very morning. Jean had certain proof of this by mail.

'I went down tae the cellars,' Hannah continued, frowning as Jean slapped another shot of brandy in the coffee. 'That nyaff Richie Powers is sleeping like the dead. Whit a cairry on, eh?'

'Was Maisie with him?'

'Aye. Sitting by his bed. So, I sent her and Lily upstairs tae their scratcher.'

Hannah shook her head gloomily. That bliddy play would give her nightmares. Poking folk's eyes out. Whit kind of entertainment was that?

'I told Maisie straight, Mistress. He leaves later this day – it's too damned perilous. If McLevy found Richie here, we would be for the high jump.'

Jean nodded. True enough, but Maisie loved her brother, so what to do with the wretched wee idiot? He was connected to that robbery somehow plus the fact that all hell was breaking loose in the parish of Leith.

That woman in the drawing was still looking out the window and might do so for a long time.

A sharp tap on the back door interrupted proceedings.

'Who the hell can that be?' muttered Hannah.

'Maybe it's the inspector,' said Jean a trifle wearily. 'Come to scrounge some coffee.'

'I hope tae God not.'

'Go and see who it is, but don't unchain the door unless it's a known voice.'

'And don't you teach your grannie tae suck at eggs,' replied the old woman grimly, patting the pocket just above her left bosom.

Out she went and Jean sighed. Perhaps it was the brandy but she abruptly felt deflated. What a night!

It seemed an eternity ago she'd had that dream. *The baby*. What did it signify?

Noises at the door; the chain being unlocked. It must be a friendly voice. Kenneth Powrie probably, arriving with some more mediocre champagne?

Then Hannah hurtled through the open kitchen door to land sprawling on her hands and knees, propelled by a savage boot in the rear. Plookie Galbraith and his wee scabby dog were next shoved in, forced to the side, the dog whining and its master white with shock and fear.

For behind him stood Niven Taggart.

Favouring his belly a little, but otherwise full of beans, a large hooked knife pointing at Jean's throat.

His almond-shaped yellow eyes fixed upon her.

Sitting was a bad idea so Jean stood up, hand still on the table near the coffee cup; the liquid would be hot enough to cause painful diversion if thrown in a face.

'You seem to have a problem with me, Mister Taggart,' she said calmly. 'Would you mind telling what it is exactly?'

Niven opened that tight prissy mouth to answer, 'You killed my father.'

Chapter 42

The lowest and most dejected thing of fortune,
Stands still in esperance, lives not in fear

You killed my father.

In the silence that followed that particular statement, Plookie blurted out his confession in a jumble of contrition.

'I'm sorry, Mistress. He knew where I lived, got me out of bed, I thought he jist wanted money but – he – he – wis going tae cut wee Raggie's throat and I was feart!'

Somehow Niven had known Plookie to have a key to the side door, maybe had had him watched; but worse than that, he had stood behind Plookie knife to the groin, forced him to answer when Hannah asked at the door, and then booted his way in.

Jean nodded. That was the least of her worries.

Hannah had sat up painfully and rested against one of the kitchen cupboards. She groaned as if at the last gasp but Jean noticed her hand had moved towards the razor pocket. Though the old woman would be too slow getting off the floor and Jean's derringer lay in a large reticule plumped in the middle of the table and therefore nowhere near enough at hand.

So, better have a wee conversation, eh?

'And who might your – father be, Niven?'

He moved closer so that the tip of his knife now rested just under her chin. This conversation might be very short lived.

Then he said a name that had haunted her life like a bad dream.

'Henry Preger.'

Her mind flashed back to that moment when, as a young girl, she had been forced in front of this giant of a man. Cruel. Rapacious. Ran a dirty low dive of the worst kind of bawdy-hoose. She remembered the instant when he looked into her face and smiled.

The eyes!

How could she have forgotten? Niven was slender, a skelf compared to Preger, but the eyes were the same.

Preger had run his hand down her face, down to her breast and squeezed it tight. Not much to squeeze in those days but he had done so anyway. To hurt. Possess. Command.

'Ye have spirit,' he had said. 'That's good. I'll enjoy breakin' ye.'

But he never had. Not inside. The hymen, yes; the heart, never.

'You poisoned him,' said Niven, bringing her back to the present with a dig of his knife to the soft skin of her neck.

'Who told you that nonsense?'

'My mother.'

Hannah had managed to get her hand near to the razor pocket but she was still trembling from the fall and would definitely not be quick enough.

Plookie just stood there like a useless lump, right beside the easel with Jean's image. Both were stock still.

'Mae Taggart?'

'When he died, ye took over. Ye threw her out on the streets.'

'She went for me with a knife!'

'Jist like me, eh?' Niven laughed mirthlessly but the hand never wavered, the blade pressing in a little deeper.

And it all made a hellish kind of sense. Preger had droit de seigneur *in the bawdy-hoose, took his pleasure where he fancied. Mae was one of his wee whores and she had high hopes to become his best fancy.*

Jean by the time was his partner. He relied on her and she hated him. When Preger had a rammy with a young constable, a certain James McLevy, the big man had been battered to bits.

In his sickbed Preger was given a healing broth. Somebody put arsenic in it. Very sad.

But his seed lived on. And here it was. Mae must have considered it an honour.

'My mother told me just before she died. She wanted tae wait till I was big enough. And then she could swear me to vengeance.'

No point in denying the poison, Niven would not believe her in any case. Preger's seed, eh? Was that what the baby in the dream meant? Surely not. That was a *nice* baby.

Niven's other hand swept at the coffee cup she had inched her fingers near, to hurtle it off the table so that the vessel crashed to pieces on the stone floor.

'I'm watching you,' he grinned. 'And I have a present for ye as well!'

A manic glint in his eye as he fished with his free hand in the pocket and brought out a wad of tissue paper.

Another jab. Forcing her head back.

'Open it!'

'I can't see to do so.'

He grinned again and slid the knife round to just below her left ear.

'Open it.'

With a slight tremor to her fingers, she did so and brought out from the paper a thing of beauty.

'Put it on.'

The necklace. Had to be. Photo in the paper. But it was coming under guard to Waverley Station.

How in God's name had this happened?

'That's the – Tholberg necklace!'

'Aye. And it's mine.'

'But this day – it's to be at the railway station?'

'A trick. Frae the police. Tae fool people. But it didnae fool me.'

Niven abruptly slashed the collar of her gown to expose the swell of her breasts.

'Put it on!'

She did so. Hannah tensed herself, she would have to try but the odds were not in favour. If Plookie would try something, that might help, but the gangling figure was rigid with fear and had been discounted entirely by their assailant. Niven was King of the Castle.

The necklace lay glittering on Jean's skin as she fastened the clasp behind her neck.

Niven leant forwards and spoke softly. 'Now I do it. The blood runs over my diamonds. I remember this all my life.'

'Ye're a mad bastard!'

'You'll be next,' Niven answered to Hannah's yell, a fixed grin, teeth bared, eyes iced in fury. This was the best moment of his life. Nothing would beat it. He'd take the necklace back of course and give it a good clean. Lick it spotless. That would be nice.

'Are you planning to kill us all?' Jean asked, stalling for time.

'Why not? But you first.'

The point pressed in. The next move would be a sideways slash, she'd have to attempt something. Hannah would try as well but it was a hopeless proposition. As Jean tensed to kick out at his groin, Raggie, sensing the terrible tension and fear, suddenly darted forward and barked loudly.

Niven kicked the dog aside, hard into the ribs, and the beast let out a piteous yelp.

And then Plookie Galbraith in terrified desperation snatched up Jean's portrait from the easel and crashed the frame over the head of Niven Taggart.

Were events not so lethal it would have been a black comedy, for the paper split apart and the small wooden frame wedged itself over the top of Niven's narrow shoulders like a shackle, pinning his arms to the side. It also aggravated a wound from the earlier fight.

Niven let out a feral scream of rage and kicked out at Plookie to batter him back. Hannah had got the razor out and swiped at Niven's leg from the floor, cutting just above the ankle-bone, and he let out another cry, lashing out with his foot to knock her away.

Then, despite the pain from ankle and belly, he prised the frame from his body, threw it off on to the floor and raised the knife again – only to find himself facing a derringer pistol. It had taken Jean a matter of moments to open the reticule on the table and pull out the gun.

The dog whimpered. Its ribs were bad hurting.

'See to your pal,' said Jean.

Plookie knelt over and comforted the animal, holding it gently against his body for warmth and consolation.

Hannah pulled herself slowly upright up against a kitchen cupboard door. The derringer did not move.

The killing light in Niven's eye was matched by that of Jean Brash. Green to yellow. Both cold as the grave.

'Put the knife down,' she said in the thick silence, 'or you allow me no option but to render you a dead man.'

A curiously formal statement, almost Shakespearean.

But Niven was king. No one could defeat a king. He looked into the barrel of the gun and behind it could see the necklace glittering upon that poisonous bosom.

His beauty. His vengeance. And he had a trick up his sleeve, courtesy of Billy Musgrave. He spat full into the bitch's face and launched himself at her. One cut. He would win. He was king.

The gun fired. Not in reflex, not in blindness; though Jean jerked her head slightly, she had not been moved from purpose.

Niven had pulled his head back to slash down and she put the shot into his exposed, scrawny throat. For a brief moment he staggered back, then he coughed, a cloudy gargle that sounded like a sink clearing.

But he was still alive. And the knife had never failed him.

Another move yet the step faltered – no – no – he would kill the bitch!

He threw his body forward, knife raised, and this time Jean shot him where she'd shot the octopus: right between the eyes.

No doubt Niven would have resented his fate being compared to that of an eight-armed cephalopod, but he was in no shape to argue that point. He lay on his back, knife fallen by his side, some blood oozing from the throat yet still a tidy enough corpse.

Beside him was Jean's ruined picture; the woman had stopped looking out of the window and the whole thing appeared as if struck by a bolt of lightning.

Perhaps Jean could have shot to wound but she had a memory of Erik de Witte's smiling face and in any case, a derringer is a law unto itself.

Plookie, who had found biscuit crumbs in his pocket, had slumped down as his legs trembled and gave way, to land beside his dog on the floor.

Raggie was contentedly chewing, pained ribs forgotten for now. The sharp crack of the derringer had scared the animal but a biscuit is good compensation.

Jean's face was white and set. Sometimes a woman can run into one too many dead bodies.

Hannah ran water from the tap to clean her razor blade and then turned to survey the scene. A dead man, a destroyed work of art, a boy and dog on the floor, plus a beautiful woman with diamonds round her neck and smoking gun in hand.

'Jist lik' a bliddy play, eh?' said Hannah Semple.

Chapter 43

Report is changeable

By the time James McLevy arrived a mere half an hour later, Mulholland loping behind, the flagstones had been wiped clean of blood by a house-proud Hannah Semple but the body remained in place.

Danny Summers had found the policemen in the wynds, told the news of seeing Niven Taggart entering a side door of the Just Land, and then headed for the Haymarket as they sped off in quite another direction.

The inspector had come bullocking in, steam rising from his nostrils, to find a scene of calm tranquillity except perhaps for the corpse, though mark you it provided little in the way of noise. It had been tastefully covered over with a blanket, however the face was left free.

Mulholland knelt by the body. 'Niven Taggart,' he announced cheerfully. 'Two bullet holes. Neat as ninepence.'

The portrait had been replaced on the easel though looking as if some cannonball had found its mark, Plookie and his dog were safely hidden away, sleeping in the stables – not exactly heroes of the hour but not too far away from that – Hannah Semple had brewed up another pot of coffee, and Jean done up her torn collar and dress.

Though it near broke her heart, loving as she did jewels of the earth, she had placed the Tholberg necklace back in its paper nest on

284

the table, while she pondered over how to get out of what might seem to suspicious minds a certain amount of involvement in this matter.

She might have eventually sent for McLevy but he had saved her the bother by turning up, as usual, not when wanted but – she had to admit – not totally unexpected.

Jean knew he'd be on the trail; no matter how it twisted and turned, he would get there in the bitter end. So after banging on the back door, being let in by the Mistress herself, his first sight was of Hannah sitting quietly at table with a priceless fortune nearby, just beside the sugar bowl.

That sight calmed him down. The corpse could wait, it wasn't going anywhere, but the Tholberg necklace was a sight for sore eyes. The day was saved.

A cup of coffee was slid in front of him while Mulholland received his customary tumbler of tap water to then stand by the sink as his inspector sat down, for he was sore fatigued, and tugged the diamonds plus paper towards him.

It would not do to look *too* eager but McLevy could not deny a certain measure of relief because even though none of this was his fault, he would have got the blame. Somehow.

So, who exactly *was* the guilty party?

A sip of much needed coffee, the night having been long and arduous, then he and Jean began negotiations. There was a certain conformity in this. How many times had they sat opposite like a pair of poker players?

At first most civilised, she explained the advent of Niven Taggart, his mistaken assumption of paternal poisoning, the witnessed and necessary shooting of same intruder and, witness also the scrapes on the skin of her throat to show what a near tragedy it had been.

McLevy, in turn, related the death of Dunsmore at the harbour during a robbery, the finding of the two tied-up and terrified keelies in the cubby-hole at the back of the tavern, adding to their terror by shaking the truth out of them as regards Niven Taggart's secret den, then the finding of a dead Billy Musgrave and a wee instinct that he ought to pay a visit to the Just Land.

No need to mention Danny Summers or his spying activities, that would just complicate matters.

Jean had also avoided mention of Plookie Galbraith's presence for exactly the same reason; unless it was necessary she would rather spare him and Raggie the ordeal of police questioning.

Too many cooks spoil the broth, as Henry Preger had found to his cost.

Of course McLevy had been told Niven may have had company at the side door, but that did not interest him too much as there might be other fish to fry.

A sizzle as one landed in the pan.

A judicious swig of coffee to sweeten the blow, then:

'Doesnae look good, Jeannie.'

'Why not?'

'Chief Constable Craddock will think the following: you organised the robbery, Niven did it, came to you for payment say; you shot him but I arrived before you could get rid of the body and plank the necklace.'

'Do you believe that nonsense?'

'Not necessarily but he will if it suits him.'

She realised that in his own thrawn way, McLevy might be trying to warn her. Craddock could have no such reservations and he would love, as Niven had tried, to stick the knife in.

Just as well she had thought all this through.

And of course McLevy was right that she was hiding something. Richie Powers for a start. Though she might just have had an idea of how to solve that.

Nature abhors a vacuum, and a stage manager had just vacated his position.

However, best deal with Craddock first. A delicate sip of coffee, ignore the awful noise McLevy made when drinking his brew, then begin.

'The papers will have a field day.'

'How so?'

'A foolish effort to deceive the public that results in a priceless necklace being put at risk and the death of an officer involved.'

'Not my idea.'

'No. But if I am brought up in court my lawyers will brandish it like a torch. Murray Craddock will be a laughing stock – in any case, the evidence you have against me is circumstantial – I shall be found innocent and he will be ruined. What a pity.'

McLevy took another gulp of coffee. It was indeed a delicious brew. He'd never find another.

Hannah winked over at Mulholland, who kept his face straight. Always a pleasure to watch this pair in action.

'So, how is all this clamjamfry solved?'

'Simple. The robbery happens, Dunsmore dies, you two go on the trail, find Niven Taggart's den – there he lies dead. Billy Musgrave's dead. The robbed jewellery lies between them. No honour amongst thieves.'

Hannah slid a bowl of sugar biscuits towards the inspector. He took one out and bit in as Jean went on.

'That's what Craddock puts out as a cover story. If he wants to save his neck.'

'Whit about the farce at Waverly Station?'

'That goes ahead. No one will be any the wiser.'

'Then whit the hell exactly did Niven Taggart rob at the harbour?'

'Smaller stuff. Part of the exhibition. Sent under separate cover.'

'And Adam Dunsmore?'

'Death of a hero.'

Silence.

'My Aunt Katie always says,' remarked Mulholland out of the blue. '*If you must lie, lie in your teeth.*'

McLevy gave him a bleak look and shovelled the necklace plus paper into the side pocket of his coat.

Jean smiled. The game was on. The cards dealt.

'Tell me the whereabouts of Niven Taggart's den – I can get the body over there in no time. Angus will do it, just a wee ride in the coach.'

'Why should I help you?'

'I'm doing you all a favour.'

'*Favour?*'

'Think of the disgrace. For everyone concerned. Once the papers get to know of it – a bloodbath.'

She smiled like the Fairy Godmother.

A neat high-class piece of blackmail, thought Mulholland. *That woman can bring home the bacon.*

McLevy slugged back his coffee and stood up. 'They'll be waiting for me at the station. Craddock and Roach. I'll wave the necklace, inform them about a bloodbath on approach and then – see what transpires.'

'If you could let me know? Time is short.'

McLevy looked at Niven's dead body.

'Not for everybody.' He shook himself like a bear. 'I'll send Ballantyne with a note frae the station. He's no' that bright but fast on his feet.'

'He'll get lost,' advised Mulholland laying his tumbler neatly by the sink.

'Not at all,' Jean admonished. 'He knows his way here fine well.'

McLevy blinked a little at that remark then brusquely signalled Mulholland to leave. Hannah took that as a cue for flirtation, crossing to link her arm with the constable.

'I'll see ye tae the door, my mannie. A big handsome fellow like you needs company.'

They exited and that just left – not for the first time – Jean, McLevy and a dead person.

'Thanks for the coffee.'

Jean put her hand on his arm. 'As regards that favour you owe me?'

'Whit?'

'For the favour I just did you.'

'Eh?'

'There's just one wee request I'd like to make.'

The bare-faced cheek of the woman was beyond belief, yet it would seem she held the aces for the moment.

'It's no' a proposal of marriage, is it?'

'Not quite, James.'

She leant forward and whispered in his ear, even though the corpse could not hear a word.

Chapter 44

Bid them come forth and hear me,
Or at their chamber-door I'll beat the drum
Till it cry sleep to death

The play had come to an end.

Jean had gone to the last night with mixed feelings. For many reasons.

Everything had worked out well as regards the death of Niven Taggart. She had even gone with the crowds to Waverly Station to watch the farcical handover of the fake necklace and been rewarded with a glacial glare as Chief Constable Craddock saw her face in the throng. Anyhow, off it went with a phalanx of police; she noticed that McLevy and Mulholland though on hand kept well out of the way.

The real necklace would then be displayed at the Castle under heavy security and therefore capitalism and culture could walk hand in hand. A rare event.

She spotted Ballantyne standing proudly in the ranks. He had indeed found his way to the Just Land that night with a two-word note from McLevy, a merciful veil drawn over the blunt exposition to his chief constable summed up along the lines of the French Revolution's famous epithet: *your head is on the block.*

As regards the two words?

Go ahead.

Below that was an address in the wynds.

The body of Niven Taggart was swiftly transferred to a different resting place, to be *discovered* later by the intrepid Inspector James McLevy. This would be fed to the papers and all would be well save for poor Adam Dunsmore, who would be granted a funeral with full honours, possibly in Paisley, the city of his birth, so that he would not have to share the same geographical location with James McLevy.

Lieutenant Roach avoided her eyes and spotting the Reverend William Baines in the crowd made swift accord for a round on the golf course.

One small hiccup in the smooth unfolding of that Waverly day occurred when, on the way back, Hannah having remained behind at the Just Land to scrub the flagstones further from sin, Jean slipped in to pay a visit with Jack Burns as she had promised. Now that she had time to spare.

It was to be a surprise.

Jack had not been at the train station and she had assumed the artist would be hard at work. Which he was indeed – in the throes of creation.

Jean had, of course, as becomes any mature woman with a younger lover, the key to Jack's studio. In she went, to a certain extent buoyed up by how well everything had gone and raring to kick over the traces. A goddess rampant and alive.

The stone representation of a modern Venus was, however, untouched at that precise moment.

Two other figures were very active under the blankets of Jack's small studio bed. One was the sculptor himself, as was only to be expected, but the other was in no way goddess, artist's model, nor muse. Unless Melissa Fortune had found a new part to play.

She was naked arising from the bedclothes not a seashell. Jack Burns equally unclothed, any burgeoning emergence on his part hiding its light under a bushel or, more accurately, the blanket.

Both bedbound combatants were somewhat sweaty despite the cold studio and was it only the previous night that Melissa's hem had been despoiled?

Time, as the man said, is the unique subjective.

A fragment from a line in the play came into Jean's mind – what was it? 'The lusty stealth of nature.' What a genius Shakespeare was to be sure. She was no match but would have to do her best.

'Is this part of the exhibition?'

Answer came there none.

'I just thought to pay a wee visit, Mister Burns,' she said in the manner of a concerned passer-by. 'Like yourself, I am a creature of impulse.'

Melissa had slid back beneath the covers.

'Peekey boo – I can see you,' was the soft call.

Jack Burns swallowed hard.

'Jean – I – I –'

'My name is Mistress Brash.' She threw the studio key on the bed. Followed by his precious straw hat, though, first of all, she did put her fist through the crown. 'Pass it on,' she said, and was gone.

Hence the mixed feelings on the last night of the play.

Beside Jean had sat Hannah, while around them flew Kenneth Powrie like an overexcited flittermouse.

'Our new stage manager is a joy to behold,' he had confided to Jean just before the performance began.

'I still don't know how you got off wi' that,' muttered Hannah.

The request Jean had made to McLevy for her *favour* was that if he would agree to drop any proposed charges against Richie Powers, she would promise never to use her knowledge about the Tholberg necklace debacle, in any way, shape or form. On that she gave her word.

In truth the inspector was quite relieved not to bring a prosecution against the youth. What would be the point? Especially when Jean promised that Richie would be leaving Edinburgh in the foreseeable future.

Of course she did not inform the inspector that the mannie in question was barely twenty yards away.

A word from Jean to Kenneth Powrie, who passed a word to Alfred Tyrone who passed a word to Barnaby Bunthorne who had been trying to cover as stage manager, that he had a new recruit on board – and it was done.

Richie was tricky as a bagful of monkeys but he was clever with his hands, had a knack of how things worked and what to do if they didn't, kept a cool head in emergencies, and, despite the black eye, was a cheerier and less baleful presence than Billy Musgrave. In a few days he had become a favourite and would travel with the company from now on.

Maisie Powers was delighted; it had got the brother out of her hair and she might now lay on the lash with a clear mind.

Lily Baxter also celebrated; their amorous activity had been a touch stunted by the cellar sibling's presence and she was a girl who liked entanglement.

Richie recovered miraculously when told the idea, so all was well that terminates thus.

And yet when a play ends its run, no matter how brief, there is always a feeling of sadness as if a life has ended. The stage is empty.

The last performance had gone well enough save for Emilia, who was curiously flat, but the audience gave a fine ovation and afterwards, at Kenneth's insistence, Jean bade the company farewell.

Performers are in the main splendid at both giving thanks and apologising – two sides of the same coin and who knows when you may come this way again? And have need of an audience – for actors crave attention like a drunkard his wine.

It was a curious moment; Hannah had flatly refused to come to the goodbyes and so Jean was on her own with only the new-fledged impresario by her side.

The cast lined up, some still in costume and part makeup, for Jean had no wish to linger. Farewells were not her forte unless induced by a derringer or a busted straw hat.

She had told Hannah that Mister Burns was no longer in the picture but spared that sensitive soul the grisly details.

And so, like visiting royalty, Jean Brash passed down the line.

John Wilde was reasonably sober as he bent over her hand, only a faint odour of whisky emanating. Barnaby also inclined his head in respect as befits monarchical reception. Melissa Fortune, part shamefaced part triumphant, was chagrined to be looked straight in the eye as if a cleaning lady of sorts.

'Is it true,' enquired Jean after a queenly fashion, 'that your real name is Mary Dowd?'

A few hidden smiles from the company, as Melissa gritted her teeth and attempted a nod.

'From Rotherham, I believe?'

Another grit-filled acknowledgement.

'How charming,' said Jean and moved on, giving silent thanks to Richie Powers who had passed her this valuable information, via Barnaby Bunthorne who loved to gossip and was charmed by his new assistant.

Emilia Fleming also managed a spasmodic nod as Jean smiled enigmatically at her.

That left the Tyrones. Brother and sister.

Bridget was equally contained as Jean, each recognising a fellow traveller.

'We must all thank you, Mistress Brash,' she said with a smile that did not quite reach the eyes. 'Not only for your support but also for the fact that – for once – we seem to have made a profit.'

'So have I,' replied Jean, aware that behind Bridget's grateful words lay an element of irony.

'Indeed? *Manus manum lavat*,' murmured Bridget.

'One hand washes the other. Seneca.'

Bridget blinked. She was not used to this level of response from backers of theatrical ventures. 'Indeed. Seneca.'

Jean nodded gravely in response before adding, 'And both hands wash the face.'

This time the smile *did* reach Bridget's eyes.

And then it was only left to Lear himself, the great Panjandrum that was Alfred Tyrone. He swooped from on high to plant a malodorous kiss upon her far from innocent hand, then spread his arms wide like the sails of a galleon.

'Mistress Brash! We shall never forget your beautiful city, your hospitality and generosity, your appreciation of our humble, homespun art—' Here he stopped to include all of the company, possibly indicating that the modest creative ability might more belong to them.

'And we shall carry with us to the end of our days, your name and your memory!'

A subdued mumble of agreement from the cast, with no contribution from at least two, ended the exchange.

Except that Alfred could never resist another curtain call. He assumed a solemn demeanour.

'Yet let us not forget the fate of poor Billy Musgrave who sadly could not rise above the darkness.'

A poetic version of the knife-wielding keelie.

'He will be sadly missed.'

'By some more than others,' said Jean dryly with the merest flick of an eye towards Emilia, who caught the allusion and flinched, her face white with anger.

How did she know?

One more effusion of thanks from Alfred as he lit the inevitable cigar and they all parted as wayfarers at a crossroads.

Jean looked back just once and saw Richie's cheeky face poking out of a curtain, the black eye making him look like a koala bear. He thumbed his nose at her and grinned. A new adventure before him. Lucky boy.

Outside the tent in the darkness of the night, Kenneth sighed. He was now solvent but what next?

'Who would have thought,' he announced in solemn tones, 'a tragedy to have brought so much – fulfilment?'

'Well, there's any amount of them coming out the woodwork,' said Jean. 'Ye can start with the Greeks.'

'The Greeks – why not?' said Kenneth Powrie. 'Medea comes to mind. I see it now. *Medea on Leith Links!*'

And on that note, they too parted.

All these thoughts and memories passed through Jean's mind as she sat in her boudoir and accomplished her morning toilette. Quite the lady. A silk dressing gown fell around her body as she brushed her thick and lustrous red hair. The jade eyes thoughtful, the skin, despite many depredations, like porcelain.

Quite the lady.

The scrapes on her neck had almost faded.

Quite the lady.

A knock at her bedroom door and Hannah's voice came through.

'Ye have a visitor.'

'At this time of the morning?'

'One o' thae actors.'

'I've already said goodbye.'

'Maybe ye still owe them money?'

Jean pulled the dressing gown to a more chaste representation and made response: 'Send this person in.' If one of the men, there was little danger of ravishment; if Melissa Fortune, then she might surrender to base instinct and skewer the bitch with a nail file.

But it was not Melissa who entered, it was Emilia Fleming – white faced and wrecked from an overindulgence of hashish the night before.

However, this morning she had broken the pipe and sworn to herself that she would indulge no more. Whether that vow would last was another matter.

Without a word of greeting, having closed the door, fingers trembling slightly, she brought out something from her coat pocket and threw it towards Jean. The missile was caught neatly enough. It proved to be a locket, not in best condition, the metal dull, a dent to one side, its chain tarnished silver.

'Open it,' said Emilia tightly.

Jean did so.

A woman's face stared up at her from a small photograph inside the metal case.

It was like looking at herself.

Chapter 45

Shall we not see these daughters and these sisters?

In the garden one of the male peacocks spread its wings and shivered its feathers. The intent was that the eyes formed by these selfsame feathers would hypnotise the female and bring her within reach so that he might, however clumsily, mount her back and despite a myriad of plumage, consummate the mating process.

He shivered again. The female pecked at the ground and paid no heed. This might be a long courtship.

In the boudoir, Emilia Fleming spoke once more.

'Our mother. Isn't she a pretty sight?'

She should have taken a vicarious and sly satisfaction at the stunned look on a face that had always been presented to her as invulnerable and smooth like a glacier, but the confusion in her own heart seemed to have found expression in the opposite being.

'I don't have much time,' she said. 'The company leaves shortly. Aberdeen. I'm told the winds are cruel.'

Jean finally found voice.

'I don't – understand you.'

'Simple. Jean Shields. Good Edinburgh stock. But she fell. Had a child by a serving man of sorts. Because of her disgrace the family moved. To Newcastle. She married there. A Civil Engineer. Daniel Fleming. Dull but safe. One offspring. Emilia.'

Jean looked down again at the image. A hint of wildness in the eyes? Some of that in Emilia, but what had Jean inherited?

Was any of this true? How could it be?

'Red hair, green eyes, tall – not an ugly dwarf like myself – clear skin. When I first saw you – it was her – a kick to the stomach, I bent over. I was sick.'

Emilia laughed. Bitter like poison.

Jean also felt sick. Hope does not so much spring eternal but torment with dreams of what might have been.

'Where is she?'

'Who?'

Jean could not bring herself to say the words that Emilia so relished to hear. *My mother.* More than the wind can be cruel.

'Jean – Shields. Where is she?'

'Asleep.'

'Where?'

'In the graveyard. Buried beside my grandparents, all in the family.'

The shaft went home. Jean Brash closed her eyes as Emilia inhaled a deep lungful of air.

'Pennies for her eyes. When I was fifteen. I left soon after. Ran from home. To London. Sold myself to this profession. Sold myself. You must know the feeling?'

Jean did not answer. Let her talk. Better that she did – Emilia knew secrets. Keep the face blank. Like a blackboard. Let her scribble all over it.

But what was truth and what was lie?

'Our dear mother. Never there. Opiates. Pills. Every day. Her little friends. Like a ghost in the house. My father always at work and me – with a ghost.'

299

Emilia's hands had clenched into hard little fists and Jean could sense the terrible pain and anger.

'And then – just to add to the fun – I found the letters. From you. In her private little drawer.'

'I wrote nothing!'

'You were left like a bag of dirt with a serving woman. Margaret Brash. She wrote to mother – all about you. What a dear child you were. A perfect life.'

Memory had brought hatred into Emilia's eyes. For Jean it was confusion. She and Margaret had lived in poverty, the old woman had told that the parents were dead and Margaret herself had died of rotgut whisky.

'On her deathbed, I asked my mother. *Did she love me?* She could not answer. *Did she love her dear little Jean – the one she had left behind?* She nodded. Smiled. Or perhaps that was just the opiates? She died – a fully-fledged addict. Passed it on to me. My inheritance.'

Jean sat there like one transfixed. Like a character in a fairy story that is stopped by a demon in the road and frozen to the spot until the spell is lifted.

Emilia relished the power she now possessed.

'She wrote to Margaret. Many letters. Sent her money when possible – not often. But then after a while the letters came back. Not delivered. Person not known at the address. What heartbreak. Dear Mother told me such, then she closed her eyes and departed this vale of tears.'

'I saw no letters. The money – it – must have gone on bad whisky. I saw no letters.'

'What a pity.'

A church bell sounded ten o'clock. Emilia threw up her hands like an actress in a frothy comedy.

'Heavens! Is that the time? One must be going.'

She turned as if to leave but it was a false exit, for she waited a question that must come.

'The letters? From Margaret – to my mother. Where are they?'

'I burnt them.'

A dreadful silence followed this remark, and then Jean let out a cry of near animal pain.

'Why?'

'Simple. I was jealous. She loved you more than me.'

'I never saw her face.'

'I did. Every day. Turned away from me.'

Jean finally stood up. Her legs were shaking but she had to make this effort.

'Can we not – try to be friends?'

'I never want to see you again. I would ask you never to approach me. Ships that pass in the night, eh?'

Emilia walked to the door as Jean made one last try.

'Why tell me all this, Emilia?'

'I wanted to see you suffer.'

'I don't believe that.'

Emilia had been facing to the door but now she turned.

Jean held those dark troubled eyes in her own gaze – she could not afford to fall. Be steadfast. Have courage. Fight. Never give in. Never. That would be death. She could see the depths of anguish in Emilia's face, and felt deep compassion for a lost soul.

Both daughters. Sisters. Both lost.

'I am so sorry, Emilia.'

The younger woman straightened herself up.

'I suppose – I owed you something. You saved my life after all. I have told you the truth. Now you know it all.'

She opened the door.

'I would ask you one thing. One favour. Never to see me again. Respect my wishes, if you please.'

The actress bobbed in a mocking curtsey.

'Goodbye, Mistress Brash.'

The door closed behind and Emilia Fleming was gone.

Jean Brash remained. She looked back down at the picture – nothing and everything had changed.

From the garden came a harsh strangled cry of triumph as the peacock finally mounted upon his hen.

Chapter 46

Croak not, black angel; I have no food for thee.

Edinburgh, September 1844

They would leave tomorrow. Father had sold the business and would start again in another city.

Now she loved her beautiful life. The opiates that took the hurting away made everything so fine.

And the baby would be happy, not to have disgrace cut into her flesh, not to have a mother who had lain with the common herd.

Margaret Brash was a good soul. Perhaps a wee bit fond of a wee bit whisky, but let he who is without sin cast stones upon – she could not remember the words to follow but was it not in the Bible? Some Jezebel stoned to death against a wall because she had a dirty life and the good folk punished the sinner, but then Jesus had saved her. With his wise words.

Who would save young Mistress Shields?

But no. She did not need saving, She had the blessed opiates coursing through her, so everywhere the blood went, they followed suit. Like a faithful dog.

Her grandfather's portrait had been taken down so she no longer had to bear the weight of his disapproval, although the wallpaper where it had rested was a blighted pale colour – a framed space to remind her of evil ways.

A knock at the door and Margaret entered, the baby in her arms.

'We are leaving now, Miss Jennet.'

'That's only right. And I will see you soon. I will come back and we will play together.'

It was a shame, thought Margaret, to see her so scattered in her wits but the servant had heard the doctor say that in time she would recover and be able to present a decent front to society.

As long as the opiates worked to calm the daughter down, keep her on the even keel of normality.

Those were his words to the parents.

Margaret had been given a fair amount of money by Thomas Shields but after that, his hands were washed. The understanding would be that she gave the child away, Margaret knew folk that bought and sold, but Miss Jennet was to believe that Margaret and the baby would live together in heavenly bliss.

And in time, time that washed memory like dishes in the sink, it would all be forgotten. Like a bad dream.

The old woman watched as the girl fussed over the baby, took it in her arms, cooing with delight as chubby arms waved in the air. Such would break your heart.

Yet it had to be done.

Margaret would do quite well out of it, at least for a while – she had rented a wee place in the wynds.

What would happen when the money ran out? She could sell the child of course. But would she? The old woman had grown fond of the little mite. Perhaps she would keep her. For a while. She had no children of her own and now – her family were leaving. She had taken on their colouration, spoke well, in a proper manner, even learned to read and write. But now they were leaving.

It had been made plain to her not to ever approach Thomas Shields again. A good settlement of money but that was it. Unless Miss Jennet took a hand?

The baby had grown restive and was mewling, while the girl looked confused.

'The child will be hungry,' said Margaret. 'I'll feed her now.' She took the baby back and it quietened at once.

A sudden thought upset the smooth process of the drugs. 'She is not yet baptised!'

'I will see to that, Mistress.'

Indeed Thomas Shields could hardly bear to look at the child, and his wife obeyed the master's voice.

For a moment it seemed as if the girl would collapse in tears and Margaret hastened to repair the cracks.

'And she has your name of course. Jean.'

A smile of sorts came on the girl's face.

'Yes! And yours to follow. Jean Brash.'

'A fine name, Mistress.'

Margaret hesitated. She would be taking a chance here but would she not be doing the girl a favour, as well as perhaps herself? The servant took out a scrap of paper.

'I have written my address here, Miss Jennet, but this must be secret between us, your father must never know for his anger would be terrible.'

The girl quickly hid the scrap. 'Of course. But I will write and you can tell me how she fares.'

'It must be secret, though.'

The girl smiled in mischief and Margaret glimpsed the child she once had been. The old woman felt a hellish pang of regret, but what could she do? Only as she was bidden.

'And I can send you money,' added the girl. 'Notes in an envelope. No one will know.'

What the servant had hoped for and music to Margaret's ears.

They both looked round the empty room, for all the packing had been done, the carriage vans already on their way to Newcastle. Soon the door would close forever.

'We must leave you now, Miss Jennet.'

The girl awkwardly hugged Margaret and then looked down at the child.

'It is all for the best, is it not Margaret?'

'All for the best.'

The girl leant her face into the swaddling bundle that held the child, and inhaled deeply. 'She smells like roses.'

'Babies have many odours.'

On that wry comment Margaret made to leave but the girl clutched at the bundle.

'One kiss!'

'As you will, Mistress.'

The girl kissed her child on the forehead. 'Goodbye Jean Brash.'

The old woman left.

The girl looked up at the rectangle of empty space.

Chapter 47

It seem'd she was a queen
Over her passion; who, most rebel-like,
Sought to be king o'er her

Leith, 1883

Three people stood in the middle of a squalid cramped room in one of the wynds.

McLevy and Mulholland had been in many strange situations but this one was an original. Jean Brash stood centre stage, her face white and chilly like a statue. The policemen had been on the saunter in the late afternoon when her carriage hauled up beside them and the woman herself had leant out.

She needed professional assistance and where better to discover such a level of expertise than a practising policeman on the streets of Leith?

It turned out she wanted a room searched and did not trust herself to do so.

Given the helter-skelter of previous events, it had been a peaceful enough day, and McLevy was already itching to ginger it up somewhat.

'Whit're we looking for?' he asked.

'Letters. Papers. Hidden,' was the terse response.

'How come you want us tae accomplish such?'

'I can trust you.'

She said no more. Take or leave.

It was not often McLevy looked to his constable for guidance, but he flicked a glance sideways.

Mulholland for some reason remembered a moment from youth, when his Aunt Katie had caught him poking into the guts of a dead badger with a long stick. *'If you're born to be hanged, you'll never be drowned,'* she had remarked. In his youthful mind he had equated this with a warning to somehow mind his own business, but since she had followed the words with a smile and then a cuff in the ear, Mulholland had been left in some confusion. 'Trust is important,' he declared.

So now here they stood. All three.

The place stank of unwashed bodies and stale food: the family who had previously occupied same had been paid to quit the premises until further notice. A gift from the gods the mother considered, and off she went to a sister's with her brood, the father having departed for Perth Penitentiary some six months previous for stealing hens to feed, as he pleaded in court, hungry dependants. The fact that he'd been apprehended trying to sell the poultry to a local flesher, the birds not decently half plucked, somewhat undermined his excuse, and so, not for the first time, he became a guest of Her Majesty.

'Johnny McGill,' said McLevy thoughtfully. 'Nae wonder he prefers the jail.'

He noticed Jean's eyes wandering round the room – various improvised mattresses on the floor with a small bed recess for the adults. Her face bore an expression he had never seen before: almost childlike and an equally unknown depth of feeling in her eyes.

'Ye know this place?' he asked.

'I was raised here. Eleven years.'

'That's nice.'

'Isn't it just?'

'Has it changed much?'

'Nothing changes.'

That cryptic remark could mean anything; from all circumstance remains essentially the same, no matter how it might seem in alteration, to a deeper darker imprint of fate that the birthbrand laid upon a child will last until the end of time. From Jean's point of view, she could not bear to stay in the place; the memories were too lethal.

'I will leave you now. Wait in the carriage.'

'Aye, well there's no' much tae search,' replied McLevy, looking at the bare walls and detritus of a family with nothing to spare. 'Shouldnae be long.'

'Might I ask you, ma'am,' Mulholland said as Jean turned to the door. 'The person who hid these – papers you say – young or old or man or woman? It would help to know – an indication of sorts.'

'Woman. Old. Very possibly drunk.'

Jean Brash left.

'Old and drunk, eh?' muttered the inspector. 'Nae need tae look at the ceiling, then.'

'Why're we doing this?'

To this sudden question of the constable, McLevy shook his head. 'I'm not all that sure. A reasonable idea at the time, it seemed.'

Or was it the look of desperation on Jean's face as she leant out of that carriage? A need he could not ignore from the depths of his own being?

And think of the coffee cups of best Lebanese he would accrue.

Mulholland fumbled in his pocket and brought out a greaseproof square of paper. He broke the contents in half and offered it over.

'Honeycomb,' said he. 'Take away the smell.'

McLevy bit in. 'Thank God for the bees, eh?'

Back to business. Walls first, then the floorboards. Of course there might be nothing to find. If Jean was eleven, that would be a fair time ago. Many folk pass through. To say nothing of floods, rodents and natural catastrophes.

Paper is a flimsy medium.

Still. Fools and bairns should never see work half done.

Chewing steadily, both men moved towards the nearest wall and began to minutely examine the surface exercising after all what was part of their chosen profession. And both were good at their job of work.

Jean waited in the carriage, her body stock still as if in shock. Some animals will freeze when under threat, pretending to death in order to avert the real thing. Just being present in that room had unleashed a deluge of memories.

Why had Margaret not told her the truth? Did she want to keep Jean for herself? Or more likely keep the money that was sent for whisky? Or was it a bit of both, for in a strange way she felt the old woman had cared for her as if her own child.

But as the years passed, Margaret Brash had spiralled downwards; White Dog whisky was her best love.

When Margaret died and Jean had been thrown on to the tender mercies of the streets that must have been when the letters started to be returned.

Emilia's lips had twisted in bitter derision when she said 'what heart-break'. But it must have been such anguish for Jean Shields as she lost the only connection that remained with her firstborn. The one thread of love.

Perhaps Margaret planned to let Jean know when she was a big girl? When she came of age?

Like Niven Taggart?

But on the streets of Leith there is no coming of age. Margaret Brash had died, whisky on her breath, mouth agape, eyes fixed on eternity.

And Mistress Shields?

She had died also.

Nothing changes.

'Jeannie?'

She opened her eyes. McLevy's big bawface was staring into the carriage like a cow looking over a dyke.

'Already?' she blurted.

'Whit d'you mean?'

'Hardly been long.'

'Three hours, Jean.'

Time had lapsed. Angus the coachman still sat above, the horses were still standing, patient, munching at the nosebags.

'We found. Whit was there.'

'The letters?'

'Whit was there.'

Something in the stillness of his face should have warned her but, fingers trembling, she put out a hand.

'Pass them over if you please.' Her voice squeaked like a child, but she was Jean Brash, Mistress of the Just Land.

McLevy put out both hands, cupped together. In the dim light of the wynd from one of the few lampposts left unbroken, she could see crumpled shreds of paper in his paws.

'This was all we discovered.'

She had to cup her own hands so that like a priest at Communion, he could drop the shreds into upturned palms.

'We found the hidey-hole. Below the bed in the recess. A loose floorboard. Been there too long. The rats must have got them.'

McLevy could not bear the awful silence and took refuge in bluster.

'I never even went tae see that play of yours,' he said loudly as if an audience was listening. 'Wha did a' the killing – who's the guilty party?'

'Family,' she answered. 'Leave me now, James.'

He nodded briskly as if he had not noticed the white bloodless sheen of her face. 'Aye. Well. Goodnight to you anyhows.' He turned and walked back to where Mulholland was standing at the corner.

'How did it go?'

'Jist dandy.'

The constable knew better than to believe the statement plus the sardonic tone in delivery more than gave a clue.

'Let us repair to the Auld Ship Tavern,' McLevy said in formal cadence. 'I may even buy you a drink.'

'A weak beer,' was the response. 'As always.'

'I may treat myself tae a large hooker o' whisky,' the inspector replied. 'I can hear it calling.'

The two men turned and walked off into the darkness.

In the carriage, Jean tried to unravel one of the scraps. A sliver but at least not stained in rat urine.

The trouble with waste products is that themselves being unwanted, they obliterate and destroy.

Two words. Could she read them?

Fond – kiss.

A sudden eruption of sound as a catfight exploded in one of the alleys. Territorial, no doubt.

A single tear ran down her face.

What was that song from the Ploughman Poet?

Aye fond kiss
And then we sever.

Chapter 48

Who are you?
Mine eyes are not o' the best

Sarah Baines frowned in the process of reconstructing her portrait. It had been a long sitting so far. The remnants of the first attempt lay in a corner, the frame buckled and the drawing completely destroyed. She had asked the cause and been rewarded with an enigmatic smile.

A wild animal. The bawdy-hoose is full of such.

When the artist had begun again, she observed before the first line was drawn that Mistress Brash had changed her outfit entirely.

The lavender gown, Italian boots, French chapeau, all were gone and now she wore a simple white dress – still with a décolletage, mind you – and round her neck a silver chain with a battered old locket. It had been polished and shone with a certain jaunty air, but it was a plain shape against the white skin. Meanwhile, the red hair was hanging loose.

And the effects of all this? The woman looked – younger – more vulnerable. As if she had been *cleansed* somehow.

However, the subject still gazed out of the window as morning light from the April sun shone equally upon her and the garden beneath their vantage point.

From her view Jean could see and even vaguely hear Hannah Semple scolding the magpies below as they played merry hell with the task of pegging out the bed sheets and pillowcases. This was the custom and spring was a fine season for airing linen of all kinds.

Nettie Dunn had not only been forced to abandon her dreams of modelling in the grand salons but also inherited a large pimple on the end of her nose; this had rendered her the butt of Hannah's caustic wit. *Knurlie neb*, she had been nicknamed by the old woman and, like a pimple, the name had stuck.

Lily and Maisie were up to their usual tricks where Maisie's strong right arm was beating hell out of some carpets a distance from the sheets, and Lily was darting around behind her like a gadfly.

Big Annie Drummond munched quietly upon a biscuit and dreamt of a demon lover as she pegged out upon the line with swift and sure hands.

The Dalrymple twins went quietly about their business, nunlike in their concentration.

The rest of the girls set up a chirling call as Plookie Galbraith emerged from the stables, a steaming bucket of manure hanging from one hand. He was heading for the compost pile and did not turn a hair. Was he not a hero of sorts? Even if sworn to secrecy and no one would ever know of his derring-do, there was swagger in his step, matched by Raggie the dog.

A new collar plus lead for Raggie, a clean shirt for Plookie, and they made a fine pair. He had been promised moreover the chance of a wee place of his own. Not in the wynds, though; in a lodging house where the landlady liked dogs and had need of a garden helper.

And to boot, his skin seemed to be clearing up. Maybe it was the manure.

As Jean mused upon all this, she saw Hannah staring up at her. The old woman gathered that something dark had happened but knew better than to pester. Perhaps Jean would never tell her. Perhaps she would never tell anyone. It was a private matter.

Jacks Burns's cat Horace had appeared again atop the garden wall. The dog saw it and barked loudly. The cat took no notice but when Plookie threw an accurate little wedge of straw and manure, it stalked off in high dudgeon.

Mister Burns had shown his exhibition. Very successful. A modern slant on the old ways. A coming man – however as far as Jean was concerned – a gone man. Welcome to travel a ways to Aberdeen and cavort in the freezing cold with Mary Dowd or the more fetching Melissa Fortune. She and Jack deserved each other.

Jean should have known better than to take a young lover. Stamina only goes so far. Mind you, it's better than nothing at all. At least she had not – as the old song says – *twa gae ups for one gae doon.*

The Tholberg necklace had been gawked at by the populace and was now on its way back to Amsterdam. A pity Erik de Witte had never stolen the thing but at least Jean had worn it round her neck. Even though the gems were intended to be covered by her own blood.

Edinburgh had revelled in cultural manifestations and who knows what might happen in the future?

No doubt Roach, Mulholland and Constable Ballantyne would be hunkered down in Leith Station awaiting the next onslaught of crime.

James McLevy would be looking out with the eyes of a wolf. God help the poor wee lambs.

With luck Chief Constable Craddock had piles.

And Jean Brash – what of her?

'Have you ever been to a New World?'

This question from Sarah Baines jolted Jean out from a long rambling train of thought.

'No. I have enough trouble with the old one.' A dry response that perplexed the artist for a moment.

'No. I meant. America.'

'I know what you meant.'

Sarah, in an odd way, as artists often do, found confession easy to an object of depiction.

'I may go to that land very soon.'

'Well, you'd better hurry up your drawing then.'

A glint of humour in the eye as Sarah went back to her work.

'My friend – Miss Lumsden – will travel there to spread the word.'

'Is your friend evangelistic?'

'For the empowerment of women.'

'Oh, I thought it might be the Bible. She looks the religious type.'

Sarah did not rise to that one.

'Suffrage,' she clarified.

'Right enough.'

'Louisa desires my – company there.'

'Desire is important.'

'I am a little afraid.'

'How is that?'

'I don't like change.'

'Change can happen. Whether you like it or not.'

Sarah nodded, eyes intent on the paper. Then she leant back. 'There! It is rough but – something.'

Jean crossed from the window to look down. It was her for sure; the girl had caught more than just a likeness. A sense of – what – longing?

Life goes round in circles disguised as movement perpendicular, up or down, or sideways, but really just a circle that leads back whence you started. How do you break free from the circle?

'You have talent,' she murmured.

Sarah flushed. 'It needs more work. I can return tomorrow?'

'I'll be waiting.'

'I may not have time for a version in oil.'

'That will be fine. I'll make sure this one doesn't get – ruptured.'

'Or to sketch the rest of the – girls.'

'They'll just have to bear it. You may go now.'

Sarah was now used to Jean's abrupt ways. She made for the door but then an imp of mischief seized her.

'Mistress Brash, would you ever be interested in – the empowerment of women?'

'I have my own version.' Jean followed this laconic retort with another. 'Now, off you go!'

Sarah Baines grinned and for a moment there was a flash of attraction between them, then she left.

Jean looked down once more at the portrait, clicked open the locket and smiled down at her mother.

'What a wee menace you must have been.'

That baby she dreamt about might have been herself, she supposed, or even Emilia, but in dreams – who knows? The past trammels the present and if you're not careful, damned well wrecks the future.

Niven Taggart brought retribution for the long-ago death of his father, but Henry Preger was a cruel bastard who deserved to die and Niven was no babe in arms.

She would respect Emilia's wishes and make no effort to resurrect the past. Let the dead bury the dead. If her half-sister came back she would be welcomed with open arms. But that was her choice.

That night when McLevy had passed over the fragments of a mother's love, covered in rat piss and so unlike the fate in romantic novels, Jean had sat inside her carriage for what seemed time without end. As if her insides were torn apart and a gaping hole had appeared in her heart. Fathomless and empty.

That pain would never leave her and she did not wish this to be so in any case. Grief has its own sanctity.

In time it may heal, but only in time.

However, in the carriage she had opened up the locket again and looked into those eyes so like her own, and seen the love.

And in the days following, something precious and unknown had emerged.

And that *unknown* transmuted into its opposite.

For now she *knew*.

Where she had come from. What she had grown to be. And what she would fight for till the very end.

Past, present, future.

Mind you, no need to get carried away, she still had a bawdy-hoose to run.

With that in mind Jean went back to the window, looked out and narrowed her eyes. Was Hannah now wearing that faded paper rose pinned to her apron? The old woman was still scolding, the magpies fluttering with mischief, the ornamental fish oblivious, and one of the male peacocks had started shivering. Which put her in notion of something else.

She delved into a pocket of the dress and brought out a post-card. Hand delivered some days ago through the letter-box and unscathed by rodents. It was a picture of a city. Paris, not Edinburgh, one of the grand boulevards, and a large arrow had been scrawled pointing at one of the buildings.

J'habite içi!

I live here, unless she missed her guess.

The words under the arrow, and on the back of the card an address precisely printed with a flourish of a signature; of course it would be fancy: *Gabriel Bonnard.*

She'd never been to Paris. It might be worth a try, who knows? Not exactly a New World but perhaps an old one reborn.

And was there not supposed to be a famous bawdy-hoose there – *Le Chabanais* – right next to the Louvre?

Two birds with the one stone, eh?

She looked out of the window like her portrait. A few clouds in the sky but nothing much to worry over.

Jean Brash.

That would always be her name.

It was spring and she was raring to go.

Acknowledgements

Not much has changed. My wife Lisa and my daughter Maddy still remain steadfast in the face of a near lunatic who bellows anguish at the computer screen. Occasionally I am instructed not to talk so loudly to myself but that's as far as it goes. Cisco the cat is never distant from his supper dish and rarely criticises my punctuation. Daisy our dog finds the odd stick but never beats me with it. What more can a man want or ask from those near to him?

I'd also like to thank my agents Val, Rebecca and the immaculate Sara for their support and forbearance, and especially thank my publisher Lisa Highton who weathers all storms and does not blink an eye. Amongst her crew, my gratitude to Fede, Yassine and the imperturbable Dominic – then Chris at Heavy Entertainment who records the audio books and keeps me in carrot cake.

All my neighbours ask politely how the book is coming along knowing the danger of a long diatribe and my special thanks to Neal Wills who prints that which I cannot and keeps company when I walk Daisy. Also thanks to Nick Jones who knows which keys to press on my slow lugubrious laptop.

Last but not least, the radio cast who gave me so much inspiration when I threw my hat in the publishing ring – Brian Cox, Siobhan Redmond, Collette O'Neil and Michael Perceval-Maxwell. Plus the original producer, Patrick Rayner and present incumbent – Mighty Bruce Young.

And so – as Bugs Bunny would say – 'That's all folks.'

The verses preceding each chapter are taken from Shakespeare's *King Lear*.

THE FIRST BOOK IN THE JEAN BRASH SERIES

Mistress of the Just Land
A Jean Brash Mystery

New Year's Day and through the misty streets of
Victorian Edinburgh an elegant, female figure walks
the cobblestones – with a certain vengeful purpose.

Jean Brash, the Mistress of the Just Land, brings her cool
intelligence to solving a murder, a murder that takes place
in her own bawdy-house (the best in Edinburgh and her
pride and joy). A prominent judge, strangled and left
dangling, could bring her whole life to ruin and she didn't
haul herself off the streets to let that come to pass.

The search for the killers will take Jean back into her own
dark past as she uncovers a web of political and sexual
corruption in the high reaches of the Edinburgh establishment,
but she has little time before a certain Inspector James
McLevy, comes sniffing round like a wolf on the prowl.

Jean may be on the side of natural justice but is she on
the side of the law? Or will the law bring her down?

READ AN EXTRACT NOW

Chapter 1

*The cattie sits in the kiln-ring spinning, spinning,
And by came a little wee mousie, rinning, rinning.*

Her bare feet hurt on the sharp cobblestones as the young girl ran for her life through the gnarled and twisted wynds of Leith.

A memory of the old woman, bent backwards, mouth agape as if trying to deliver a last word, burnt into the girl's mind – a candle throwing pointed shadows on the wall as she had tried to shake some life into the dead body.

But Margaret was gone. The old woman was gone. On the table a bottle of cheap White Dog whisky lay on its side, last dregs soaking into the rough wood. It was Margaret's custom to send the girl early to bed, then mumble her memories over a chipped glass before slumping into her own recess to snore the night away.

Jean Brash usually lay upon a thin mattress on the floor. Hers was a lonely, restless sleep, but this night jumbled dreams and desperate emptiness – a private emptiness she fought to keep at bay; fought to keep any unwanted tears from sliding down her cheeks to dribble salty drops into the corner of a mouth – all that had been arrested by a crack like a bone breaking. She sat up in an old dress, yellow now that had once been white, to see Margaret had jerked back, a baleful, harsh croak shooting out from her chapped lips. Dead as a doornail.

*   *   *

Where to now? Jean was running blind; the wynds she knew so well had been left behind and these wormy, slimy clefts, with a cold, dark Edinburgh night, the east wind driving a sharp, cutting rain, were unknown territory.

She stumbled and crashed up against the rough wall, scraping some skin on her bare arm, but there was no going back. With one fierce action, she had burnt her boats.

'Buggeration!' she shouted, and then told herself off for such. Bad manners to swear and Margaret had tried to instil some manners into the child of her keeping.

She had also managed to teach Jean the rudiments of spelling and numbers, for Margaret, as the old woman never tired telling, once worked as a housekeeper for a wealthy Edinburgh family and had been taught the bare bones of learning and kitchen craft. Margaret never said why she had lost the position, only that the family had moved from the city, leaving their faithful, loving servant behind.

They were both a cut above the riff-raff that swarmed outside their grimy tenement, pronounced Margaret. But that was not so. The old woman drank like a fish and Jean ran wild with the feral street-children.

Though she always held something back. The boys called her Queen Bee. They caught the other girls and had their wicked fun and games, but not Jean.

She never ran. Just stood her ground. And even Dirk Martins, who shook his mop of flaxen hair and grinned his grin, and then wee manky Jeb Summers like a rat up a drainpipe – a pair of dirty devils – hesitated to shove a questing hand where there might be plunder.

They had tried it once, mind you.

Only the once.

She attracted men and she could sense it. Even at her eleven years, she could sense it. Red hair, porcelain skin, green eyes, thin as a rake – but she attracted.

Jean could smell it coming off them like a dank spoor.

And on she ran, a small figure in a dark landscape, the faded yellow dress flapping like a broken wing.

She wrenched open the door of the tiny, cramped room and fell out into the narrow landing of the tenement, calling for help. No one answered. All the families, ten or more to a room, were asleep or pretending to be so. There were many screams and cries at all hours of the night up and down the landings, cutting through the thin walls, and it was better to pull a ragged sheet over your head and render the outside world beyond sight and sound.

One door opened. The one she did not wish to see. Alexander Moncrieff stuck out his head. A cadaverous lank figure, his age was hard to guess: about thirty or so but he seemed older. As if his blood ran thin. Cold and cruel.

Moncrieff ran the tenement, collected rents for the landlord, had the one swivelling eye and a habit of licking his lips incessantly. It was said he had once been in the army and he affected a military bearing – straight back, instant obedience – which went down well with those in command. In fact, he had recently been offered a better position at another establishment by the landlord in recognition of his many virtues, and he was puffed up with the resultant power. No one ever saw the landlord – he was like God in heaven, hidden in the clouds.

The man shoved past her into the room and leant over the remnants of Margaret Brash. She had given Jean her name but was not kith and kin.

There was no mother, no father, just a procession of the dead. According to Margaret, Jean's mother had died at birth and her father had been up to no good and nowhere to be found. Jean had sensed a lie in these words, but the old woman would not be shaken. Now she was still as the grave.

'Well,' said Moncrieff. 'That's a peety. Drink is a terrible curse. I rarely touch the beast.' He turned and drew back his moist lips in a liverish smile that froze her to the bone. 'Nevertheless – the rent is owing and will have tae be paid. All things must be paid. One way or the other.' A hand was held out, palm up. 'Have you the money?'

Jean shook her head.

Moncrieff moved forward till he loomed over her. 'I can take care of it. I can take care of you. I can take care of everything.' His large, raw-boned hand came to rest on her shoulder and she could feel its heat through the thin material.

'I am your lord and master now,' he declared, his one good eye boring into hers like a demon in the fairy tale. 'I am your lord and master.'

For a moment Jean felt something inside twitch in response. It must have shown in her face because Moncrieff grinned and his hand tightened, the fingers digging into her flesh like claws rooting her to his beck and call. Would she have been lost? Swallowed whole, like the child in the evil legend?

Then her leg swept up and a hard, bony shin hit into his groin like a hammer.

In all Jean's life to come, no matter what hardships and dangers were dealt, no matter the evil on hand, this feeling would never leave her. A voice that said 'Wait for your moment, then strike the blow. There will always be one moment – one chance to take – don't miss. One chance.'

Alexander Moncrieff yelped, hunched over in the most excruciating pain and when after some time he looked up again, the room was empty save for him and the corpse. The girl was gone. The agony, however, was only too blindingly present, and his eye swivelled wildly to signal such condition.

One chance. One blow.

As she stumbled onwards, the breath catching raw in her throat, Jean could see some slivers of lamplight up ahead, faint in the mirk. Perhaps a street of some kind – she would be safe there.

Safe? Something had slid deep inside her when Moncrieff had spoken, an evil, insidious imprint that would always be there, waiting for a sign of weakness.

The devil's calling card, and many men take on his countenance.

Her bare foot slipped on the slime of the cobblestones and Jean fell headlong, jolted face first, wind knocked out of her body. Through the buzzing in her ears she could hear footsteps coming towards where she lay.

Was it *him*? Or some other fiend from hell?

Two women looked down at Jean. One sported a bright scarlet feather boa to disguise her wrinkled neck, skin stretched like parchment over the sharp bones, and the other had flat features, almost primitive, with jet-black hair and a jaunty emerald-green bonnet perched perilously on the back of her head.

Both wore garish cheap gowns under nondescript shabby coats, one a bright blue, the other faded pink set off by a slash of livid orange.

Faces painted white like masks, red markings like a signal in the dark.

Nymphs of the Pavé, Fleurs de Nuit whose petals often opened at night, cowclinks in Edinburgh's coarser tongue. Their names were Jessie Sheridan and Nan Dunlop.

Jessie was the older – men had passed below her like froth under the Bridge of Leith. Like paper boats.

From her and Nan's point of view, they saw a small figure crouched like an animal on the stones – hard rain beating down to soak deep the thin, discoloured dress.

'How come ye're running wild, wee girl?' asked Jessie. 'Have ye cut a throat, maybe?'

The figure shook its head, auburn hair plastered to the skull.

'Where are ye going in such a hurry, then?'

An answer came finally.

'Nowhere, thank you.'

Nan grinned, revealing wide gaps in her teeth. Unlike Jessie, there was a primitive, unstable quality to the woman, eyes dark and shiny like a mongoose. She was yet young enough that her body still cradled a sensual challenge and invitation.

'And whit are ye leaving behind, my wee chookie?' she asked, green bonnet dancing with the movement of her head in the cold, damp air.

'Nothing.'

The women looked at each other. A story would emerge eventually but this was not the time – it had been an unproductive night, the rain was getting heavier, and in Jessie's case the beginnings of a consumptive cough were already stirring in the fragile casing of her chest.

They could leave the girl to the tender mercies of rats and bigger beasts – or take her in hand – yet what had they to offer?

Only a profession that ran out of hope, like water down the drain.

The girl scrambled to her feet – feet that were bruised and bleeding from reckless flight – and faced them with a spirited defiance undermined somewhat by the shivering in her body.

'Whit is your name, wee girl?'

'Jean. Jean Brash. And I am a Queen Bee.'

Nan let out a roar of laughter at this response to Jessie's question, as the older woman smiled thinly.

'Well, we better take ye tae the hive, then.'

Jessie and Nan shared a room and had done so for the past two years – they could squeeze her in somewhere.

At least she was skinny, Jessie surmised. Maybe she could sleep standing up.

There was an element of calculation in Nan's eyes – if the lassie filled out, she might yet pay her way.

Everyone must pay their way. In this world, whatever you have to offer is always for sale from the moment you're born.

The girl stepped between them and the trio turned to go with the women leading in front. As they walked on, Jean, impulsively, put slim, delicate hands into theirs.

And so the three figures departed, moving towards the glimmering rain-streaked lamplight ahead, like ghosts disappearing from view towards an uncertain future.

Chapter 2

This is the way the ladies ride,
Clippety clop, clippety clop.

The New Year bells clanged resoundingly from various pious pulls as Jean Brash shifted in her sleep. She had stumbled into bed in the early hours of that morning after her palatial bawdy-hoose, the Just Land, had entertained what seemed like half the professional ruling classes of Edinburgh city.

The medical and legal gentleman's clubs, having drowned their sorrows at the passing year and then greeted with appropriate conviviality a new arrival from the loins of Old Father Time, had descended upon the Just Land with appendages aquiver.

They joined forces with a number of Bristol businessmen who were up to finance a deal with the powers that be of the city council and, having haggled with some success but not quite enough, had called it quits for the moment, thrown caution to the wind, and led by a merry but totally bald round-faced fellow, Sammy Deacon, and his equally boisterous but taller, more handsome and fully thatched colleague, Joseph Tucker, had brought some of the more adventurous councillors along to slake their carnal thirst.

Who knows?

A satisfied man faintly redolent of a smudge of French cologne might look more kindly upon funds and figures. Satisfaction is a fine financial bedfellow.

8

A wild party had ensued where many a purloined legal wig had decorated many an unveiled evidential body, and the magpies for their part knowing by rule of thumb that medical men tend to strive longer than advocates who are all talk and no great pith, clove to choice of profession in accordance with their preferred or pecuniary desires.

The Bristol boys would no doubt be a mixed bag of sweeties as men inevitably are – dip your hand in a brown paper poke, trust they don't stick together, pop it in and hope for the best.

Amongst the gathering were also a number of wild young bucks of a more artistic bent, one, a sculptor, Jack Burns – a handsome devil whose high cheekbones set his face in conflicting sharp planes – had leant over Jean and most earnestly requested that he might immortalise her naked form in an innovative version of Pallas Athena.

'You see, Mistress Brash, a woman unclothed is the most powerful weapon of any artist,' he asserted, eyes blazing into hers part fuelled by creative intent, part by a fairly decent champagne. 'I would consider it a great honour to mediate between your earthly flesh and the immortal goddess. Athena presided over the finer elements of man. Courage, strategy and heroic endeavour.'

Jean nodded at this deific description, aware at the same time that one of the artistic champagne guzzlers was staring at her from the corner of the room.

She indicated the onlooker, who for some reason was dressed as a dusky-hued Arabian prince – many of the artists had affected exotic display, two had even come in extravagant ostrich plumes.

'The small, dainty fellow from the Mysterious East: who is he?'

Jack smiled briefly. 'Solomon Baines. Shows promise.'

'In what?'

'Portraiture.'

Jean inclined her head in a friendly fashion towards Solomon, who managed a jerky bob in response, then she and the sculptor got back to business. It could not be denied that a certain attraction was in the air along with the cigar fumes and aforementioned cologne. Art is a great leveller.

'And how do you see the goddess in human form?'

The sculptor took a deep breath. 'Lean-flanked, fertile-breasted,' he ventured. 'A long, slim body.'

'Was she not also virginal?' asked Jean. 'I fear that might compromise me somewhat as a model example.'

Her green eyes were open and candid – for a moment Jack felt a tickle at the back of his throat.

The woman before him was in her prime. Indeed fertile-breasted as far as he could see from her discreet décolletage, red hair lustrous in the glittering candlelight, green eyes with a mocking glint echoed in the smile of her full lips, a porcelain complexion – all contained in a complex, withheld quality that radiated an almost feline powerful attraction.

But don't mistake magnetism for invitation, that would be foolish.

'Just give me the chance,' he said hoarsely. 'I will uncover your essential innocence.'

'That's what worries me,' replied Jean, aware that music was stirring once more in the background as their one-eyed fiddler, Finlay Craigie, laid down his drink with a deal of regret to loose ancient fingers for other matters.

'And once your garments are thrown to the four winds, it's a devil of a job to gather them back up again. A *devil* of a job.'

She smiled at the sculptor suddenly and Jack felt a spasm of masculine response that had little to do with artistic leanings.

Then the music began, she had disappeared into the throng and he was left cursing the fact that champagne is, now and again, not quite such an all-embracing aid to seductive strategy as portrayed in fiction. It may oil the tongue and fire the blood, but does not necessarily provide sufficient speed of verbal response.

Jean turned in the sheets, smiled in memory at the man's impudence and regarded her image in the long mirror beside the bed – red hair tousled from sleep, skin clear and innocent as a newborn babe.

In fact, was it not James McLevy, the thief-taker himself, who had muttered over a cup of the finest Lebanese coffee, 'Tae look at you, Jeannie, ye'd never guess what you've done and where you've done it.'

Always wanted to be a muse, she thought. *But I might end up as a mere plaything.*

And yet she could not help but notice the strength in the sculptor's hands, blunt powerful fingers that would no doubt exercise a strong and steadfast grip and a rough-hewn physicality that might have its own unclothed attraction.

Like Hercules unchained?

Certain licentious images were put carefully to the side but not completely forgotten as the Mistress of the Just Land reviewed the rest of that evening.

Couples had sped headlong for upstairs rooms to reappear later happily replete upon the fruits of Venus – a slippery goddess at the best of times – and then revelled in impromptu reels and jigs while the fiddler stamped his boots and big Annie Drummond shifted plump but dexterous digits over piano keys as if toying amongst so many cream buns.

While smooth legs emerged from flounced chemises and an exposed bare foot flexed itself in the dance, it would have been a cold fish that did not feel the blood-heat.

But hot blood can lead to hot deeds. Like murder, for instance.

A bang of sorts and then the bedroom door burst open to reveal Hannah Semple – Jean's right-hand woman, keeper of the keys of the Just Land, old as the hills, with a basilisk stare that might arrest many a rampant satyr.

But now her eyes were wide open in shock.

'Mistress, there's a deid body in the cellar, hinging over the Berkley Horse, a big knife in the back!'

The New Year bells kept ringing.

Ding-dong.

Ding-dong.

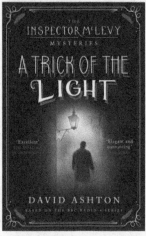
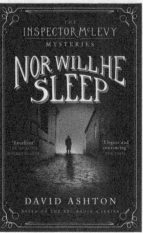

Shadow of the Serpent

An Inspector McLevy Mystery

David Ashton

1

The Diary of James McLevy

There is a legend that after Lucifer had been cast into hell, God granted him the one wish to make up for what must have been a severe disappointment.

Satan thought long and hard, then averred that he would wish to grant mankind the gift of desiring power.

God could see no harm in that: He Himself had possessed supreme omnipotence for all eternity and see the good job He'd made of it.

So, God granted the wish.

And Satan has been laughing ever since.

I have reached my third coffee. The cup has left a yellow ring at the top of the page where I write but nothing is perfect. Not even myself.

I am James McLevy, inspector of police. I record in this wee book what the French call my 'pensées', or what the Scots would term 'whatever passes through a body's mind'.

My existence is a struggle between personal human frailty and the desire to serve justice. An exactitude forever compromised by the very people who framed the laws they now wish to bend.

I look back to see the anguish and pain I have caused for others and caused to myself by the unyielding pursuit of justice. I look ahead and see much the same prospect. So be it.

Break the law, high or low, I'll bring ye down. Suffer injury, high or low, I will avenge ye. To the best of my compromised ability.

I'm down to the dregs now. Coffee is like blood in my veins.

Out of my attic window, I can see a thousand torches flickering in the sky from the direction of Waverley Market.

They light the way to power. Politics. The dunghill upon which many a cock has crowed.

I turn the other way and look out over my kingdom.

2

Who finds the heifer dead and bleeding fresh
And sees fast by a butcher with an axe
But will suspect 'twas he that made the slaughter?

WILLIAM SHAKESPEARE, *Henry VI, Part 2*, 3, 2

Leith, March 1880
Sadie Gorman shivered as the cold east Edinburgh wind bit into her bones. No place to hide. She looked down at her dress, dirty yellow like the lamplight and thin as a winding sheet. What kind of life was this? She should have decent drawers, keep her old bones warm and cosy, but no, she had to be accessible to all comers. Shed her shanks to liberal or conservative. All comers.

She laughed suddenly and the sound echoed in the silence of Vinegar Close. It was late, past midnight, other folk in bed, ten to a room, drunk men snoring, children clenching knees to keep the contents of their wee bladders at bay, and the women?

Well, whatever they were, at least they were spared standing on a corner in Leith on a dank March night, hoping for some mortal old fornicator fuddled with drink on his way home from the big meeting. On his way home, but, Christ Jesus this wind was cold, just enough blood in his veins to prove that a standing cock has nae conscience.

The gaslight flickered and she caught sight of her image on the other side of the street, reflected in the oily glass of one of the half-uncles, the wee pawn shops, dotted round the closes. A shop she'd been in many a time herself, the door well locked, window empty save for this daft soul in a yellow dress slavering back at her.

Look at the sight. The woman was *ancient*, for God's sake, if she was a day. A single white feather stuck in the back of her wispy hair added a gay touch to the shipwreck.

What year was it now? Soon she'd be coming up to fifty. Sadie shared a birthday with Queen Victoria, May the 24th. That day Her Gracious Majesty would be a sight older but better preserved. People would kiss her hand, kiss her backside if they could find such under all those skirts and petticoats and God knows what else. Aye they'd get lost in there, choke on all that flannel guarding the Queen's private parts, choke, kiss her backside and sing the National Anthem. All at the same time. On their knees.

She walked across the street and looked closely at herself in the glass. By God, she was a treat to behold. Face white with powder and chalk, eyes black as pitch, cheeks rouged up like a paper doll and her mouth a big red gash. Not exactly a shrinking violet but what's a shop without a sign? She opened her lips, and pouted comically at herself. A big mouth. Her speciality.

In the silence, faintly, the sound of a child whimpering from one of the black, grim, warren of houses in the close, then it was quiet.

Set out with high hopes this night, high hopes. Some palaver-merchant had been blowing up a storm at Waverley Market, big crowds, men getting demented over politics. That was good, good for business; they would spill down the hill to Leith, lash out their money and their love-drops; that baby's howling again, must be her teeth coming through, poor wee soul. Born tae suffer.

None of that for her, no cuckoos in the nest, she sheathed the custom up, and if not, a sponge-and-vinegar girl. Not a seed born of man survived that barrier. A sponge-and-vinegar girl. In Vinegar Close.

Sadie's face went slack for a moment and her eyes, looking deep the other in the glass, seemed like a child's, full of pain and vexation. Her white plume moved in the cold wind as if waving goodbye.

What was it McLevy had said to her? All these years ago, all these years.

She'd dipped a mark in the Tolbooth Wynd, while the man was standing to attention, him being an officer of the guards, and slid the wallet over to her then fancy boy, wee Dougie Gray.

Dougie had taken off round the corner while she gripped the mark fast in pretended passion. The man discovered his loss but she gave gracious pardon, it must have fallen from his pocket or perhaps it was at home with the wife, never mind settle up the next time, eh?

He cursed her something fierce as a rancid wee whore, but the smile froze on her face when Dougie marched back round the corner, arm in arm with Jamie McLevy, prime thieftaker of the parish of Leith, in the city of Edinburgh.

The policeman was limping though, puffing for breath; wee Dougie must have kicked the clouds but the ploy had not worked. Not well enough.

God bless wee Dougie, took it right on the chin, said he'd delved in regardless, nothing to do with her, no proof, she was free of scath. But, even though, even though, McLevy turned those slate-grey eyes on her, wolf eyes in that big white face that looked like it never saw the light of day. He smiled and her bowels lurched, then he reached out and gently flicked the feather which even then she wore as her proud emblem.

'One day, Sadie Gorman,' he said, and his voice pierced in deep. 'One day, your wings will be broken and you shall fall to earth at my feet.'

Well, he could kiss the devil's arse because here she was alive and kicking. But still. His voice echoed in her mind. All these years.

And wee Dougie had died in the Perth Penitentiary, defending his honour against some brute from Aberdeen. He did not deserve that. Nae justice.

The east wind nagged her back to the present. She turned and looked at the dead street. Not a hunker-slider in sight. That

4

bloody wind must have frozen the randy boys where they lay.

Sadie shivered and glanced around again. This dark time, the evil hour, played tricks upon your mind. Satan might be watching, long black nails and big red eyes. She had felt him on her trail these past nights.

She dare not go home empty handed. Her pounce, Frank Brennan, was a big Irish lump with hands like a navvy's shovel, genial enough save in drink but, by this time of night, he'd be steaming like a horse dollop and looking for his due reward. Her face was safe but God help her belly from his fist.

For a moment she felt a sense of panic, desperation, as if she was sliding away from what she knew into the darkness, some pit where only monsters waited. She'd seen a drawing once, a woman drowned at sea, a great big octopus dragging her under, the mouth open, screaming, hair wrapped round her face, breasts naked, dress ripped from her by the slimy tentacles. Of course it was to ginger up the clients in the Holy Land, the bawdy-hoose where she'd first been on the bones. Should have stayed there, Jean Brash would have seen her right, but no, she was too young, too restless, she liked it free and easy. Free and easy. Look at her now.

A hard shake went through her whole body. It was cruel and cold. No mercy. She'd have to go home. Take her licks.

She could stand the panic now. It was like a dull ache but a thing she knew.

But then the fear charged in again, like a black mist. She heard something in the shadows, a rat chittering; what if the beast scuttled right up her leg? She detested rodents. Now wait. What was that? God's mercy on a cold night maybe?

Footsteps, coming towards her, through the narrow wynd, heel and sole on the cobbles, a fine firm masculine step.

Aye, there he was now, oh definitely on the prowl, ye could tell. Under the tile hat, a furze of white hair shone in the gaslight, a patriarch, even better, might settle for a wee flutter of the fingers, gentleman's relish, but see the light grey frock-coat – that's quality, that's good money, that's more than promising.

Sadie licked her lips and pulled a touch back into the shadows, distance lends enchantment. She laughed softly, the man's head turned, slow, ponderous.

'Well, my braw gallant,' Sadie spoke low, inviting, she had a fine organ for that, whisky tonsils. 'Is it company ye're searching for? I'll wager you could tremble me, I can tell just looking. I know a strong man when he comes a-calling.'

She laughed, kept in the shadows, extended a white arm; her arms were her best point these days, elegant, long, supple fingers waggled saucily.

He also kept out of the light, but she could see, straining her eyes, that he was a fair age and height, white sideburns, eyes deep set below craggy brows, shaded by the brim of the hat. The mouth worried her, it was not a kind cut. And there was an odd smell in the air. A hospital smell. Coal tar.

This might be slow fruit and it would help if the auld bugger might think to say something. Now, wait. She knew that face surely, she'd seen it before but not in a serving capacity, no, that mouth the downward set of it, in the newspapers maybe? Not that she could read but the photos, or was it somewhere else? The man fumbled inside his jacket; if he brought out his wallet then to hell with what she knew or didn't know, business was business.

She pitched her voice soft and throaty. 'I can see a man of substance, a man of style, a man whose wishes must be met. I can satisfy you, sir, satisfaction is my aim, tell me your heart's desire.'

She risked coming forward a touch more, threw back her head, thrust out her chest, maybe her titties would take his eyes off the state of her teeth.

'Tell me your heart's desire.'

Sadie's first lover had been a flesher's assistant; he would present her the odd mutton chop when chance arrived.

She loved to watch him at work, a butcher's boy; his big meaty hands wielded the cleaver with surprising delicacy. He had a delicate touch with many things. The flash of the blade

6

through the air always excited her as the edge bit into the lamb's neck. A flash of steel.

The axe blade hewed straight through her collarbone, crashed through the ribs and only stopped when it reached the heart. Sadie fell like a stone. The man, with gloved hand, carefully wiped the sharp edge of the weapon clean on her yellow dress and put it neatly back inside his coat.

The plume still clung to her hair like a last vestige of life, though the top had snapped off. He picked up the fragment, placed it into a side pocket then walked off with measured tread.

Above her sightless eyes where she lay was a motto carved on one of the doors. *In Thee, O Lord, is all my trust.*

Her blood flowed out in a hot gush. A rat scuttled in the shadows but Sadie didn't mind. It was the first time she'd been warm all night.

The white feather had been broken. The east wind blew it from her hair, and cast it out into the darkness.

Stories ... voices ... places ... lives

We hope you enjoyed *The Lost Daughter*. If you'd like to
know more about this book or any other title on our list,
please go to www.tworoadsbooks.com

For news on forthcoming Two Roads titles, please sign
up for our newsletter.

enquiries@tworoadsbooks.com

TwoRoadsBooks